THE MURDER

M K Turner

127 Publishing

This book is dedicated to Molly, the dearest little Bichon.

I will miss my bundle of fur supervising my writing.

And, of course, to

YOU, the reader, for giving me a reason to keep making stuff up.

Acknowledgements

Edited by Sharon Kelly & Jill Buss

Cover by: https://www.behance.net/lwpmarshala1e9

And of course my wonderful beta readers

Paperback ISBN	978-1-7398165-8-2
Hardback ISBN	978-1-7398165-9-9

CONTENTS

Also by M K Turner
Meredith & Hodge Series
The Making of Meredith
Misplaced Loyalty
Ill Conceived
The Wrong Shoes
Tin Soldiers
One Secret Too Many
Mistaken Beliefs
Quite by Chance
Family Matters
Not If You Paid Me
A Measure of Guilt
Meredith & Hodge Bear Witness
Web of Deceit
Error of Judgement

Bearing Witness Series
Witness for Wendy
An Unexpected Gift
Terms of Affection
Meredith & Hodge Bear Witness

Little Compton Mysteries
The Murder
The Abduction
The Burglar

Others
Who Killed Charlie Birch?
The Cuban Conundrum
Murderous Mishaps
The Recruitment of Lucy James

THE BODY

Had Emily called on time, Tom Large wouldn't be staring at a dead body. The body of Denise Knight, a fellow volunteer librarian. Denise Knight, who liked to tease him, and whose nails were too long. Certainly too long for most tasks required at the library. But she wasn't a bad woman. She had atrocious fashion sense, yes, but she didn't deserve to be dead. Dead and lying half in and half out of the stream. Tom couldn't see her face, but he knew it was Denise because she was wearing her faux fur coat, the dalmatian one she tried to keep for best. The hand he could see certainly had her long nails. Although they weren't the deep red they were yesterday, today they were a pale and sparkly pink.

Careful not to step too close, he leaned as far as he could towards her body and used the torch on his phone to look around. It was difficult to be sure, but the part of her that wasn't in the water appeared to be dry. She probably hadn't drowned. There was a dark patch of blood on her temple, which had stuck her regularly dyed blonde hair to her face. She'd had her hair done too. Yesterday her salt and pepper roots were a good inch long. They were gone. He didn't need to see the face obscured by that hair, because the coat, nails and the hair all told him it was Denise.

"Poor old Denise," he muttered, taking several steps back onto the elephant track path which ran parallel to the stream. Then, realising the implications of his discovery, he cursed. "Bloody hell! Now I'll have to call the police, and a pound to a penny, that's when Emily will call. Not bloody good enough!"

He pondered his next course of action. Dithering was one of his latest habits. But not tonight. Tonight, he was decisive. He wouldn't wait. However long it took the police to arrive, be it minutes or hours, he wouldn't stay. Simply thinking about them with all their paraphernalia, and all those people milling around put his head in a spin, and he knew he couldn't wait. Mumbling to himself about the police, paramedics, and forensic staff, Tom took several photographs of the scene. They might be useful if someone else passed by, they might not be as careful as him. They might trample over potential evidence.

Job done, and standing almost to attention with his eyes closed, Tom nodded a formal goodbye to Denise. Turning away, he started his journey home, trying to think up a defence for leaving the scene. He knew one shouldn't leave the scene of a car accident. This was bound to be the same.

"Ha!" He nodded as a cracking reason came to him. Only last week, Liz, his cleaner, had told him about her neighbour catching a burglar in his garage and trapping him in by switching off the power so the electric door at the front wouldn't work, and locking the previously unlocked backdoor from the outside. The police had known he'd caught the burglar, but had still taken three hours to arrive. By which time, of course, the burglar had smashed his way out of the side window. Hopeless. Cuts and more cuts had made everything useless until the country could barely function.

Tom Large had a lot of opinions, most of which he kept to himself, because other than Emily and Liz, neither of whom were very interested, who was there to discuss them with? Certainly not Denise, not now. That wasn't the reason he was leaving, but it's the one he would use.

Increasing his pace, Tom headed for home, his eyes searching the area around him as best they could with the light from his phone, for... for what? Clues? Evidence? He didn't know. He just felt he should. But other than an empty gum wrapper, a screwed-up cigarette packet, which he thought was Marlboro, but he could only see half so that was a guess. He'd never smoked, but knew all packets looked the same these days. He assumed the pack was empty. A couple of feet away lay a torn betting slip. He photographed the three items but saw nothing he thought would be of interest.

Once home, he slammed the door behind him and leaned against the hall wall to steady himself, knocking the framed photo of a five-year-old Emily askew in the process. His shoulders relaxed, but his heart continued to pound.

The shrill beep of his phone warned of a low battery and prompted him into action. First a dead body, now a dead phone. This was Emily's fault. Had she phoned on time, he would be asleep. Dead to the world, not facing all the trauma that was about to come. Marching into the kitchen and through to the diner, he lifted the cable and nodded at the satisfying vibration which told him his phone was charging. He should call the police, not watch the battery bar get bigger. Pulling a chair from under the table, he called nine-nine-nine. After what seemed like far too long, his call was answered, and he cleared his throat to answer the questions thrown at him.

"Police, please. I've found a dead body. Little Compton, half in the stream, I was on the path by the side of the stream. High street end, a couple of hundred yards at a guess. No, I'm at home now. Why? Um, because I had to call you. Yes, yes, my phone was at home charging. Couldn't sleep, was awaiting a call, went for a brisk walk. Tom, that is Thomas David Large, Pendry's Bungalow, Lower High Street. About ten minutes ago. Yes, yes, I do. I volunteer at the library with her. Did, that is. Denise Knight. No idea, nope, no idea where she lives either. We weren't really friends. As sure as I can be. Because she was laying half in and half out of the stream, with blood all over her head. I wasn't going to touch her. Didn't want to compromise any forensic evidence. No. no. When? Oh, I'll just wait then, only I'm expecting a call from my daughter. Any idea how... oh, okay. I'll keep the line clear. No, I don't have a landline. Thank you."

As he hung up Emily called.

"Hello Dad, so sorry I'm late. It's been a day and a half. But I'm here now. How's things? Have you done anything different today?"

"It's too late. I can't speak to you. And different? I'd say so. I've found a dead body. Denise, from the library, it's her who's dead. I must keep off the phone in case the police call. We'll have to leave it until tomorrow."

"A dead body? A real one?"

"Yes, of course. Don't be stupid. How do you have a false dead body?"

"And you knew her?"

"Yes. Emily, I said, I really should get off this phone."

"When did you find her?"

"About half an hour ago, maybe a little less."

"You were out?"

"I was waiting for you to call. You were, are, late. I was restless, so I went for a walk. Wish I hadn't now. I often walk at night." Tom crossed his fingers. Often, was not a word to replace 'It was the third time since I moved in twelve months ago.'

"Not during the day, though? Still, it's out. That's good. Another step forward. Well done, I'm proud of you."

"Emily, it's why I found a dead body. I don't think it's a cause for celebration. I'm hanging up, the police might want me. We'll speak tomorrow." He hit the red button and tutted. "She speaks to me like I'm a child, not a grown man, not her father." Further complaints were halted by the doorbell.

After giving the two detectives the identical run-through of events he'd given the woman who'd taken his call, the two detectives went off with their growing ensemble, most shouting into mobile phones, to find the body. He wasn't asked to go with them, and he certainly didn't volunteer. He was told to wait inside for them to come back and not to go out. As he closed the door, he wondered where on earth they thought he might go at this time of night. Blinking against his tired eyes, he rubbed his temple and thought longingly about the contents of his bedside cabinet.

Less than twenty minutes later, one of the young detectives returned. Tom had no choice but to invite him in. He didn't offer tea.

"Explain to me again how you knew the deceased and what you were doing up on the path so late at night." DC Patrick Connor sat on the opposite side of the table to Tom.

"I was waiting for a call from my daughter, Emily. She's in Australia. She always calls between ten and midnight. I'd prefer ten, but sometimes she can't get a break. You know, from work. I got fed up with waiting, and I thought, why not go for a walk? It's a bit nippy out. It'll keep me awake."

Tom watched the detective flip back through several pages of notes. When he'd done so, he looked from Tom to the telephone, still charging on the table next to him.

"Says here you didn't take your phone because it was charging. Surely if you were awaiting a call, you'd have taken it with you. Wouldn't you?"

Tom wanted to curse at the stupidity of lying. Instead, he furrowed his brow, nodding slowly as he considered the implications of that lie. He'd had to get home. He couldn't have been with all those people, shouting and asking questions. Who knows what might have happened? What to say now? Compound the lie, or tell the truth?

The officer rose to look at Tom's phone. "How's that charge doing?" He looked at his watch. "Seems to have been charging for a long time."

"Since I came in. I did have my phone. I thought I told her, the girl on the phone. My battery was so low I knew it would run out the minute I used it. It was low before I left. I should have left it at home charging. So I came home, it's only a few minutes away, as you've just discovered. Put it on charge, there, and called sitting here. Was I wrong?" He twitched his finger between the two locations.

The detective was nodding, but his expression said he wasn't convinced. "Okay. We discovered the victim's ID in her handbag, it was Denise Knight. I understand you knew Mrs Knight."

"I did. Didn't know she was married though. That's a surprise. She never wore a ring."

"Were you interested in her, then? Romantically? I'm guessing so, enough to notice she wasn't wearing a ring." DC Connor looked around the kitchen-diner. "Is there a Mrs Large?" he asked, as he tilted his head and looked at the reasonably attractive middle-aged man he was questioning. Large had all his hair, although it was a bit on the long side, and was tidily dressed in black jeans and a V-neck sweater, underneath which was a checked shirt with a button-down collar. Quite smart for a late-night walk. A divorcee might be interested in him. This bungalow was worth a tidy penny.

"Not anymore. She died. And no, I wasn't interested. Denise had a very complicated life as far as I could make out. I kept as far away from it as possible. Her nails are the reason I noticed. She was forever having them painted. Came in with little gems stuck to them one day, then couldn't do a thing in case she knocked the gems off. In fact, she never did much at all because of her nails. But I digress. It was because she was always showing off her nails. No ring. You see?" He held out his own hands, wiggling his fingers. Although he, of course, had a wedding ring.

"How did you know it was her? We were told you didn't approach the body. What do you mean by complicated?"

"I recognised her coat, her nails, her hair. All Denise. It would have been a major coincidence if it hadn't been her. There couldn't possibly be two people who dress that way. As to the complications, she was always doing things. Quizzes, shopping, cinema, cafes, restaurants, and Zumba, whatever that is. I doubt she was ever home. I'm... more of the quiet type. Good film on the telly type of man. I'd never keep up with someone like Denise."

This time, when he nodded, DC Connor looked more convinced of Tom's answer. It didn't help Tom relax, though. He wondered if his anxiety was showing. Was his brow dotted with perspiration, was there a wobble in his voice, had his hands been shaking? All these things had happened in the past when he was anxious, and he didn't need them today. Not now. He waited for the next question, drawing air in through his nose and then out through barely parted lips. He didn't want it to be obvious he was trying to relax, that could be another tell of his guilt. Not that he was guilty, but they didn't know that. Closing his eyes, he let his head fall forward and blew out a noisy huff of a breath.

"Are you okay, Mr Large?"

"Yes. Well, no, of course not. It's not every day you find a dead body. Particularly one you know. I'm exhausted. I've had to tell my daughter I can't speak to her and," Tom threw his hands into the air, "to be quite honest with you, it's all a bit much."

"I'm sure. Can you tell me what you were wearing tonight?"

"Wearing? This." Tom held his hands out as though revealing his attire. "Why? Oh, I see. You want to check me for forensic evidence? Is that it? That's easy. Charles's Bungalow, last bungalow on the row. They have one of those cameras that follows you. At least I think it does, it moves. I've never worked out what it would do if two people walked in opposite directions in front of it. That'll show you. At least I think it will. I had my coat on, though. The one on the banister, and the wellies in the porch. You can take them to do a cast if you need, but I only took one step off the path. I knew not to contaminate the scene." Tom allowed himself a small smile of smugness.

"Will do. I think that's it for now, Mr Large. I'll leave you to get some sleep. We'll need to take a full statement tomorrow. Can you come into the station after nine?"

"Do I have to? Go to the station, I mean. Can't you come here?"

"Is there a problem coming into the station?"

"Yes."

"Why?"

"Because... I'm expecting someone. Not sure what time."

"Okay, it's a bit odd. But I'll be in the area. I'll pop in. You won't be going out at all, will you?"

"Oh no. I'll be here all day."

Tom unplugged his phone and saw DC Connor out. Immediately the door shut, he turned off the lights and hurried up the stairs to the dormer bedroom. On hearing voices, and careful not to knock his head on the slope of the ceiling, he looked out of the window through the crack in the curtain.

"All done in there? How is he?" The second officer had returned and was speaking to DC Connor.

"Yep. Done for now. He's a bit shaken, and weird. He's weird in a gentle sort of way. Not ruling him out at the moment. How's it going up there?"

Tom didn't want to hear any more. He was weird, he knew that, but he didn't want it confirmed by strangers. He hadn't always been weird. Bloody people.

He dropped onto the bed with a sigh. Tonight, he opened the drawer before he'd even got undressed. Lifting out the glass and bottle, he poured a generous measure. Popping two sleeping tablets from the blister pack, he worked them to the back of his tongue and washed them down, emptying the tumbler. That was better. He was going to stop this reliance nonsense, but not today. No, certainly not today.

As he got himself ready for bed, Tom sipped another generous nightcap, and then finally lay down. If he were lucky, he'd have oblivion until at least nine o'clock. He liked oblivion. He couldn't be weird if he were oblivious.

THE MURDER?

"So, tell me what you want, what you... Argh!" Her singing interrupted, Liz Thorne's scream was shrill, and she jabbed her feather duster towards Tom. "You nearly gave me a heart attack." She pulled one of her earphones out. "What are you doing in there?"

Heavy eyes looked at Liz. "Taking a shower. What does it look like I'm doing? I was sleeping. Why are you here so early? Is it even your day?"

"Yes. Wednesday. And I'm not early, I'm late. It's ten thirty. Had to go into... I won't bother you with that. Then they had the top of the road taped off. I hope it's not another unexploded bomb. That took an age to deal with last time. I thought you'd gone out, although that would be strange. Have you not got to work today? You usually just grunt from behind your screen."

Liz Thorne waved the duster as she spoke. Tom sometimes thought he should have a word with her about the lack of respect. But he liked her attitude, her zest. Liz was never rude, not really, she simply told it how it was. She was refreshing, if somewhat irritating.

"I have, yes. Ten thirty, bloody hell." Tom threw the duvet back. "I'll jump in the shower. Don't suppose you've made tea, have you?"

"Nope. Because you weren't there to ask for one. I'll go and put the kettle on and do downstairs first. I only came up out of habit. Don't you get moaning at me for doing it first. Did you have too much?"

"Too much what?" Tom flicked his hand back and forth, indicating she should move out of the way. He knew exactly what she meant.

Leaning around him, she pointed at the glass. "Too much."

"No, I didn't, and I resent the accusation. If you must know, last night..." Tom's hand flew to his mouth, and he mumbled into it, "You knew her."

"What? Knew who?" Liz grinned. "You dark horse. Have you been on a date? Is that what you're really doing on that computer, dating sites, not boring old accounts?"

"Don't be ridiculous. I found Denise Knight's body. She was dead. I'm so sorry."

"Dead. Denise? Oh my God. She's been murdered, hasn't she? That's why the tape's there. How did you find her? Were you meeting her?"

"I know it's a shock, Liz, but really. You've met Denise, you've met me. Why would I be meeting her?"

"I don't know. Stranger things have happened, like you being out and finding dead bodies. Dead bodies belonging to people who were being stalked."

"Stalked? Have you told the police?"

"I've only just found out she's been murdered. Oh God, I need a drink. I'll put a drop of this in our tea." As bold as brass, she opened his bedside drawer and took out the almost empty bottle. She held it up as though inspecting how much had been imbibed. "Hmm."

"Hmm! How did you know that was there? Have you been going through my things?" Tom's hands were on his hips.

"No I have not! And I resent that accusation. I clean for you. Properly. Behind stuff. On the first Wednesday of every month I do the bedrooms, properly. I move stuff to clean behind them. That cabinet always chinks. Glass on glass. I didn't need to look to know what it was, because I also see your recycling." She was jabbing the feather duster at him again. "It's obvious you have an issue."

"What? Liz, you have just overstepped the mark. I might have issues, but drink isn't one of them, and even if it was, you are not the person to tell me. I'm going for a shower."

"And I haven't got an issue with it either, but I'm having some of this in my tea. Hurry up. I want the details, then we must call the police." Liz was already on the stairs. "Don't stand there gawping. Get in the shower."

"Even my wife didn't speak to me like that. You are overstepping the mark. Again."

"So you keep saying, hurry up, Mr Large. I've got to do Harry Burnham after you. I don't know what he's going to say. He was her neighbour, and he liked Denise."

When Tom came down, the tea tray was in the middle of the table, and a coaster sat ready and waiting for his mug. Liz was clasping hers in two hands as though she were cold. He looked at the biscuits.

"I haven't even had breakfast yet."

"I'll get it. Is it cornflakes or Weetabix today? Two slices of toast?"

"I'm quite capable."

"Yes, but slow. Sit down, I'll be two ticks. Start talking because the food will get in the way."

While Liz prepared his breakfast, Tom told her how he had happened across the body of Denise Knight. "I took a couple of photographs and virtually ran home to call the police. It was awful."

Liz placed his breakfast on the table and her hands flew to her hips. "You did what? Why would you take photographs? That's weird. What did the police say?"

"Because of what you said, and I didn't tell them. It didn't come up."

"What I what? I've only just found out. You really aren't making much sense." Her eye shot to the near empty bottle on the tray. "Do you need some paracetamol?"

Tom rolled his eyes as he huffed. "I did not have too many, I do not have a hangover, and it was you who told me about the three-hour fiasco with the garage burglar. I wasn't going to stand there for three hours with a dead body. I took the photographs in case anyone else came along and disturbed things." He bit into his toast.

"Ah. But they wouldn't take three hours for a murder. How long were they?"

"About twenty minutes. But we don't know that it's murder."

"She had a stalker. She was scared, I told you that. How did she die then? I think she's only two or three years older than me. Mid-forties at the most. You don't drop dead in your mid-forties."

"I don't know how she died, but an educated guess would be a knock to the head. She had blood here." He moved his hand around the side of his face, watching Liz's nose wrinkle.

"Knock or blow? That's the question. The thing is, Mr Large, when I saw her on Monday morning she was really rattled. I couldn't stop for long, I had to get our Gemma to the dentist. But she said the night before someone was spying through her windows."

"Did she tell the police? When I saw her in the library on Monday afternoon, she seemed happy enough. She was complaining about the cost of dry cleaning. She had that spotty monstrosity cleaned."

Liz smiled for the first time since she arrived. "You mean her Cruella de Vil coat? It was a bit over the top. But back to the stalker. She saw a face, screamed, and it disappeared. What could the police do? She said someone had been knocking on the door and leaving, someone had scratched her car, and someone had cut all the heads off her dahlias and just left them lying around, and—"

"Kids. That could be children. Did you never play knock-out-ginger? You know where you knock and run away? We did all the time, especially in the winter."

"That's not the point. What about the scratches on the car and the flowers? I did none of that."

"Progress. In a backward way, of course. Everything moves on. Not all progress is good. Now, I'd better get... I'll go." Tom left to answer the door.

"Hello, Um... DC Connor, isn't it? Come in. I expect you want to take my statement. I was just having breakfast, a bit late, but it was a late night."

Connor followed Tom through to the diner and looked at Liz. "Morning." He gave Liz a smile. Large had told him he wasn't married, perhaps she was the girlfriend, although she looked a little too young for him, it couldn't be his daughter, she was too old. "Are you off to the gym?"

Liz looked down at her clothes. Her shapely figure was encased in the same as usual. Today it was pink leggings, white trainers, and an oversized floral tee-shirt. "No. I'm the housekeeper, although I don't live in. Have a seat, I'll put the kettle on. Mr Large has just been telling me about Denise. Such a shock. I only... but that can wait. How was she murdered? Mr Large thought a blow to the head, and he said she had blood all over here."

"Murdered?" Connor pulled a chair out. "They don't think she was murdered. Misadventure is most likely, they're doing the PM now. But it appears she was walking along the path by the stream, lost her footing and hit her head. What with that and the shock of the cold water... not nice. But they don't think there's been foul play at this stage."

Forgetting about the kettle, Liz took the seat next to him. "But what about the stalker? Being followed, being troubled at home, the damage to her car."

"I told her it was probably kids. Thinking it's funny when it's not. I'll put the kettle on, shall I?" Tom wandered back into the kitchen and filled the kettle as Connor flipped open his notebook.

"She had reported damage to her car, because she wanted a crime reference for the insurance company, but nothing about being stalked. Are you sure about that?"

"No, because it wasn't me. I only know what she told me, and she was scared. Properly scared, not a bit worried, really frightened. Kept looking over her shoulder as if she were being followed. What are you going to do about it? Now I've confirmed it, I mean."

"Had she told anyone else about this?"

"How would I know that?" Liz looked at Tom and shook her head as though Connor wasn't up to the job. "Isn't that what you do? Finding out what happened, when, who knows, et cetera."

"Only if we know about it, but we don't. Still, I've got you now." Connor pulled his pencil from the side of the pad. "Name, date of birth, and address, please."

"Why? I haven't done anything?"

"Because you're about to make a statement. It's required."

"Oh. Elizabeth Ann Thorne. 25a Hyacinth Close. Third of June 1984. A statement about what?"

Tom put a fresh pot of tea on the table. "I don't mean to be rude, but one, I must get some work done, so can we do me first, and two, I'm paying my clean... housekeeper by the hour. This seems like it will take a while. Can you do it later?"

"Mr Large, a woman has been murdered, a friend of ours. As if I'd charge you. Now, inspector, a statement about what?"

"It's detective, DC Connor, although thanks for the vote of confidence, and we don't know it's murder. I'll need a statement about the stalker following Mrs Knight. Who, when, where, et cetera, we might be able to get some CCTV."

"I don't know. I didn't have time for the detail, I was taking Gemma, she's my daughter, to the dentist. I was going to catch up with Denise on Friday."

"We've not been able to trace any family. Only the ex-husband, Andy, does she have any other family, or any close friends we could speak to?"

"She has a sister somewhere, not local. I'm surprised she didn't mention it to Andy, about the stalker, I mean. They're speaking again now. Perhaps Mrs Francis could help. She's one of the architects in the office next to the dry cleaners. Amery & Cheriton. Nice lady, I do her on a Tuesday. Denise worked there four days a week. Or perhaps her neighbour, Mr Burnham, Harry Burnham. They got on well because he was a friend of her mum's."

"I thought she worked at the library. Didn't you say that, Mr Large?"

"Have you been to the library, DC Connor? I'm guessing not. If you had, you would know that it's the room behind the village hall. A large room, not much smaller than the hall, but a room with mismatched bookshelves, two of the vicar's old sofas, and tables and chairs which were probably used on the Ark. It has a small budget, very small. All of which is spent on new books. Government cuts. If they carry on cutting, they'll run out of things to cut. But you know that. When was the last time you had a decent pay rise or saw a bobby on the beat?"

"But you both work there?"

"Not as such, all the library staff are volunteers. If we wanted wages, there would be no library. I do two afternoons. Monday and Thursday for a couple of hours. Denise also did Mondays. Mrs Lambert, the vicar's wife, organises it if you need more detail."

Connor jotted this down. "So you also saw Mrs Knight on Monday and she didn't mention a stalker to you?"

"She didn't. Not a word. She seemed quite chipper, and started to tell me why, but we had a couple of school children come in, and she spent most of her time with them."

Liz checked her watch. "Oh blimey, look at the time. I'd better ring Mr Burnham. I do him after Mr Large. I'm going to be even later now."

Tom rubbed his temples. "Don't worry, Liz. You can skip me today. I'll pay you for your normal hours. It's all been a bit much, hasn't it?"

"If you're sure." She smiled at Connor. "Panic over. No rush." She glanced at Tom who'd given a little groan. "What shall I do about Denise?"

"In what way?"

"In the 'I'm supposed to be going to hers tomorrow', way. I went every Thursday for a couple of hours while she was at work. She wouldn't do certain things because of her nails, not even with gloves. She had beautiful nails."

"So I understand. I don't suppose it's worth it. You won't be paid, not unless the executor agrees, and we've not got one yet. Not found a will."

"You've been to the house and looked?"

"We have. Very neat and tidy... and clean. All her important stuff was in the bedside cabinet. No will I'm afraid."

"She might not keep it at home. It might be with her solicitor." Tom suggested. "Mine is. Did she have a solicitor, Liz?"

"I don't know. She would have for the divorce, perhaps she made one then. But what about the fridge? It will need emptying. She was doing her shop when I saw her on Monday. The stuff in the fridge will go off. Should I get rid of it?"

Connor was losing the will to live. "I don't see that that could do any harm. Don't touch anything else though."

"I don't think I like—"

"Liz. Please. Let the man do his job. DC Connor, it's clear Liz can't make a statement other than to give you hearsay. I do think you might investigate it, perhaps once you've finished with me, you'll pop in and see Denise's employer and neighbour."

Connor agreed, and Liz said she'd just do the bathroom and get off to Mr Burnham. Tom regurgitated his account of events the night before, read through what Connor had written down, and signed it. As Tom closed the door behind him, Liz came down the stairs.

"He doesn't believe me, you know. How bad would it be if they didn't investigate her murder? Poor Denise."

"Indeed. Are you off? Because I really must get some work done. I've got two VAT returns I was hoping to finish today."

"I am. Thanks for letting me get away. I've not prepared anything for your tea tonight."

"Not to worry, I get my own dinner on the days you don't come in, I'm sure I'll manage."

Tom breathed a sigh of relief as he opened his laptop. Peace and quiet, everything was back to normal. He worked without interruption for the next two hours. Having completed the first return, he allowed himself a break, made coffee and ate the biscuits still sitting on the table. He'd just started the second when there was a knock at the door, and Liz called to him.

"Only me." She appeared in the kitchen. "I've done Mr Burnham, I was right, he's devastated. DC Whatsit showed up, so I suppose that's something, but Mr B didn't know about the stalker, nor did anyone at Amery and Cheriton. Why did she tell me and no one else? He thinks I'm lying. I'm not."

"I'm sure that's not the case. Was there something you'd forgotten?" Tom hit the save button.

"No, I'm after a favour."

"Really? If I can help, of course. What?"

"I knew you'd come. Thanks, Mr Large. Only can we do it now? I have to pick Gemma up at half three."

"Come? Come where?"

Liz told Tom she didn't want to go into Denise's house alone. Firstly, she was a little scared, but secondly, and more importantly, she knew Denise kept the drawer in the sideboard locked. Denise had been rummaging in it while Liz was there once, and when finished, had waved the key at Liz and said, 'I don't know who I think would be interested. But I can't break the habit.' Liz hadn't given it any more thought, but what if the will was in there? She wanted to look, and she wanted someone to witness that. She thought Tom could do that as he was connected.

"Go to Liz's house? Now? Look in a locked drawer, how? Do you know where the key is? I think this is a job for the police, not an accountant. I'm not connected either. If Denise had been found by the usual dog walker, you wouldn't be asking them, would you?"

"But the police don't believe me, and I'm going in anyway, to do the fridge. I thought you'd be interested."

"I am to a point, but not so much I'd... Oh, I don't suppose we would be breaking in if you have a key. But surely they looked everywhere. They would, wouldn't they?"

"Who knows? And it's a sort of secret drawer. Not obvious if you don't know to look. How interested do you think he sounded? I'm asking you, as my employer, and, yes, as my friend, to help me make sure, if we can, that our mutual, Denise, wasn't murdered."

"I'm flattered you think I'm a friend, but how will finding out what's in that drawer prove murder one way or the other?"

"We won't know that until we look, will we? Perhaps she has a will and she's left the money to someone who's now bumped her off for the inheritance."

"This isn't a TV show, Liz. But I get your point... I think. It's just... I have this VAT return to complete, and it's only two thirty."

"What's the time got to do with it? Other than the fact I need to pick our Gemma up, so we need to get a move on. Shall I get your coat?"

Tom couldn't tell her it was because he didn't want to go out. Couldn't go out. Not in the day, not with so many people moving about. If it were later, it wouldn't be so bad. He looked at his feet. "I've got my slippers on."

"Then I shall get your shoes. Thanks, Mr Large, you're a star."

Before he could say another word, Liz had rushed off to get his things. Beads of sweat dotted his forehead and he drew deep draughts of air in through his nose to calm himself. Liz was coming back what could... he snatched up his phone.

"Yes, I can get that to you by six. Is that okay? It's not. Why? Ooh, I see. It's a bit inconvenient but I'm sure I can move things about. Thank you. I'll call later." Putting the phone down on the table, he turned to Liz and shrugged. "I can't come, not now. I've got to get this report done, crucial apparently, even the VAT return will have to wait. Sorry. Perhaps tomorrow?"

Liz made the right noises and left, but he could tell she was miffed. He was bloody miffed. He was a grown man. What was he frightened of? He knew what. Making himself look a right prat again, that's what. He couldn't do it! Walking to the bottle Liz had left in the kitchen, he snatched it up. There was barely a measure left, and for the first time ever, he unscrewed the lid and drank it straight from the bottle.

Having completed the VAT return, he made himself an omelette and washed up, still chewing his last mouthful. Wiping down the drainer, he hung the tea towel on the door of the oven. What, if anything, Liz might have found was bothering him. He couldn't concentrate. Perhaps he'd look at the stuff Wilkins had sent in for his end-of-year.

Tom got caught up in his work, and the evening disappeared. But everything was done by ten o'clock. He'd even showered and shaved. He'd watch a bit of television while he waited for Emily. To his surprise and delight, the phone rang before he'd picked up the remote.

"Hello love, you're nice and early tonight. How are you?"

"I'm okay, Dad. Hope you're okay. What've you been up to? More importantly, what's happened about your dead body?"

"Not mine, I'm glad to say. Interestingly, Liz, my cleaner, who promoted herself to housekeeper for the police officer, thinks Denise was murdered." Tom gave her a resume of the day's events. "And I couldn't bloody do it. I made some excuse about having to get a report off to a client. But I promise you this, I'm going to work on it. I'm going to make myself go out every day, even if I only get to the end of the street."

"Oh dear. That's such a shame, and when she thought you'd support her too. She sounds like a good sort. Was she very disappointed? Perhaps if you'd powered on through, you know, put your coat on and gone for it, you might have been okay." Emily sighed. He'd been like this for years. It was time he admitted he needed help.

"And what if I wasn't," Tom snapped. "What if I became a gibbering wreck unable to move? Sweating and jerking about all over the place? What then? I'll tell you what, everyone would think I'm weirder than they do already. I'm bloody working on it, small steps, but I go for walks at night, and at your insistence I took the job at the library." He didn't mention that he only took the job because it was less than five minutes away, and

British wintertime was kicking in. Luckily, the library opened odd hours to accommodate the working community, and he'd insisted he could only work from three thirty due to his business commitments. That way it was dusk when he left, and dark when he came home. Although he enjoyed it, if things didn't improve, he was packing it in next year when the clocks changed.

"Have you thought about speaking to someone again? Perhaps a different counsellor might help."

"No. Absolutely not. They're all the same. Too fluffy, too patronising, and standing at the gate taking deep breaths is not going to help me go to the shops at ten thirty in the morning. It's just going to convince me that I shouldn't. I'll do this my way. I'm getting there. Have you got anything else to say, or are we just going to rehash how useless I am?"

"Dad. That's not what I'm saying. You only went once. And that was two years ago. I am pleased you're going out for walks, albeit in the dark, and that you took the job. But I looked it up on Google Maps, and I know if you hurried, you'd barely know you were out, but it is something. Ten years, Dad. Ten years of being a virtual prisoner. For me, please. I can tell from your voice that you're interested in finding out more with Liz, and that you were disappointed you didn't feel able to go. What I'm saying is—"

"I'm a weird wreck of a man. I'm sorry about that, Emily, truly I am. I am doing something about it. But in my own way, in my own time. And before you ask, because I know you will now that you're on a roll, yes, I'm sleeping, no, I'm not having nightmares. So that's also positive."

"Yet, you still sound cross. Would you like me to go?"

"If you haven't got anything else to say, perhaps you should. Because you sound cross now, and I don't want a row."

"Please yourself. I'm only trying to help, Dad. Goodnight. Love you."

Tom switched the lights off and went upstairs, pulling the new bottle from the drawer he poured a hefty measure and drank it down. Then, popping two pills into his palm, he poured another. Pills taken, he got under the duvet and switched off the light. Ten minutes and he'd be at peace. Sweet oblivion. He hadn't lied about the absence of nightmares.

THE BREAK-IN

T hursday morning was bright and frosty. Tom walked to the end of the garden and looked back at the bungalow. Amy would have loved it here. She never much liked living in the city, and he knew she'd have insisted on wrapping up and going on a brisk walk. He'd have enjoyed that. Not so much enjoyment found walking in the dark, unable to see his surroundings and the wildlife. But it was a start. He knew today wouldn't be the day he walked down to the shop, so there was no point in considering it. He needed to get his work done and do his stint at the library. Without Denise. Not that she did Thursdays, but if it had been a Monday, she wouldn't have been there, trying to protect her nails. As he walked back in, he realised he was going to miss her.

At three o'clock, he sent his last email and closed the laptop. He gave his casserole an extra sprinkle of dried herbs for luck before popping it in the oven, because whether or not his casseroles were tasty, was always down to luck. He locked the back door, put on his shoes, pulled on his coat, and looked around. Everything in order. As he hurried across the road to the church hall, he wondered who, if anyone, would be working with him.

Kathy Lambert, the vicar's wife, greeted him. "Hi, Tom. Come on in out of the cold. I've put the heater on, the cost can be worried about by someone else. Aren't you an accountant? We were looking for someone to do the hall accounts, Mrs James can't see well enough, and if I got involved it would be horrendous."

"Do you mean would I like to volunteer to do the accounts, or am I taking on new paying clients?" Tom smiled at her as she filled the kettle.

"Transparent, aren't I? Yes, volunteer, I'm afraid. I won't be offended if you say no. After all, you're not a member of the church. Do you not believe, or are you one of those, I only pray when I go to bed, types?"

"A bit of both. Common sense and science tell me it was all a ploy to... I don't know, control people, or give them hope, perhaps a bit of both. But I still hope there's something else, you know, once one has been snatched from this world."

"That's a common desire for people who have lost loved ones. Rest assured, whether you believe or not, your wife is in a better place. I truly believe that."

"And I thought it was your husband who was the vicar."

Tom had made a joke, and he paused as he hung his coat on the hook. It was a long time since he'd done that, and he hadn't flinched when she mentioned Amy. Another step forward?

"Ha! Very good. Got to do my bit, you know. I'll make you this cup of tea, then I must slip off for a while. I'm not expecting a rush, but I'll be back."

"No problem. Anything you need me to do, or more of the same?"

"There's a box of books which have been donated, under the desk. They need to be logged, ticketed, and put on the right shelf. You could make a start on those. I was meant to do it yesterday, but I had to do a mercy dash to my sister. She went into early labour, so it was all hands on deck with her other children. I love them dearly, but I was glad to get back this morning."

"Will do. So you weren't here yesterday. That being the case, I take it you've not heard about Denise?"

"What's she done now? Broken a nail? She's such a funny lady, she does have the ability to make you smile. I saw her on Tuesday, just as I was leaving. She saw me with my overnight bag and asked if I was leaving the vicar. I told her not at the moment, and we had a giggle. Tell me, what has she been up to?" Kathy handed Tom his tea.

"Bad news, I'm afraid she's dead. I found her up by, or more accurately, half in, the stream on Tuesday night. Police think it was misadventure. Liz thinks it was murder because Denise had told her she was being stalked. Did Denise say anything to you about that?"

"Dead! Oh my goodness. How awful, poor old Denise. A stalker? No, I saw her on Monday and Tuesday, not a word. In fact, as I say, she was very chirpy on Tuesday. Joking about as only she can... could. Gosh. How awful, I wish we had a little tipple to pour in here. What a shock for you, too. Are you okay?"

"I am now. Such a shame, as you say, poor Denise. Let's hope the police investigate what Liz says properly. She's worried they're going to close the case and Denise's murderer won't be brought to justice. Do you know Liz?"

"I think everyone knows Liz. She seems to 'do' for half the parish, and she's always running around in those brightly coloured Lycra ensembles. Is she scatty? By that, what I mean is, is her judgement likely to be sound? What do you think of her claims?"

Tom didn't know that Liz was a runner. He's seen her brightly coloured Lycra outfits, of course. That was her standard garb. She'd never mentioned she was a runner, but why would she?

"Scatty? Hmm. Not scatty, no. In fact, the opposite, I suppose. She calls a spade a spade. She can hold her tongue though, I know she's wanted to throw a few comments my way now and then but decided against it. On balance, with regard to Denise, I'm torn. I've been thinking about it all day. Liz wouldn't have said anything if she didn't believe it, but she was upset. It could be an emotional thing getting in the way. You know, wanting it to be someone's fault, not an accident."

Tom turned away and went to the desk. Pulling the box out, he grunted as he heaved it up. Shocked at what he had just said, he needed to be busy. Because that's what he had wanted, someone to blame.

"In which case, I hope the police do the necessary. If you don't mind, I'll pop out now. I'd better update the vicar before I do my errand. Did she have any family, do you know? I can't recall her mentioning anyone, but he'll want to pay a visit."

"Only the ex-husband as far as I'm aware. I'll get on with these."

Thirty minutes later, Tom had catalogued and stuck the tickets in half of the books. He decided he'd shelve them to make more room before he started on the rest. He separated the murder mysteries, which were the most in demand, leaving a Val McDermid he hadn't read to one side. As he slotted the first one into position, one of his regulars, Jane Bairstow, came in. Mrs Bairstow was an old girl, and short. She couldn't see past the third shelf, and always wanted recommendations. She read three books a week. He called a greeting as she walked to the desk.

"Hello, Tom, I ran out. Finished the Agatha yesterday morning. So clever, although I've read it before, of course. Oh. New books? Anything I'd like?"

It took almost an hour to check her books back in, discuss the new ones she might be interested in, and stamp them out. There was something satisfying about stamping the date on books. Less than an hour to go, and Kathy hadn't come back. He hoped he didn't have to lock up, he didn't like the responsibility. Returning to his task, he was startled as Liz came flying in through the door.

"Right. This time you've got to come. I'm not waiting there on my own." Liz paused to look around.

"Good, no one here. Come on, let's go."

"Go where? And anyway, I can't. I'm on my own."

"Do you have a key? Yes. Lock the door. Come on, Mr Large, it's urgent."

Kathy Lambert arrived back. "The door's open and the heating is on. That's not good. We've got a planet to save and bills to reduce," she grumbled as she entered. "Oh, is everything okay? You look out of sorts." Closing the door, she hurried over to Liz.

"I am out of sorts. Someone has broken into Denise's house. The police want me to wait. But for how long? Gemma's at her nan's, so that's not a problem, but I couldn't find anyone else, so I thought of him." She jerked her head towards Tom. "Can he come with me? I'm not waiting on my own."

"Yes, yes. Of course. Off you go. I do hope you're not hanging around too long." Kathy lifted Tom's coat off the hook. "There you go. Don't come back, I'll lock up."

As Tom shrugged his arms into his coat, he gave a silent prayer of thanks that it was dark. He had no excuse not to go. "Where does she live? Did she, I mean." He asked as he struggled to keep up with Liz.

"I can't believe you don't know that. Lower High Street, but right down at the bottom."

Liz spared little thought for the fact that he wasn't a runner. He was barely a trotter these days. "Slow down. The burglar's not still there, is he?"

"I don't know. I didn't stop to find out. I phoned the police on the way to get you."

"Could you not have knocked on the neighbour's door?"

"Old Mr Burnham, don't be silly. He's ancient, he'd be no use."

Tom was now feeling two things, breathless because he was talking and trotting, and impressed that Liz thought that he, Tom Large, would be of use in a crisis. He didn't answer, mainly because he couldn't.

Liz slowed as they neared the end of the road. "They came in through the back. I opened the front door and thought, oh, that's chilly. But it wasn't until I got to the... you'll see. Come on." She led the way up the path and opened the front door. "You go first."

"Thanks." Tom walked into the hall and looked around, nothing seemed out of place. When he entered the kitchen, he saw the open back door and the glass on the floor. Several of the drawers had been opened. He pointed to the door on his right. "This way? Don't touch anything!"

Liz snatched her hand up off the breakfast bar and nodded agreement. When they entered the dining room, everything was in place except for the sideboard. The two cupboard doors were open as were the two large drawers, it was clear that the contents had been rifled. It was an odd piece of furniture; it had a lid, under which was a drinks cabinet of sorts, and inside there was a narrow pelmet which when pulled down revealed two small secret drawers. One drawer had been pulled from its slot and left upside down. The other was still locked. A kitchen knife and scratch marks showed how the burglar attempted to gain access.

"Nice piece, is it walnut? I've not seen one like this before. Is this the drawer you mentioned? If it is, whoever it was didn't get in. Surprising really, it's only a small lock. A bit of brute force should have done it."

"It was her mother's, a family whatsit, heirloom I think, like the house, she left everything to Denise. Where do you think she kept the key?"

"How would I know that? Come on, let's check the rest of the house."

Every room had been searched. There was some mess, but other than the back door and the drawer in the sideboard, no damage had been caused. Tom came back down the stairs, repeating his warning to Liz about touching anything, and he looked around. It had been a home. A welcoming, cosy home. He thought about his bungalow. It was warm, but not cosy, it was perfectly neat and tidy, and of course functional. But was it welcoming? He doubted it was. Another thing women were good at. Poor old Denise. He checked the time.

"It's only been twenty minutes. If they take three hours, we'll freeze to death. Shame we can't make a cup of tea."

"We could go next door and see Mr Burnham. That way, we can let him know what's happened and find out if he saw something. Tell me she wasn't murdered now."

"I don't know Mr Burnham. Do you think he'd mind? As for murder, could have been opportunistic. They heard of Denise's demise and knew the house would be empty. I don't think you should join up the dots quite yet."

"You're not listening or seeing. I'm not sure if that's intentional or not. And how would you know Mr Burnham? You never go anywhere. You should get out more. It's not good for you being cooped up."

"Have you been speaking to my daughter?"

"No. But I'm glad she nags you, too. A twice weekly flit over to the library is not a social life. Humans are social animals, we need interaction with others."

"Have you been watching David Attenborough again?"

Liz laughed. "Yes, something like that. I'd better knock, not use my key." She tapped on the door, the curtain twitched, and the hall light came on.

"Hello, Liz, what are you doing here? Who's that you've got with you?"

"Hello, Mr Burnham. This is Mr Large, one of my other clients, he's being a hero. I popped into Denise's to empty the fridge and there's been a break-in."

"Come on in. Was this about three o'clock?"

Harry took them through to the sitting room. Once he'd settled them, he told them he'd heard a noise from next door late afternoon. He'd gone to investigate, although he confessed that he was being nosy as much as anything else, but he couldn't see any lights on, and no one answered the door. Then there was the sound of breaking glass, but when he looked around, he saw Mrs Henry putting out her recycling, so he assumed it was that.

"Is there much damage? Poor Denise, she'd be turning in her grave if she had one. Do we know when the funeral is? It's not right, a young 'un like that being taken. I've been on this earth for nearly eighty-one years, by rights it should have been me. Not that I'm in any hurry, but you know what I mean. I'll miss her. Poor old Denise."

They didn't answer his questions. There didn't seem to be any point, but they agreed it certainly was poor old Denise. Having made tea, Liz drew back a curtain and perched on the arm of the chair to keep an eye out for the police. She was pleased when ten minutes later, a car pulled up and DC Connor got out. She tapped on the window and indicated they'd come out to him. Pulling on his coat, Tom thanked Harry and followed her out.

"You too. Did you come to help?" Connor asked as he spotted Tom.

"Help? No, more to make sure no one was still here. Liz came to get me. We waited next door because it's freezing in there and we didn't know how long you'd be. We've heard it can take quite a while."

"You were lucky, I'd just got back in, they gave it to me because of whose house it was. Have you had a look around? I hope you didn't touch anything." Connor snapped on a pair of gloves and entered the property first. Pushing the doors open as he went, he gave it all a cursory glance, telling them to wait downstairs while he checked the bedrooms. When he returned, he didn't seem very interested. "Probably someone taking advantage of knowing the house was empty. She had quite a bit of jewellery upstairs, and it looks like it's gone. I've got forensics booked."

"You're still saying that she wasn't murdered, that she had an accident, and by coincidence she was also burgled. Look, DC Connor, I know how strapped you are on manpower, I know all about the cuts, Mr Large keeps telling me about them, but murder is murder. Is this really what you think a good policeman should do?" Her arms akimbo, Liz was not taking any prisoners.

Connor's smile was forced. "I did listen, yes. I've told my boss, and we've asked the pathologist if it was possible. For your information there is a possibility that she was hit with a stone, because whatever her head collided with had an uneven surface, so not a baseball bat or the like, but yes, she could have been hit and the weapon and body rolled into the stream. BUT, and this is a big but, it could also possibly have been misadventure. There was no evidence of anyone being down near the stream, no footprints leading to or from the body, and about a million on the path. If a stone had been used and thrown into the water the forensic evidence would have been lost. But we can find no motive to kill Denise. Everyone we've spoken to has been shocked at the suggestion it might have been murder. Denise appeared to have no enemies. There's little to go on. But we are looking. I'm seeing her sister tomorrow. She tells me she's not seen her for a while, but you never know."

"Thank you for that, I'm glad to hear it. Now, can you break into this drawer for me? Denise kept it locked for a reason." Liz crooked her finger and led Connor into the dining room. She pointed at the drawer. "You see. He, or I suppose possibly she, tried to get in and failed, but I want to know what's in there. It's bugging me. I'm guessing no one looked when you lot were searching."

"I can do better than that. I think I know where the key is." Going back into the kitchen, Connor opened the green pastel tin on the windowsill and held up a small key. "I wondered what it was for. I didn't do the dining room. I have no idea if whoever did looked in the drawer. I'm guessing not because you had to know it was there."

Back in the dining room, he inserted the key, he turned the lock. It took some wiggling, probably due to the effort with the knife. Once open, he slid the drawer out. There were two items in there. A slim envelope with Last Will & Testament in an elaborate font, and a birth certificate.

"I told you," Liz said triumphantly. "Who gets what?"

"I'm not sure that it would be appropriate to tell you that."

"You what! You wouldn't have that if it weren't for us. Open it now or I won't tell you what else we've found out."

Tom looked at Liz from the corner of his eye. They hadn't found out anything else, had they? He nodded anyway. "I do think that's only fair. We have been doing your job for you."

Connor was desperate to know himself. If he could solve this one, he might be in line for promotion. He didn't care if it took these two to get it. He wagged his finger before walking to the table. "Not a word to anyone." Sliding the document from its envelope, he read aloud. "I, Denise Bertha Knight, blah, blah, blah. Ah, here we go, leave all my worldly goods, in their entirety, to Alana Matthews." Connor looked at them. "Any idea who that is?"

"Bertha. Poor old Denise, who would give a child a name like that? But, no. Never heard of her."

"I should have known it wouldn't be that simple." Connor looked over his shoulder. "That sounds like forensics have arrived. Remember, not a word." He slid the will back into the envelope. "You can go now. I know where to find you, but before you do go, what else have you found?"

Tom looked at Liz who shrugged. "Absolutely nothing. But we will, and you'll get the call. Whose birth certificate is it?"

Connor unfolded the certificate. "Daisy Mills."

"Relative." Liz announced. "Mills was Denise's maiden name. We'll let them in on the way out. See you later."

The journey back home was at a more leisurely pace.

Liz was thinking out loud. "We must find out who Alana Matthews is. I know the police will look, but they won't tell us, and if they don't, we won't be able to keep an eye on them. I'm not going to let this drop, you know."

"I didn't for one moment think you would. I admire your tenacity, you know, and I am happy to do my bit."

"Thank you, Tom, I'm not sure what that means, but I know it's a compliment. There's Sally, she knew Denise. I wonder if she knows who Alana is. Yoo-hoo, Sally. Hang on a minute."

Tom didn't have time to ask who Sally was as Liz sprinted off past his house, and to a young woman lifting shopping out of her boot. He trotted to catch them. They were mid conversation.

"I know it's terrible. I didn't know her that well, she came into the bank sometimes, and we both went to Blow Your Top to have our hair done and she did the Zumba class before mine. She was so cheerful and happy all the time. A pleasure to deal with at the bank. Oh hello, you must be Mr Large. Nice to meet you, neighbour. I don't think we've met before. How long have you lived in Pendry's? I'm Sally." Sally Ellis held out her hand.

"Nice to meet you. Call me Tom, about a year now."

"A year? How come I've never seen you?" Sally asked as she slammed the boot.

"Umm..." Tom became flustered. A stranger, and *that* question.

"Busy. He's an accountant, never stops work, unless he's volunteering over at the library." Liz jumped in and Tom nodded his thanks.

"Ahh. Do you know how the police investigation is going? They asked for my security recordings."

"Ahh, right back at you, as the Americans would say. Charles's Bungalow, I take it." Tom pointed at the last bungalow on the row.

"Correct. Look, I'm freezing because the heater on my car is playing up. Can we catch up another time, or you can come in and have a coffee while I unload this lot?"

"We'll come in," Liz announced.

"Will we? I thought you had to pick up Gemma."

"She'll be fine at her nan's. I just want to ask Sally something."

"How intriguing. Come on then. Grab a bag, Tom."

Tom smiled as they entered. This was something Emily could stick in her pipe. Called to a burglary, tea with Harry, now tea with Sally. He'd been out for hours, and he was quite enjoying himself.

Sally lifted the kettle, but Liz told her not to bother as she really did have to pick up Gemma. "I just didn't want you to get colder, which is what would have happened if you knew," she explained without explaining anything.

"You have to tell her what, and probably why." Tom shook his head and explained very simply that Liz believed Denise had been murdered, but the police weren't taking it very seriously, so they'd decided to do some investigating themselves. They were doing well so far. "Which brings me to what should have been Liz's question. As you knew Denise, did you know or hear her speak of anyone called Alana Matthews?" His eyes widened as Sally went beetroot red from the chest up. "What? Why are you blushing? Do you know Alana?"

"I'm not. Bit of a flush, that's all." Sally's hand shook as she lifted a tin from a bag.

Liz took her by the shoulders. "Sit down. You're too young for flushes. What do you know?"

"If I tell you, you mustn't say anything. Promise. I was going to tell them, and I got so busy with cashing up, I just forgot. You know how it is. Before I do say, you must tell me why. Who is Alana, and why is she part of your investigation?"

Tom liked it being called an investigation. It was so much better than snooping. Which was, after all, what they were really doing. He decided honesty was the best way to get more information out of Sally. "She's the sole beneficiary of Denise's will. But you must keep that to yourself."

Sally gripped the table, her eyes darted from one to the other. "I don't know whether that's a good thing or bad. I don't know if I should tell you."

Liz plonked herself on a chair. "Our Gemma's going to have to have a sleepover at this rate. I'm not going until you tell us."

"The police came into the branch today and asked for the last three months' bank statements on Denise's account and confirmed her death so the account could be frozen. I printed them off and updated the account. I was so shocked she had died. She wasn't that old, was she? Anyway, I was thinking about how awful it was and just scrolled through her account, my finger clicked the mouse by mistake. It was on a payment. Guess who to?"

"Alana Matthews," Tom announced. "And... because I know there's more to come."

"When you do that in the bank, it brings up all the transactions to that payee. Denise has been paying two or three hundred pounds to them every month for over a year. That's a lot of money, Denise earns... earned, reasonable money, but she had to keep topping up her current account from her savings to cover it. Do you think it's blackmail?"

"No. Definitely not," Tom said with conviction. "It doesn't mean that Alana isn't our killer though."

"Ah, so now you agree with me. How do you know she wasn't being blackmailed?"

"Because you wouldn't leave everything you had to someone who was blackmailing you. However, the beneficiary, Alana Matthews, might have wanted her legacy a little earlier than Denise's expected expiry date. We need to call the police."

"No. You can't, I'll lose my job. I shouldn't be discussing confidential stuff like this with my neighbours." Sally was visibly shaking. "I couldn't afford my mortgage without my job."

Tom considered this for a moment. "What time is it? Ah, just gone seven, all is not lost. Come over to mine, and we'll... Damnation!" Already walking away, Tom called back, "My place, ladies. My place. I must try to save my casserole."

"Just do the frozen stuff." Liz pointed at the bags. "I'd better call my mum. I thought I was joking about that sleepover. I'll see you at Mr Large's."

"Why do you call him Mr Large? He clearly doesn't mind his first name being used."

"Professional distance. I'd find it difficult doing men's personal stuff if we were on first-name terms."

"But he called you Liz?"

"That's because I'm his housekeeper. It's allowed the other way around." Liz left a bemused Sally to stock her freezer.

In Pendry's Bungalow, she found a very happy Tom. "Cat's got the cream then. What's made you so happy? Have you had a House moment?"

"A what? I'm chuffed because that extra hour made all the difference to my casserole, that or the just for luck herbs."

"House was that genius doctor chap, who always had a moment of clarity when trying to diagnose what was wrong. You know him, he played that daft Wooster bloke. Mum used to let me stay up to watch it. That smells lovely. Our Gemma's had her tea with her nan. I don't suppose there's enough for more than one, is there?"

"Always do too much, would you like to join me for dinner, Ms Thorne?"

By the time Sally arrived, had raved over the smell, and bemoaned the fact she couldn't remember the last time she'd eaten a freshly cooked meal that hadn't come via a takeaway, Tom was heating three plates while Liz set the table.

"It's all very simple," he told them as he dished up. "All you need to do is say that you remembered you hadn't called them while you were at the supermarket, but you'd left their card at work. As it might be important you contacted me because I'd found her, to see if I had the contact number. Simple. There you go, take those through. I think I've got a bottle of red at the back of the cupboard. Will you join me? This is turning into quite the dinner party," he added as they agreed.

An hour later, a very tired and grumpy looking DC Connor rang the doorbell. "This had better be good, Mr Large. I've been working for twelve hours straight and there's a pint with my name on it and I'm starving."

"I don't know. Sally came round for your number, and we ended up having dinner and avoiding the subject. She's very prim and proper where rules are concerned. She wouldn't discuss confidential information with us."

"Who's Sally?" Connor wiped his feet and yawned.

"My neighbour. Charles's bungalow. The one with the camera. Oh, that pleased you," He added when a smile lit up Connor's previously miserable face.

"It did indeed." Connor stepped past him and into the sitting room. "Miss Ellis, thank you so much for taking your own time to contact me, some people would have waited until tomorrow. Very conscientious and much appreciated."

"You're welcome." Sally's blush was back, and Liz nudged her.

"Don't go all doe-eyed. Tell him what you need to, we've got homes to go to." Sally retold her story. Connor's smile got wider, and he looked at Liz.

"Fantastic. You could be right, you know. This appears to give us a lead. Definitely not blackmail, or why would she be in the will, doesn't rule out murder though."

"I know, that's what Tom said," Liz announced happily. "What happens now?"

Tom groaned and covered his face as Conner's smile fell away, and Sally gasped as Liz gave the game away.

"It's okay, Sally. May I call you Sally? I know what these two are like, very persuasive. We'll forget Ms Thorne said that. What happens now is we must find Alana Matthews. Check if she has an alibi and ascertain why Mrs Knight was leaving all her money to her." Conner tried to give Sally a reassuring smile, after all it was only a small thing, and she was gorgeous. He wouldn't mind taking her out.

"I've just had a thought. Why don't you ask Andy, her ex, he's working tonight. I saw him going in The Swan when we were coming up from Mr Burnham's," Liz suggested.

"I'm too tired. Need to run this... actually, would you like a drink, Sally? A way of thanking you for putting yourself out." Connor grasped his chance. If she said no, it wouldn't be saying no to a date.

"Does that offer include us?" Liz asked. Tom barked out a laugh, and Sally nodded, her neck a worrying shade of beetroot again.

"That would be team handed and silly. You two are lucky you're not being cautioned for interfering. We'll go alone. I can see no reason why I would be, but I'm convinced I'll be talking to you tomorrow. Behave yourselves. Come on, Sally. I'm on an early start tomorrow." Connor ushered a beaming Sally out of the door.

"He's a cheeky whatsit," Liz said pulling on her coat. "Interfering indeed, he'll probably get a promotion by the time we've solved this case for him. Now, get that laptop open and start searching for Alana Matthews. With any luck we'll find her before they do."

"What are you going to do?"

"Me, I've got to go and get Gemma. It's past her bedtime. 'Night, Mr Large. See you in the morning. It's your day tomorrow."

When Emily called, Tom was still trawling through search results. He wasn't very adept at searching for people, and he closed his laptop as his phone rang.

"Hello, love, how are you? Am I glad you called. Gave me an excuse to shut the laptop."

"I'm fine, hope you're having a good day, although possibly not, I'm guessing. Are you still working?"

"No, I did a bit earlier, then went to the library. You'll never guess what?"

"Someone donated a first edition of something really valuable, and the vicar is going to flog it to do up the vicarage." Emily giggled.

"Don't be daft, although I wouldn't put it past him." Tom proceeded to bring Emily up to date on the latest happenings following the death of Denise Knight. "Then DC Connor asks young Sally if she wants to go with him. Had nothing to do with finding out who this Alana is, Sally is a good-looking young girl in a skinny sort of way, he just wanted to take her for a drink. And she went. So I had my shower, got ready for bed, and I've been searching for Alana Matthews ever since. I'm exhausted, truth be told, such a busy day. For the record because you're counting. I've been to the library, to Denise's house right down at the bottom of the High Street. Into Harry's house, he's a nice old gent, and into Sally's house. Then had Liz and Sally to dinner. They loved my casserole."

"That's fab, Dad. Well done. You'll sleep well tonight. I heard you yawn just now. But why are you searching for this Alana girl? Aren't the police doing that?"

"They are, or he says they are. Who knows, Em, they've been pretty useless with everything else."

"Well, be careful. You don't want to get yourself in trouble by obstructing the police. This could be a murder inquiry. Don't interfere."

"We're not interfering. If it weren't for us, Liz mainly to be honest, they would have her demise down as death by misadventure. You know, walking along the path at night in those heels..." Tom fell silent.

"Are you still there? Hello, Dad?"

"Sorry. Yes, I'm here, something just came into my mind and left just as quickly, I was trying to bring it back. Never mind, it couldn't have been important. How's things with you?"

"Same old. Although I'm applying for a new job. Better money and extras, I'd get health insurance for... you know. Just better. I'm filling in the application now, it's very complicated. In fact, I'd better get on with it. Sleep tight, Dad, By the way, I meant to ask, do you still take the sleeping pills, or are you weaning yourself off them now you've moved and you're getting out and about?"

Tom bristled. Why did she have to keep checking up on him? It was she who buggered off to university and then Australia, if she was that worried she should have stuck around. He took a deep breath. "I take them when I need them."

"That's good. Well after today's events you certainly won't need them. If you think you do, read a book or something, that always sends me off. Right, I'll leave you to it, and don't interfere on this Denise murder thingy. You'll get yourself worked up and probably into trouble with the police. 'Night, Dad. Love you."

"Goodnight."

Tom was still bristling when he cleaned his teeth. If Emily weren't so far away, he'd have a stern word. But she was, and it wouldn't do to fall out with her.

Sitting on the bed he stared at the drawer in his cabinet for a moment, then opened it, poured a small measure which he used to wash down the pills.

THE PUB

Tom had been working for a couple of hours when Liz arrived.

"Sorry I'm late. I'll do the bedrooms properly today, but before I do, you'll never guess why I'm late."

"Go on, surprise me. And as you've interrupted me, put the kettle on."

As Liz prepared the tea, she told him that Harry Burnham had called and asked if she could pop in. He'd remembered something about Denise and needed to tell her. Especially since Denise's death was now officially suspicious, and he didn't want to waste the police's time unnecessarily.

"I think he wanted a bit of company as much as anything else, but I went. Do you want biscuits? Don't bother answering, I'm already doing a few. Anyway, talking about company, you could always pop down and see him. You know, when you're not working, two birds and all that."

"All what? How old do you think I am? Fifty-four, that's how old. Harry is eighty-one, what on earth do you think we'd have in common?"

"In common? Loads. You're both lonely, and don't deny it, I know. Neither of you leave the house from one day to the next. Going to the library twice a week doesn't count. You both like football. Ooh. Remind me to come back to that. You both have kids on the other side of the world, his are in New Zealand though. And, of course, you're both widowers. Age doesn't come into it." Liz put the tray on the table and pulled out a chair. "Do you want me to tell you what he said, or are you going to be grumpy now I've pointed all that out?"

"I don't get grumpy. I do offended and occasionally shocked. Never grumpy. What did he want?"

"A couple of days before she died, Harry saw Denise arguing with someone by her gate. He couldn't hear what it was about, but Denise was wagging her finger at the man, and he kept leaning forward in an aggressive way, putting his face into hers. Apparently, Denise tried to push him away and he grabbed her wrist."

"Blimey, that sounds promising. What am I saying? I mean, it's good if we're looking for suspects. You know what I mean. What did he look like?" Tom closed his laptop and took a biscuit which he dunked in his tea.

"Mr Burnham was a bit wishy-washy on that because for the best part he only saw him from the back. But he's young. Which means anything below fifty. Short or no hair, and he was wearing a baseball cap backwards. And here comes the big clue, it was an Arsenal cap." Liz's eyes widened knowingly.

"And..."

"And what?"

"And, are you going to tell me you know who wears one? You said it was a big clue."

Liz deflated. "Oh. Big as in accurate. I don't know any Arsenal fans, I don't think. You've depressed me now. I thought I was getting somewhere."

"Sorry. But it's a bit like saying he was wearing Skechers trainers."

"No, it's not. Only middle-aged people wear those trainers." Liz looked at the latest addition to her footwear wardrobe. "I wouldn't wear them. Do you?" She grinned at him as she took another biscuit. "But before I go and get on with upstairs, or it will never get done, what do you think we should do?"

"To follow it up? My daughter thinks we should stop interfering and should leave it to the police. You could try calling DC Connor, he said he knew he'd be talking to us."

"But what do you think? Because I think we should carry on doing what we're doing just in case they miss something again. If it weren't for Sally, they'd not have known about the regular payments to Alana, whoever she is."

"I agree. Talking about Sally, I wonder how they got on last night? I tried for hours and couldn't find Alana Matthews. Do you think the ex knew who she was?"

"Not heard. I'll message Sally." Liz pulled her phone from her pocket and tapped it several times. "Oops, wrong button. I'm calling her." Holding the phone in front of her face, she tidied her hair as though she were looking in a mirror.

"What are you doing? I—"

"Hello, Sally. Sorry, I was meant to message you. Didn't think you'd answer."

"I'm on my break. Be quick, I've only got a couple of minutes left."

"Will do. Did DC Connor find out who Alana was last night? How did you get on by the way? He fancies you, you know. Ahh, you're blushing again." Liz turned the screen to face Tom. "Look, how sweet is that?"

"Liz. Don't be... Hello, Sally." Tom gave a wave as Liz turned the phone back.

"Hi, Tom. Behave, Liz, although I do like him. He's taking me for a meal tomorrow. But no joy on Alana, Andy Knight didn't know who she was. Look, I've got to go. We'll speak this evening. Bye."

"Don't you think that's odd," Liz put her phone back in her pocket, "that his ex is making monthly payments to someone and has been for over a year and he's never heard of them? I do."

"Not really. My wife had standing order payments to three different charities I never knew about. Don't know why she didn't tell me. Probably thought it wasn't important."

"Exactly. But leaving everything you have and paying a decent sum of money out every month is." Liz got to her feet. "This isn't going to get a proper clean done upstairs. When I'm done, perhaps we'll go to the pub. He's working this lunchtime, saw him go in on the way up."

"The pub? At lunchtime? No. Why? I'm all for poking around, but I'm not going to question someone about why they didn't know the ins and outs of their ex's life. No."

"Are you ashamed to be seen with me? And we're not going to question him, I only know him by sight, I just want to check him out. I'll buy your dinner."

"I have no idea what check him out means without questioning, and it's lunch. Get those bedrooms done, I must get on."

As Liz tutted and left the room, Tom wiped his hands on his jeans, and took a deep breath, which he held for a count of thirty. There was no way he was going into the pub, especially during the day. Disappointed in himself, he opened his laptop, but he couldn't concentrate. Quite apart from the noise that Liz was making, he was more than a bit concerned that Liz was getting too attached to him. She never mentioned a partner. Only her mother and Gemma. Although he had found the body and therefore broken the news to Liz, why was she dragging him into investigating it? He wasn't a bad looking bloke, he knew that, but he had a good fifteen years on Liz. Where she was firm and fit, he was soft and lazy. She liked to be out and about, he didn't. He rapped the table in frustration. Why was he even thinking about it? His only interest in Liz was professional. In her housekeeping capacity. His smile appeared. Housekeeper! She did make him smile, he'd give her that, but that was as far as his interest went. He wondered how to put her off. No rarely worked with Liz.

"Look at you away with the fairies. You've finished then. Good. Grab your coat, you've already got your shoes on. I'll put this away and I'll even buy you a sandwich to go with your pint."

"I am not having a pint in the middle of the day. I do have work to finish. Leave well alone, Liz."

"An orange juice and a pie, then." Liz called as she banged the door of the under-stairs cupboard shut. "Here you go."

Tom looked up as Liz appeared in the doorway, she had one arm in her own coat, and his coat in her free hand. She launched it at him. Tom caught it and looked from the coat to Liz shaking his head. "I really can't."

"Can't spare the time. Or can't walk out of that door in daylight? I know, you know, I'm not stupid."

"You know what?" Tom demanded.

"I know that you've lived here best part of a year. I don't think you left the house at all for the first six months, did you? Anyway, I've been reading up on it, and—"

"Enough. You're starting to sound like Emily. You're wrong, both of you. I'll come to the bloody pub with you, but I do have work to do. Thirty minutes, and I'm not hanging around if it's busy."

"Done."

When they left the house, Tom's lungs dragged in a deep draught of the cold air. He looked up the High Street towards the pub. It wasn't as far as Harry's had been. Minutes if he got a move on. He could do this. He shoved his sweaty hands in his pockets, and taking another deep breath, he set off. Liz linked her arm in his. He paused to look at it in amazement before shaking her off. "Get off! Are you mad? People will talk. Unnecessarily."

Liz grinned and skipped a few steps to catch up with him. "You are ashamed of me. And what people? There's no one about. Look around."

That was exactly what Tom didn't want to do. Who knew what would happen then. No, he had to keep focused. He looked back at the Swan on the sign outside the pub and set off at a steady pace, counting his strides as he went. A smiling Liz matched him step for step.

"I like a man who can get a stride on. I do hate dawdlers, don't you?"

Tom looked at the group of men smoking outside the pub as he paused at the zebra crossing. "I hate busy pubs, that's what I hate. If it's busy, I'm going home."

"It's Friday lunchtime, there will be a few in I expect, but it's lunchtime and not on a Sunday, so it won't be jammed, I doubt. Can't say for sure, I don't drink during the day either."

Tom knew she'd turned to look at him, probably wanting confirmation he didn't hit the bottle during the day. He didn't, but he wasn't going to tell her that, she was getting far too familiar for his liking. A joke and a bit of teasing was one thing, but she'd started to interfere in his private life. Not acceptable. Pulling back his shoulders, he marched across the crossing. The four men looked up as he headed their way.

"Excuse me, gents. Coming through."

Tom nodded and smiled a greeting as he walked through the middle of them and pushed the door open. The brass of the handle felt cool against his palm, and his smile returned as he looked around the bar. It was a proper pub. Not a themed bar, not a restaurant pretending to be a pub, but a proper pub. There was a dart board, a pool table, and a door next to the gents' which told of a snug beyond. It had been over ten years since he'd been in a pub and that hadn't been a proper one. As a bonus, there were also only about half a dozen people in there. His smile was almost a grin as he stepped up to the bar and looked around at Liz as the barman asked what he could get him.

"What do you want?"

"Lime cordial and soda water. Lots of ice and a slice of lemon. They don't do lime. I said I'd pay."

Tom's look told her she was doing no such thing, and he turned back to the barman. "And a half of... what ale do you recommend?"

"Strangled Badger. It's a new one. On draft, lovely woody flavour."

"A Strangled Badger? Dear me, go on then, I'm feeling adventurous." Liz climbed on the bar stool next to him and he looked at her. "What are you doing? There are a dozen empty tables in here."

"I know that, but I like sitting at the bar." Liz made a face as her eyes darted along the bar where Tom's beer was being pulled. "Pull up a stool." She lifted two menus out of a box to her right. "Looks like they have quite a choice, my treat, because you did my tea last night."

"Dinner. It was gone seven, we didn't have cucumber sandwiches, cakes, or tea. We had wine, it was dinner. But thank you."

"Well, where I come from, which is a couple of hundred yards away, we had breakfast first thing, dinner in the middle of the day, and tea when the news was on. If we were lucky and or still hungry, we had supper before we went to bed." She grinned at him as she pointed to a glass cabinet at the end of the bar. "Those pies look nice. Mr Burnham was telling me he had a lamb and mint one the other day and it was delicious. The baker on Church Road makes them."

"That does sound good." Tom scanned the menu as the drinks were placed in front of them.

"That's what I'm going to have. And a lamb and mint pie for me, and for the lady..." He looked at Liz.

"I'll have the same. But can I have a bowl of chips as well, please?"

"You can have whatever you like, darling." Andy Knight smiled at her as his finger jabbed at the highly coloured tabs on the till. "I'll get the pies out once the chips have arrived. Anything else?"

Tom had a quick argument with Liz, who gave in and said she'd pay next time, before handing a note to the barman.

"Blimey, that's cash three times in a row. Unheard of. Not seen you in here before, are you visiting?"

"No, I live up the road in one of the bungalows. Why is cash unheard of? People don't buy drinks on cards do they?"

"Of course they do. I don't think anyone under fifty carries cash anymore. My nephew reckons it's so they can keep tabs on us all the time. Where we go, what we spend, you know, Big Brother's watching and all that. Cash will become a thing of the past. In town, there's a load of places that won't even take it. Started with Covid, of course, and they've never gone back." Knight handed Tom his change.

The Covid pandemic had brought mixed blessings for Tom. If you could put the devastation caused to just about everything to one side, everyone and his mother had started doing home deliveries and that had stuck around too. You had to stay in, you would be breaking the law if you ventured out without good reason, so that all suited him fine. But Emily had been planning on coming over for a visit and that all went by the way. Tom fancied himself as a modern man, but he wasn't sure he liked the demise of cash. Even though he rarely spent any, he always kept at least fifty pounds in his wallet. "What if they only want a packet of crisps?"

"Card."

"What must their statement look like? Just a string of minor numbers. Well I never." Tom shook his head and looked at Liz who shrugged and showed him her phone case and how it contained little pockets, each one containing a card. "You too?"

"Habit now. Great in the summer, no carrying purses about. When I leave the house, all I need are keys, and my phone which has the cards. I can carry them if I haven't got a handy pocket. Easy." Liz turned her attention to Knight. "Condolences, by the way. I know you weren't together anymore, but I liked Denise, it must have been a shock."

"It was. Horrible. Like you say, been a while since we split, but I'll still go to the funeral. Pay my last respects."

"Funeral? Has that been arranged? I'd not heard anything about that. Who's organising it? I thought the police were struggling to find any family?"

Tom swigged his beer. Liz was being too forthright, he'd leave her to it.

"I meant when there's a funeral. Better serve that lot." The smokers had returned and were standing by the pie cabinet. Knight asked what they wanted as he turned away.

"He avoided the question," Liz whispered. "Did you notice that?"

"Not really."

"I said the police were struggling to find any family and he didn't say she's got a nephew or a great aunt or whatever, just ignored it."

"I don't think so. You didn't phrase it like a question, more a statement of fact."

A young girl in a striped apron appeared behind the bar carrying a bowl of chips and two sets of cutlery wrapped in napkins. "Are these for you?" She placed them on the bar as Tom nodded his thanks. "I'll get your pies."

"I'll have another go in a minute," Liz decided as she popped a chip into her mouth.

They ate in silence, only pausing to agree with Harry Burnham's opinion, that the pies were indeed delicious. As she placed her knife and fork down, Liz glanced at Tom's glass and waved to Knight.

"Another half of Strangled Badger, please."

Andy nodded and lifted a clean glass down.

Tom nudged Liz. "I didn't want any more. I told you that. Why didn't you get yourself one?"

"I've got too much left. You're nearly finished. I want another word." She looked at Knight as he brought the drink to them, and she handed him her card. "Have one yourself."

"Thanks, I'm on double whiskey." He grinned and winked. "Just kidding. Ta very much. I'll put it in the book for when I've finished." Handing her back her card, he pulled a notebook from under the bar. They watched as he turned to a page with his name underlined at the top and wrote down the amount for half a pint of Strangled Badger. He seemed to have had quite a few drinks purchased for him the day before.

"You're popular." Liz tapped the list. "You must be drunk most days."

"I wish. I have a couple when I've finished, but mostly I take the cash. Everyone needs more money."

"Agreed. I see you around quite a bit. You will let me know when Denise's funeral is, won't you?"

Knight thought Liz was interested in him, and nodding, he leaned on the bar, effectively putting his back to Tom. "I see you about too. Running here and there, you're certainly fit." He looked pointedly at her chest.

"I do my best." Liz, smiled and tried to ignore the sweat stains under the arms of his T-shirt, and the hair that could have done with shampooing. "Poor old Denise. I don't think we've had a murder in Little Compton before, have we? I wonder what they'll do with the house and stuff if they can't find any family."

As though she'd slapped him, Knight pulled his body away from her. "What are you talking about, murdered? She wasn't murdered, the police said it was misadventure."

"Oh. Did they? I hadn't heard that. I heard it was murder, sorry, I didn't mean to upset you. Well, that will make it easier when they track... was it a sister?"

Tom watched Knight's shoulders relax as he swiped the back of his hand across his brow before answering.

"No harm done. Bit of a shock, that's all. Yes, she's got a sister, Karen, not that she'll get anything, they didn't like each other. I was with Denise for what, seven years, never exchanged so much as a birthday card. Even though her and her son only live in Greater Compton. But that's families for you."

"Such a shame, I haven't got a big family but we're very close, and Tom here, his daughter lives in Australia, but they still speak every day. Blimey is that the time? I've got to be at Mrs Green's at two. Drink up, Tom."

"But I've only just got it. I'm not rushing it." Despite what he said, Tom took a big gulp.

"Okay. I'll leave you to it and speak to you later. To let you know what Sally says."

"You're not going to wait?" Tom hoped his face remained impassive, but inside his heart rate had trebled.

Liz turned to face him, linking her fingers together. "Do I need to?" she asked, her eyebrows raised.

It was at times like this that Tom wished he could be a little more forthright. She'd dragged him out against his will, having been far too personal. Now she was going to abandon him in some sort of challenge. Had she orchestrated it? He shook his head.

"No, of course not. I thought Mrs Green lived up my way."

"I need to grab my supplies first. Do you know Mrs Green?"

Of course he didn't know her. How would he? Most of Liz's clients were ancient. Tom thought he was the youngest until he found out she 'did' for Denise. She really was the most annoying woman. He wouldn't rise to her bait. He shook his head.

"Not really. You carry on. I'll finish this."

If it were possible, Liz's eyebrows rose still further, giving her a startled look. She slid off the bar stool. "Great. I'll be in touch. 'Bye, Andy, have a good weekend."

With a wave, she was gone. Tom watched the door close behind her and turned back to his drink. He took another large gulp as Andy leaned over the bar.

"I don't want to step on any toes, but are you two an item?"

Tom spluttered out some of his beer, and, dabbing his jumper, shook his head. "We are not. Whatever gave you that idea?"

"Just checking. Only she's fit, isn't she? Got a spark about her too. Is she spoken for?"

Tom looked back to the door before returning his gaze to the grinning barman. "I have no idea, she's my clean... housekeeper."

"Hopefully no, then. I'll have to keep an eye out. Think I'll have the drink now. Cheers." Knight walked away to the Strangled Badger pump.

Tom ate the last cold chip in Liz's bowl as he pondered this. Why had he never asked? Because he wasn't interested, but he should know that, surely. He knew about Gemma's verruca, and Liz's mum's diabetes, but not that. Strange. Liz must be single, she talked non-stop about everyone else, there couldn't be a partner. He didn't like the thought of her knocking about with Knight, though. Not her type at all, he wouldn't have thought. He took another swig of his drink as the door opened. Tom was dismayed to watch a dozen or so men, most wearing overalls, come in.

"Look out, the factory's closed for the weekend. Things are going to get lively. Who's first?" A cheery Knight placed his own drink back on the bar.

Tom slid from his stool as the men crowded around the bar. They were loud, overly cheerful, and overpowering. He didn't stop to finish his drink, and pulling his coat on, he exited. Now in the street, he closed his eyes and drew in a breath until his chest wouldn't expand any further. He blew it out as he looked up the road, ready to focus on his bungalow. There it was. All he had to do was cross the road and march at a decent pace. He turned back to the crossing and looked either way for traffic. His head swam and he held on to the lamppost, his eyes closed.

"You had one too many, dear? Bit early to be drunk."

Through one eye, he peered at the tiny woman swamped in a padded winter coat standing in front of him.

"No, I only had a half, thank you. Just went a bit dizzy."

"That's what my husband always said. Only had a half." She cackled. "You're the new bloke in Pendry's, aren't you? Saw you leaving with Liz earlier. Edna Pendry was a game old bird. But you wouldn't know that. She's long gone. I'll be joining her soon, no doubt. Are you going home?"

"I am. Edna Pendry? Was the bungalow named after her then?"

"Yes. I live on the way. You can carry this. I'm Alice Green. Nice to meet you." Alice handed Tom a bulging shopping bag and flexed her fingers. "Onions and vinegar. Blooming heavy. I'm doing my pickling this weekend."

Tom peered into the bag. "That's a lot of pickled onions. I like a pickled onion."

"Come on, all clear." Putting her arm in Tom's, Alice stepped onto the crossing. "I take orders. Small, that's the size of a jam jar, medium, and large. Large is a three-pint jar. I have them back because they're proper storage jars, with the rubber seal and the clip lid. Only three pounds, though. Do you want to order some? I could probably squeeze another one in."

"Go on then, I'll have a medium. How much are they?"

"Two pounds. What's your name?

"Tom, Tom Large."

Tom smiled. He wasn't marching, he was almost dawdling along. Alice couldn't walk too quickly as her bunions were playing up. On his journey home, he found out that the row of five bungalows had all been named after the first purchasers, mainly because number one Lower High Street was the next house along. The Pendrys had been a nice couple, lost their son in the war, but had a daughter who produced five grandchildren for them. Alice couldn't swear to it, but she thought Tom was the third owner.

"She was such a lovely woman, as loud as her husband was quiet. This is me. Don't worry about coming in. I'm on the ground floor. Moved in when my Jim died. Got a nice little garden out the back."

Alice had stopped in front of a modern block of four flats which had been squeezed into the gap between the old post office and the old livery stable, now an Italian restaurant Giuseppe's Pizza Parlour. He handed back her bag.

"When shall I collect my onions, and do you want me to pay you now?" He shoved his hand into his pocket.

"Don't worry, I'll pick that up when I deliver them. It'll be Sunday I expect, although you won't want to eat them for a few weeks. I recommend having them with a bit of extra mature cheddar from the cheese shop over yonder."

Tom looked across the road. A charity shop, garden and pet store, and a rather posh looking establishment with a shiny glass and polished brass frontage called Prendergast & Winstanley. A rather upmarket delicatessen. He smiled. "I've not been in the cheese shop before, is it any good?"

"Bit pricey, but the extra mature is worth it. I don't know who they sell all those different kinds of olives to, though. Stuffed with all sorts they are. I tasted one once. Disgusting. Now stop keeping me, Liz is coming, and I've got to get on with me onions. People like them in time for Christmas."

Waving as she closed her door, Tom headed for home. His pace had quickened, but his hands were dry, almost, and he didn't feel like his chest would explode at any moment. Baby steps. He couldn't wait to tell Emily.

As he approached his house a delivery van pulled up outside of Charles's Bungalow. The driver jumped out with a package in his hand.

"She's at work," Tom called. "Would you like me to take it for her?"

"You're alright, gov. I'll leave it by the pot again."

Tom watched as the driver dropped the package next to the potted hydrangea. This was another new post-pandemic practice. Delivery men never knocked anymore. You simply got a text and found, a sometimes soggy, package sitting on the doorstep. He was deciding whether he should take it in for Sally when his breath caught in his throat. The man was wearing a baseball cap. An Arsenal baseball cap. Hurrying forward on the pretence of collecting the package, but intending to get a better look, Tom stopped halfway. He'd noticed too late, the van was driving off. He'd have to get Sally to check her recordings, and update Liz. But these thoughts were lost as a client called, and Tom ended up in an in-depth conversation about what constituted capital expenditure.

Tom ate his dinner and settled down in front of the television, he was surprised to find himself waking up at nine thirty, halfway through the new detective series. That had never happened before. Not without a drink or a heavy meal. Three quarters of a pint of Strangled Badger didn't really count as a drink. By ten o'clock he had showered and was watching the news headlines in his pyjamas.

Emily called at half past.

"Hi, Dad, I did it. I sent that application off and guess what? I have a Zoom Interview next week. I'm well chuffed."

"Well done, love. I'm so pleased for you. How's things other than that? By the way, Liz called Sally this morning, and ended up on some sort of video chat by mistake. Can we do that? I don't think it was Zoom because she only intended using the telephone."

"Same old here. Yes, we can do that. There are loads of apps that do it. WhatsApp or Messenger are probably the easiest. Download them and text me which one, then I'll use it tomorrow to call you."

Opening the drawer in the coffee table, Tom pulled out a pad and jotted down the names. "Are they expensive? Especially with you in Australia."

"Free. Actually, I don't know why we haven't used them before. Probably because you didn't have the internet for so long when you moved in. Good thinking, Batman. What have you been up to today?"

Tom talked Emily through his day, smiling when she squealed with delight at the fact that he'd gone to the pub for lunch, and laughing with her at being talked into buying home-made pickled onions from an ancient dwarf.

"I'm so glad you're getting back to some sort of normal. I'm proud of you. Who knows, I might try to get over for Christmas, and you can take me to the pub for lunch. I'd better dash now. Speak tomorrow, boozer."

"Ah, Emily love, that would be wonderful. I'll even take you to Giuseppe's, it looked nice in there. Never noticed before."

Her father sounded so happy that she didn't point out that was because he'd not ventured down there before. Instead, she bade him goodnight, told him she loved him, and hung up with a smile.

Tom whistled as he went up to bed. What a day. Despite his impromptu nap he felt exhausted. Pulling the duvet over himself, he reached out and switched off the lamp. No drink, no pills, and Emily might be coming home for Christmas!

The Sister

It wasn't until Tom was putting his washing in the machine, that he remembered the delivery driver with the Arsenal cap. He hit the start button and went in search of his phone. It went straight to Liz's answer service.

"Hi, Liz, it's me. Tom or Mr Large as you insist on calling me. I was just coming in yesterday when Sally got a delivery, I was about to pick it up for her when I realised the driver was wearing an Arsenal cap. I couldn't see his face but Sally's camera might have. I'll give her a ring and let you know how I get on."

As he hung up, he realised he didn't have Sally's number. He walked to the window and looked up the road. Her car was there. It wasn't raining, and the street was empty bar a little of traffic. He could pop up. It was only ten thirty. Sally wouldn't mind, would she? He tapped his phone on his hand as he considered if he wanted to venture out for the third day in a row. He had promised himself a short walk every day. Day being the operative word. He looked at his phone. The app. He had to download the app. It might be twelve hours before he was due to speak to Emily, but he might run into difficulty. Taking a seat in the armchair he looked at the names of the apps and decided to check the reviews out. Messenger was connected to Facebook it appeared, he'd never had time for social media, a load of nonsense about nothing for the best part. He opted for WhatsApp. Once done it all seemed straight forward enough. He settled back into his chair and thought about the delivery driver. Liz was bound to give him the third degree. Mind you the recording would reveal all, or it certainly had the potential to. He'd wait until Liz called back. If she called back, she might go straight to Sally.

"I'll download Messenger too. Just in case," he muttered lifting his phone. He watched the little circle spin around as it considered his request. "Now to see what this is all about." Tom knew he was talking to himself, but he didn't care. No one could hear. "So to call all you need to do then is tap. Clever." A ringing tone sounded. Tom looked at his phone in surprise. Had he tapped it?

A young boy's face appeared.

"Hello," Tom said, smiling at the top half of the boy's face

"Who are you?" The boy asked before yawning, allowing Tom to see his chin and neck.

"I'm Tom. I thought I was calling Emily, and that was a mistake, but I got you."

"My mum is in the bathroom."

The boy's face disappeared to be replaced by a dark wooden floor. Tom could hear voices in the background. They weren't clear, but he thought it would be rude to hang up without apologising. He watched the boy's journey through the house via the flooring. Then he heard Emily.

"What are you doing? I've told you about messing about with my phone. Give it to me and get back into bed. Oh no, you've called someone, haven't you?"

"It's Tom. He's nice."

"Bed. Now. Hello."

Emily's face appeared. "Dad! What's wrong? Is everything okay? Why are you smiling? It's... I don't know what time it is, but it's not time for our call. You look okay. Very well in fact."

"And you look beautiful. So nice to see your face. I hit the button by mistake when I was setting it up. Easily done. That young boy answered, who is he?"

"Oh phew. My heart is pounding, I thought something was wrong. It's late, Dad, I was just going to bed, I'll call you in the morning. Love you."

"Okay love. Who's the boy? He was a surprise."

"Eddie. He's having a sleepover. Dad, I really must go, if there's nothing wrong that is."

"Ah babysitting. No problem. I'll see you later. Sleep tight."

Tom was smiling as he went to move the washing into the dryer. Chores done, he put the kettle on, deciding he'd have coffee and cake and then worry about Sally and delivery drivers in Arsenal caps.

He'd not taken the first sip when Liz called.

"Come up to Sally's, I'm here now."

"Hello, Liz. Would do, but I was just about to—"

"Please yourself, but we're going to get on with solving this murder. With or without you." Liz hung up.

Tom took a sip of his coffee, then a bite of his cake. Then he left them both on the coffee table and put his shoes on. When Sally let him in, she took him through to the kitchen where Liz was sitting at the breakfast bar, Sally's laptop open in front of her. Liz looked over her shoulder.

"I knew you'd come. Not much luck here, I'm afraid. But I do have news."

"Your hair's wet, did you come straight from the shower? It's not raining."

Liz's normally flowing auburn locks had been hoisted into a damp ponytail on the top of her head.

"I took Gemma swimming at the sports centre. She's gone to the cinema with her nan now. Look." Liz had the recording ready and hit the play button.

The blue van pulled up. The door opened, a torso appeared and then a cap. An Arsenal cap. The man looked to the right and an ear appeared before turning around. Then he walked back to the van and drove off.

"Oh dear, that's not a lot of use." Tom sat on a stool next to Liz. "We don't know much more now than we did before we looked at it. Only that he wears a track suit to work. And trainers."

"Ah but we do. He's not very old. I reckon mid-twenties at most."

"How do you know that, because the trainers aren't middle-aged?" Tom peered at the screen. "Can't see what brand they are."

"No, although yes as well. Look at his joggers. They are halfway down his backside. He's not fat, so it's not the builder's bum thing. He's young and showing off his boxers."

"Ah yes, you should have been a detective. You'd do a better job than DC Connor. Sorry, Sally, no offence but the police have been awfully slow. Why do young men like showing off their underwear these days, and I suppose more to the point, are young ladies really attracted to it?"

"No idea. Not my cup of tea, and none taken as it's not Patrick's detective abilities that I'm interested in. Did I say we were going for a meal tonight?"

"You did yes, where are you going, anywhere nice?" Liz replayed the recording without looking at Sally. "Do you think we could get a still for Mr Burnham?"

"Giuseppe's. I love their med-veg pizza, and we can both have a drink or two."

"I have no idea what that is. I might order a takeaway one to try. Does DC Connor live close by then if you can both have a drink?" When Sally's neck turned its usual embarrassed shade of red, Tom held his hands up. "Apologies, sorry, sorry, sorry. I didn't mean to pry. Just slow on the uptake. I'd better be getting back."

"No problem, Tom. I'm easily embarrassed. Liz, I don't mean to be rude but I've got to leave in a minute. I'm having my hair done. Thought I should make the effort. First date, and what have you."

"No problem. Just let me have a printout of that. If Mr Burnham can confirm it's who he saw, then your bloke can have a quiet word, now we know where to find him. Not today, of course. Monday. Monday when he's back at work."

Sally took a copy of the still and gave it to Liz. She saw them out and did a little dance in the hall. For one moment she thought she'd be stuck with them questioning Patrick all evening.

Outside, Liz turned to Tom. "Do you want to come and see Mr Burnham with me? I've got nothing on until early evening when our Gemma gets home."

"No, I promised I'd have a look at some stuff for Emily. She's applying for a new job, better pay et cetera." Tom found he could lie easily and wondered why he didn't do it more often. He'd fooled the police about charging the phone, and the nod of acceptance from Liz meant he'd fooled her too. It would make his life a lot less stressful when these women were badgering him. "Anyway, don't you have someone waiting for you at home? Husband, partner, you know?"

Liz stopped walking and took hold of his arm. Speaking quietly, she patted it as she spoke to him. "I'm single. Have you ever heard me mention I had a bloke? No. Look, Tom, that outing to the pub was to get information from Andy Knight. It wasn't a ploy to be with you. You're a nice-looking bloke and all that, a bit weird, in a nice sort of way, and a bit old for me, but I'm happy as I am. I don't—"

Tom shook his arm free. "Get off me you mad woman. I was just being friendly, I'm not interested in you romantically, or any way really. You're just my cle... housekeeper. Have I ever given you any reason to think otherwise? No. If you want to know who is interested in you it's Andy Knight. He was questioning me about you. So, no, not interested. Now we've sorted that out I'll go in. Have a nice afternoon."

Liz clamped her teeth together and gave the oddest smile he'd ever seen. He guessed that was her showing she was embarrassed. Whatever it was, it was weird, and she'd only just thrown that little accusation at him. He shook his head and hurried up the path. Once inside, he went into the kitchen and banged about making himself a bacon sandwich. With no butter. How did he forget to put butter on his order for delivery? "Of course," he muttered, "normal people would have just popped to the shop on the corner. But I'm not normal. I'm weird, aren't I? Everyone clearly thinks so." He banged around a little more. He bet even the beetroot-necked Sally thought he was weird. She was probably sitting in the hairdresser's telling them all about him. Well, they could all stuff it in their pipes and smoke it. He was happy.

As he took the first bite of his sandwich, he realised he actually had been happy for the last few days. Being busy and getting involved with other people. Before, not so much. Being forced into this possible murder investigation had given him something to think about, other than what to have for lunch, and why a VAT return hadn't balanced. Dry bacon sandwiches were not good for soothing one's soul. Even with a generous dash of Daddies Sauce. Throwing half of it into the bin, he pondered going to the corner shop. "It's like I'm trying to fool myself." He was mumbling again as he went in search of the cake he'd yet to finish. "And now I'm talking to myself again. Weird!"

Sitting in his chair he switched the television on. Arsenal were playing Chelsea at home, it should be a good match, but his mind was still on the events of the last few days. Was it murder? He asked himself. Closing his eyes, he went back to the beginning. He was walking along the path, and he spotted Denise's coat. He'd leaned over, put the torch on, and...

As he went back over the details of what they'd found out, he knew he was missing something. Something obvious, but crucial. It was there, dancing around in his mind, but just out of reach. Perhaps if he had a little nap it would come to him. Reclining his chair, he tried to clear his brain. The sleep technician had given several options on how to empty one's brain. Sleep technicians! They had a name for everything these days, she'd been useless too. If she had been any good, he wouldn't need the pills and he wouldn't need the alcohol.

Sleep technician or not, Tom nodded off.

"Mr Large, it's me. I'm sorry to wake you." Liz touched his hand. "Mr Large, don't be shocked, but I need your help." She gave the hand a little shake. "Tom Large, wake up. Have you been... Don't look so worried. It's only me."

A foggy brain moved his eyes from Liz to the clock. It was only half-past three. He blinked. She was back. He tried to sit up, but realising he was reclined, his arm dropped down beneath the arm of the chair and pushed the button. Slowly he was raised to a sitting position. His eyes on Liz.

"What do you want? Why are you back?" Picking up the remote, he checked the score before switching off the television.

"I need another favour. Mr Burnham said she was aggressive or agitated, or something. I've been thinking about it, and I don't really want to see her on my own. It's getting dark. I thought you might like to come."

"You do know I have absolutely no idea what you're talking about, don't you? Start at the beginning, who did Harry say was aggressive, and what are you trying to drag me into now?"

"Karen Parker, Denise's sister. She went to see Mr Burnham to see if he had a key. He told her about me and took her number, saying he'd get me to call her. He said she was most put out that he didn't have a key, because she had been told that he did. She then tried to insist he call me straight away, I don't know how he fobbed her off, but she didn't like it and got quite uppity with him. When she'd gone, he called me. Said he didn't want to give my number out to strangers."

"Uppity isn't really aggressive, is it?" Tom stretched his arms above his head and yawned. "When are you supposed to be meeting her?"

"In about twenty minutes."

"Give me a ring if she gets nasty. I'll come then."

"What use will that be? She might have overpowered me by then."

Tom started laughing. It began as a coughed laugh of disbelief, but the more he thought about it the more it amused him. "Oh dear, dear, dear," he managed to gasp. "I'd like to see someone try." He dabbed at his eyes with the sleeve of his jumper and looked out at the murky grey sky. It was nearly dark. "Get my coat then."

Grinning, Liz disappeared into the hall and minutes later Tom was winding his scarf around his neck and walking down the misty damp High Street, trying to keep up with Liz.

"Why didn't you knock? I know I said to use the key, but that's for when you're due to come. Not to pop in and out at will, you know," Tom asked, although there was no edge to his voice.

"I did knock, I also tapped on the window. You were dead to the world. You looked dead, that's why I came in. I could see you lying there, but I couldn't see you breathing. You wouldn't have been the first client I found who had popped off. It wasn't until I came into the living room I could hear the snoring."

"Oh. But what if I wasn't there? I might have been out, or I could have been having a nap upstairs."

"Out? Don't be daft. If you weren't there, I mean if I couldn't see you, I'd have phoned. Now stop worrying about stuff that's not important. What do you think she wants?"

"You didn't ask her? What if she starts going through stuff, or worse, she wants to take it away? Everything in that house belongs to whoever this

Alana is." Tom shook his head and tutted. "Is that why you asked me to come? Did you think I'd stop her?"

"I didn't ask her why. I just wanted to try to get some information out of her. About Alana as it happens, but I never thought further than that."

"Well, you should have. When she arrives, we need to establish what the visit is for. If necessary, we'll have to tell her she can't remove anything."

"Agreed."

As they neared Denise's house, they caught up with Harry Burnham.

"Hello, Harry. Nice to see you again. Bit nippy isn't it," Tom greeted him.

"It's not bad. At least it's not raining. It was nice and warm in the Swan. I went up to watch the football, I haven't got the channels to watch it at home. Three - nil. Arsenal are not on form this season. Nice crowd in though. Bit of tea now, and I'll be ready for bed. Always am if I have a bevvy during the day. Suits me fine. Won't have to have the heating on. Where are you two going?"

"To meet Denise's sister. I phoned her," Liz told him. "Now we're worried she might want to take something."

"She was in the pub. Take what? What would she be entitled to? I don't know what happened there, but she disappeared completely, ages ago. Her mother hadn't seen her for a good ten years by the time she died, and she's been dead, what? Five years must be. So that's fifteen years she's not been about that I know of, could be longer. She didn't come to the funeral. Their mother left that house to Denise. I'm sure that Denise didn't even consider her sister. If she made a will of course." Harry stopped walking and nodded. "Might be hers though. Deserved or not, she's probably next of kin, what with Denise being divorced. Hope she sells it if she gets it. I didn't like her, don't fancy having her as a neighbour."

"Don't worry about that, Harry. Denise did leave a will, left everything to one person. Can't say who, the police have asked us to keep quiet about it," Tom explained.

"Who was she in the pub with? I know Andy Knight said she lived in Greater Compton, so it's not her local, is it?" Liz joined the conversation. "Might have been waiting for us I suppose. But the football was on. Was she with anyone?"

"Yep, a young lad. A proper ginger, or it would be if he hadn't shaved it so short. Tattoos all up his arms, He was watching the football, she was on her phone. What do you youngsters find on those things? Never out of your hands. Do you want to come in and wait?" Harry stopped at the gate.

"No thanks, she's due in a couple of minutes. You go and get your tea." Liz looked at Tom. "You see, Mr Burnham has tea just like me."

"I'm saying nothing. 'Night, Harry, see you around."

Liz snorted as Harry closed his door. "Around where? I don't think Mr Burnham uses the library, does he? Oh, that might be her."

A small blue car pulled up at the curb, the tyres squealed as they collided with it. A woman heaved herself out through the passenger door. "Wait here. It won't take long."

She walked up the path, looking them up and down. "I'm Karen Parker, you must be the cleaner. Who are you?" she demanded of Tom.

Tom sensed rather than saw Liz stiffen as he watched the woman approach. Karen Parker was on the large size. The buttons on her coat strained to stay fastened, its belt flapping on either side of her, and her ankles seemed to overlap the practical flat brogues. A ladder in her tights ran from said ankle, up her calf and disappeared into the coat.

"Tom Large, I was a friend of Denise."

"Why are you here?"

"We've been out together, not that it's any of your business." Tom could see why Harry had taken a dislike, and although it went against the grain, he decided he could be rude too. "May I ask what your—"

"My what?"

"Your business here."

"How dare you? This was my mother's house. My sister has just died, and I have some stranger questioning me on the doorstep."

"I wasn't a stranger to Denise, and she never mentioned you. Not once. Mr Burnham has kindly explained that you were Denise's sister, albeit her long estranged sister, so we thought it best to meet you. But we are wondering why, and whether we should allow access."

Karen Parker's hand flew up, and a nail bitten finger pointed at him. "None of your business, mate." Dropping her hand to her side she looked at Liz. "Open up. This is nothing to do with him. I'm the next of kin, I want access to my mother's house. Now."

Liz's mouth opened but Tom stepped forward answering on her behalf.

"I'm not sure that you are the next of kin, as I understand it from the officer investigating Denise's murder, the will specifies only one beneficiary, and that's not you. You might want to speak to the police. Perhaps they'll give you access."

"Murdered? Why did you say that? She fell over and hit her head, that's what I heard. You're stirring up trouble for the sake of it. Who are you again? Because it seems to me like you're interfering in my family's business. I don't like that." The nail-bitten finger was jabbing the air again. "You'd better not cross me. And you," she looked Liz up and down, "you, have wasted my time. I don't like that either. I won't forget it."

Once again, Liz opened her mouth to answer, she even took a step forward, but Tom grabbed her hand.

"You're a very unpleasant woman, do you know that? Do you even care? You won't be going in there tonight, but rest assured I'll let the police know of your interest. Goodnight." Still holding Liz's hand, he pulled her forward, but Karen blocked their way.

"You let whoever you want know whatever it is that you're making up in that weird little brain of yours, but I'll tell you this. That house is mine. She was my mum, and our Denise might have wrapped her around her little finger, but she's not here now, is she? And I'll tell you another—"

"Everything alright, Mum? What's happening?" The driver's door of the car opened, and the head and shoulders of a young man appeared. He was wearing an Arsenal cap. "You having some bother?"

"Get in the car. We're going," Karen snarled, and looking back at Tom, added. "We'll be back." Turning, she waddled back to the car, grunting as she climbed in, before slamming the door closed. Seconds later the car screeched away.

"She trapped the belt of her coat in the door. That'll be filthy when she gets out. Horrible woman. Shall we go?" Tom realised he was still holding Liz's hand, and letting it go started down the path. Liz didn't move, and he turned back. "Are you coming?"

"What just happened?" Liz's hands were on her hips. "You went all chest beating, macho on me, and well done, by the way. Then our prime suspect got out of the car. She knows she's not in line for that house, you could tell, and she threatened us. Aren't we going to discuss any of this?"

"Probably, I doubt you'll sleep on it, but I'm freezing, I'm not standing here to do it."

"I told you she was a bad 'un." Harry appeared on his doorstep. "I was watching. Well done, Tom. That told her. Glad he didn't come nearer, he was mad enough in the pub. I reckon he could be trouble. Told Andy he'd lost some serious money. Fancy betting on a football game. Madness, anything could happen in a game of football. Are you off?"

"Hang on a minute. Harry, did you just say he was talking to Andy Knight?" Liz walked down the path and went to Harry's gate.

"You called me Harry. About time. Yes, him and her were sitting at the bar, chatting to him. I was on the table next to 'em. His language was disgusting. In front of his mother too, not that I knew that's who she was then."

Tom joined them. "You told Liz you saw someone arguing with Denise a while back, did—"

"It was him! How did I not work that out? No wonder she didn't leave her family anything. Rotten bunch." Harry shivered. "I've got to go in. My tea's nearly ready, and I'm freezing. See you next week, Liz, might catch you around then, Tom. Have a good night."

They called goodnight and headed back up the High Street.

"We need to speak to the police. The question is, does it warrant ruining DC Connor's night, not to mention Sally's, or do we leave it until tomorrow?" Tom asked. "After all, there's nothing they can do, other than question them. We've got no proof of anything, and Harry will be kept from his bed until all hours if they decide it's worth following up. I wish we had more to go on."

"I think you're right. We should leave it until tomorrow. If they have done anything, or they did murder Denise in the hope of getting the house, they're going nowhere. They don't know we're onto them. And, of course, being horrible isn't grounds for arrest." Liz stopped walking. "I need to turn off here. Got to go and get the car to pick Mum and Gemma up.

Mum's turn to do the roast tomorrow, I might pop over, but if not, I'll see you Monday. If you've got time, have another look for Alana. I will too once I've got Gemma to bed. She'll have been sugared up to her eyeballs. 'Night, Mr. Large."

"'Night Liz."

As Tom walked away, he wondered what sort of car Liz had. He didn't even know she could drive. He missed driving, he'd got rid of his car years ago. Wasn't worth paying the tax and insurance on as he never used it. Perhaps he'd get a new one once he sorted himself out. He was getting there, after all, here he was out for the... He realised he'd lost count of how many days he'd been out in a row. Shoving his hands in his pockets, he whistled as he continued his journey. He glanced into Giuseppe's as he passed. The restaurant was still in semi-darkness, they hadn't opened for the evening yet, but the light was on by the pizza oven. Two men in overalls were moving about behind the counter. No doubt preparing delicious toppings for the pizzas. His stomach rumbled at the thought. Half a dry bacon sandwich was not enough for a growing man. For the remainder of his journey, he thought only about what pizza he would order, and where he'd put the discount leaflet he'd received.

As he had napped that afternoon, despite polishing off a huge and very tasty pizza, Tom didn't feel tired as he got himself ready for bed. He stared at the drawer in the cabinet as he pulled on his dressing gown. He had hoped to give that a miss again tonight. Snatching up his phone he went back downstairs. If Emily was going to make a video call, it would be better if he wasn't in bed. He flipped through the channels and stopped as the face of Joan Hickson appeared in a black felt hat. He liked a good Agatha Christie, and Hickson was without doubt the best Miss Marple. He'd put it on hold when Emily called.

As Miss Marple questioned the vicar, his phone beeped. It was a message from Emily saying she was tied up and wouldn't be able to call for at least two hours, and to let her know if that was too late. He told her that it would be fine and reclined his chair. He remained like that until Emily called and he switched off the television.

"Hi, Dad, sorry about that. Couldn't change things around today. How are you? You look good. Is that the dressing gown I bought you last year?"

"It is. Cosy, and I need cosy at the moment. You look well, love. So nice to see you, can't believe we didn't do this before. What've you been up to?"

"Just errands, but all had to be done this morning. What about you?"

"Been quite busy for a Saturday. Did the washing, popped into see Sally, she's the neighbour up the road, and she's got a hot date tonight with the DC investigating Denise. Then Liz asked me to go to Denise's with her, and I had to see her sister off. Horrible rude woman, but her son wears an Arsenal baseball cap, so we'll speak to DC Connor once he's finished his date with Sally, which means tomorrow as he was staying the night so they could both have a drink. Then I had a pizza for dinner. Ate the whole thing, and I've just watched a Miss Marple. This solving murder game is all a case of hearing what's not being said, reading between the lines, and picking up on seemingly innocent actions. I'll have to up my game."

"You should step away from the murder, is what you should do. Don't get me wrong, I'm glad it's getting you out of the house, but I doubt the police will thank you."

"We're not interfering, just following up hunches, which as I mentioned, we'll pass over. I'll tell you what I did think about tonight though."

"Will I be excited?"

"Don't know it won't really affect you, what with you being over there, but I think if things carry on as they have been, I'm going to get myself a car."

"Wow. That's brilliant, you haven't had a car for... six, maybe seven years? Ah, I'm so pleased, Dad. You'll be coming over here before you know it."

Tom's stomach lurched at the thought of being trapped on an aeroplane with all those people, but he smiled. "You never know, stranger things have happened. Have you been preparing for your interview? I know that used to stress you out."

"Yep. Keep your fingers crossed. It's going to be a challenge. It's a long time since I had an interview. But the money and the benefits are too good to ignore. I can't get a decent paying job around here. Too small a town, so I've got to shake things up a bit."

"All you can do is give it a go, if it doesn't work out you can change again."

"True. You just yawned. I'll let you get to bed."

"No, no. It's okay. Unless you're busy of course."

"I am today, sorry, but hold on to your hat. Might have a surprise for you tomorrow. 'Bye. Love you."

She had gone before Tom could question her. He smiled as he made his way to bed. It could only be a good surprise, or it would be a shock. Opening the drawer, he took out the pills and swallowed them. He had to sleep, but perhaps not with the bottle tonight.

The Daughter

Tom was looking in the freezer when Liz arrived. He was sure he'd ordered a ready meal. He wasn't in the mood for cooking and was sure he had a giant Yorkshire pudding filled with beef and gravy with which he could have some fresh vegetables. He turned to look at her.

"I heard you knock that time. Looking for something that's not there." He shut the freezer door. "Tea, coffee, or are you here to drag me off somewhere?"

"Would you come?"

"Depends on why and where?"

"Nice to know." Liz walked through to the dining room and pulled out a chair. "Coffee, instant will do. I've prepared the veg, the meat's in on low, and Gemma has gone to the park with next door. I thought we should run through everything and work out how to get the police to act on Karen and her son."

"I ran through everything last night. Without more clues, we're not going to solve this. The best we can do is keep on at the police to do something. Find Alana for instance. I didn't try again last night, didn't know where to start."

"Get a notebook and sit down. We'll write everything down in the order that it happened. Tick off stuff that we know about and make a list of what the police need to do. He's still up there by the way, his car is still parked next to Sally's."

"We are not going to badger him on a Sunday. No. Quite apart from anything else, it will ruin Sally's day too."

"I never said we were. I was just passing on information. Get a pad."

"You never *just* do anything, madam. I've come to realise that."

Coffee made, pen and pad at the ready, Tom looked at Liz. "Where do you want me to start? Monday or Tuesday?"

"Monday, although it all started before that of course, but that's when she told me about her stalker. Ten o'clock by the bakers. She was frightened."

"Monday, ten am, Denise is worried about a stalker." Tom wrote the reasons in brackets before moving on. "Monday pm Denise seems normal. Her nails are red, her roots are showing."

"What does that mean?" Liz looked like she was sucking a lemon. "I don't know what relevance that has. Why did you notice that?"

"Didn't I say? Because when I found her, I noticed her nails were pink. It was the blood I think, it was so dark. Same colour as her nails I thought, but when I looked at them, they weren't red anymore, they were pink."

Liz's eyebrows shot to her hairline. "And her hair? Why did you notice that?"

It was Tom's turn to resemble a gargoyle. "Because of the blood. It had stuck her hair to her face. I couldn't see her face, but her hair was very blonde against the blood. I noticed her roots, which she'd been complaining about the week before, were gone. I was well informed of Denise's beauty routine. We didn't have much in common, so she did all the talking. She hadn't mentioned them on Monday though, probably because the children had come in."

Liz's finger beat out a tattoo on the table. "You're mad. Have you not worked it out?"

"Worked out what?" Tom had been wondering whether he should show Liz the photos he had taken of the body, he hadn't looked at them, but thought he might have to show her so she could see how obvious these details were. He was relieved when it appeared that wouldn't be necessary.

"One she gets the Cruella coat cleaned, two, she gets her hair done, three, she's had her nails done, four, she goes from terrified of a stalker, to happy enough at work." Liz was counting the clues off on her fingers and held up her thumb. "And five... are you there yet?"

"No. But Kathy, the vicar's wife, did say Denise was particularly jovial when she saw her on Tuesday evening. That would only have been hours before... you know, whatever happened to her. I'll note that down." Tom jotted down: Hair, Nails, and Happy under the heading Tuesday.

"I'm going to give you another chance because I know you're an intelligent man. Ask yourself why?"

"Why she was happy, or why she got her nails et cetera done?"

"Both."

Tom thought about it and shook his head. "Nope. Nothing."

Liz rolled her eyes. "Men. Why was Sally going to have her hair done?"

Tom frowned. "Because... Oh my God. She had a date. All thoughts of a stalker forgotten. But who? And, more importantly, did he kill her?" Tom clicked his fingers and pointed at Liz. "That was what I couldn't recall. Heels."

"What about them?"

"She was wearing ridiculously high heels. And in your words," he held his hand out to make a counted list, as Liz had done, "one, she only told me the week before she'd bought some wedges because her ankles couldn't cope with heels anymore, and, two, why would someone go for a walk along the stream in heels? It's the end of November. I wore my wellies because that path is muddy without all the rain we've had." Dropping his hand onto the table, he shrugged. "That's it, I only had two."

"But even more relevant, how could anyone explain that away? Mind you, whoever did this had to get her up there. Why would she have gone? In heels, I mean. Hmm. Make a to-do list too. We need to go to the hair salon and the nail bar. Neither of which we can do until tomorrow. I wish it wasn't Sunday."

"Hang on a minute, we should hand this over to the police, they should be doing that, not us. I'm beginning to agree with Emily. That said, of course, they're supposed to be trained in this stuff. Why has no one brought it up? Do we know if they've traced her movements that evening?"

Liz looked under the table. "Get your shoes on, although the rain's stopped, you could wear your slippers." Getting to her feet, she picked up her phone. "Come on, chop chop. I might have done my bit, but Mum will still be cross if I'm late. Who knows how long this will take."

"What will?" Despite having no idea where he was going, Tom went to the hall, and sitting on the stairs put on his shoes. Going out was bad enough, but in slippers, no.

"Sally's, of course. DC Connor is still there. He can start giving us some answers."

"Oh, don't you think we should check if they—"

"Nope. My life is being disrupted, yours has been turned upside down. This is his job. It's a murder, they should be on it twenty-four seven, not out eating pizza and... I'll leave that to your imagination, I don't want to make you blush." With a laugh she was out of the house and knocking on Sally's door before Tom had locked his own.

Sally had seen Liz march past the window and knew she'd be knocking. She looked over to Patrick Connor, who was getting ready to leave. "Your amateur meddlers are here." Wincing, she wondered if Liz had heard her. But it's how he referred to them. She quite liked them, all her friends lived in the city. It was nice to have someone you could chat to closer to home. Smiling, she opened the door.

"Hi, Liz, I saw you coming. No Tom... Oh, hi, Tom. Is it me or Patrick you're after?"

"DC Connor, we've got crucial information and we want answers." Liz looked up the hall as Connor appeared from the kitchen carrying a holdall. "We need a word. We can go to Tom's if Sally would rather..."

"I was just leaving." Connor pulled his coat from the banister.

"Good, because that will save us bothering Sally, you can pop into Tom's first."

"I can't, not if this is about Denise Knight. I'm not working that case any longer, I've been transferred to another one. Hit-and-run in Dursley."

"Why? What did you do wrong?" Liz's stood arms akimbo, looking like she wanted a fight.

"Nothing. Another incident occurred and the team had to be split. Sorry, Ms Thorne, but I follow orders, I'm not allowed to pick and choose."

"Who's in charge then, and how do we get hold of him?" Tom stepped closer to Liz. "It is urgent."

"I was never in charge. Only of the legwork. That would be my DI. DI Truscott. Phone the local number tomorrow, they'll put you through."

"Tomorrow! Tomorrow! This is a murder investigation, Connor. Do you do that part time now?" Tom's arms mirrored Liz's.

Connor's chest rose with the deep sigh. "Only you think it's murder. We are following up on all information that comes in, but nothing at the moment, or up until yesterday lunchtime anyway, gives rise to it being a murder."

"So, you've only just been taken off that murder, to deal with another one, and yet they let you clock off and bugger off for the weekend. Damn jobsworths the lot of you. No wonder your success rate is so low, this country is ruined. Have none of you got a shred of pride in your work, a shred of compassion for the families who have lost someone they loved?" Tom had raised his voice. "Disgusting."

Connor put his coat back on the banister. "For the record, Mr Large, I have worked the last eleven days, twelve, fourteen hours sometimes, I needed a break. I'm back on at six tomorrow morning. No, we haven't got enough staff, and yes, someone, not me, will be working on both cases. It doesn't change the facts about what happened, to whom, or when, or why, because I had a day off."

"Are we coming in then?" Liz tried to lighten the mood. "You put your coat back, you want to know what we know, perhaps we could swap information."

"I'm not swapping anything, but come in, if that's okay, Sal? Tell me what you think you know, and I'll point you in the right direction."

"I don't mind. Haven't got anything on today. I'll put more coffee on."

Sitting around Sally's table, Liz walked Connor through what they'd found out, and what they believed. "So, you see," she concluded, "Denise thought she was on a date. What we don't know is with whom? What have you lot found out about her movements that evening?"

DC Connor shook his head as he chewed his lip. "Nothing, absolutely nothing. She left work at two o'clock and disappeared. Mr Burnham didn't see her come home or go out again."

"Well, she did, because she was joking with the vicar's wife. Although that could have been when she finished work of course. What was she wearing at work?"

"When was this? I don't know about that, and off the top of my head I don't know what she was wearing." Connor looked at Liz's arms, they were challenging him again.

Tom jumped in. "We can't expect you to know everything, and I don't know what time she saw Kathy. I didn't think to ask."

"Let's leave that there for a moment." Liz blew out a breath as though releasing the unsaid. "What have you, they, found out about Alana?"

Connor's mouth opened and shut as though he couldn't decide whether to tell them or not.

"Nothing?" Liz's eyebrows were up in disbelief. "How hard can it be with all that you have at your disposal, cuts or no cuts?"

"They do know. They've just not spoken to her yet. Have you?" Sally tried to defend her new beau.

"That's good, what did you find out?" Liz looked at Sally with her most encouraging smile.

As Connor said he couldn't reveal that, Sally jumped in. "She's Denise's daughter."

Connor allowed his head to hit the table and Liz, for once, was rendered speechless. Sally's neck transformed.

"I shouldn't have said, should I? Oh, no, I'm so sorry."

Pulling back his shoulders, Connor reached across the table and took her hand. "Don't be. They deserve it, they've done better than we have. The thing is, although we found her via that birth certificate, Denise had her adopted, hence the change of name, we can't find her. Not yet. Her adopted parents divorced. Her father ended up working in Canada. We've spoken to him. Mother died about three years ago, and Alana went to see her dad, then went off travelling. The last time he heard from her she was in Greece and planning to come back to England. That was over a year ago, and he found out via his sister. He and Alana fell out while she was there.

He'd not spoken to her since. But we spoke to the aunt, and she says Alana was going to look for her real parents."

"Hence the payments to her account. You see, Patrick, you have done something." Liz smiled at him.

"And before you suggest it, yes, we checked the address registered to her bank account, it's still the family home. Now sold. She never changed it, maybe because it was an online account. But rest assured, we are looking."

"Alana isn't Andy Knight's daughter, so the big question is who's the father? What did the birth certificate say?"

"Nothing. No father named."

"Blimey. She might find out who if she did one of those DNA tests. Would Harry know, do you think? There must have been gossip, this is a small village, and he lived next door," Tom suggested.

"I don't think so, wouldn't he have said when he was going on about the next of kin? I think he would. Where was she born, Patrick?"

Patrick smiled. "You're good at this. Birmingham. That's all we know. Born and adopted within months. Look, I do have to go, I'm playing football this afternoon, haven't for months. I don't want to miss it. But I will call my DI and tell him about Craig Parker, that's Karen's son's name, and your theory about the date, and hair et cetera. I promise if I hear anything I'll let you know."

"Okay. Thanks. Sorry about earlier, I get quite passionate. Thanks, and sorry, Sally."

Liz was opening the door before Tom got to his feet. She was standing by his gate as he closed the door behind him.

"You move so quickly, do you know that? I was surprised you left without further comment. Thought you'd at least want another question answered or ten."

"I must... Oh here comes Alice. Probably got your pickled onions. Her flat stinks now. Ask her in. She'll like that."

"I'm sure she would, but you're up to something. What?"

Liz didn't answer as she was already greeting Alice Green. "Hello there. Are you making your deliveries? Here let me take that." She rushed forward and relieved Alice of her shopping bag. "Blimey, that's heavy you must have muscles like Popeye."

"Not any more. Only two more to deliver now. Tom and the vicar. I deliver a personal one, and they collect the little ones for the Christmas fete. You can have yours when you come next week."

"Looking forward to it." They'd almost reached Tom and Liz winked at him. "Mr Large was just going to make me a cup of tea. Do you want to join us?"

"Yes, go on then. I'm a bit early for church."

Greeting her with a smile, Tom opened the door. He knew Liz had been intending to go home. She was obviously after some information. Once Alice was settled at the table and the kettle was on, she looked around.

"Nothing like it was when Edna was here. But then it wouldn't be. She had stuff everywhere. There was a glass-fronted cabinet there, choc-a-block with china. It was her grandmother's, must have been ancient. There were shelves above it, and one day one of her grandsons, Bill I think it was, was looking for something, probably food, he was a chubby lad, and he climbed onto it to have a look in the tins on the shelves. His mother came in and caught him, don't know how he managed it, but the whole thing went over. Not one piece left whole. He got a hiding for that. Couldn't sit down in Sunday school. Funny what you remember."

Liz cut to the chase. "Which is why I wanted to speak to you. You have the best memory of anyone I know. I wondered if you could help us."

"If I can. Help you with what?" Alice put three spoons of sugar into her tea and stirred.

"I met Denise's sister yesterday, you'd know her as Karen Mills. She wasn't very nice, and I know they hadn't spoken for years. What do you remember about her?"

"Always had a chip on her shoulder that one. Led her mother a right old dance, their father died when they were young, and Jean had a job keeping control of them. I remember going to the fair with Jean late one night in search of them. They used to set up on Jenkins' farm. They'd gone up at tea-time the pair of them, it was gone ten and they'd not come home. Found 'em on the dodgems with a load of young lads. The mouthful that Karen gave her mother was disgusting. She got a piece of my mind, I can tell you. I wasn't scared of her. She never spoke to me again. If we happened to pass, she'd look at me like I was dirt on her shoe. Didn't worry me, but it embarrassed her mother. Denise got on with Karen alright when they were younger. But Denise was the good girl, she'd apologise for Karen, always made up an excuse for her. I don't know what happened to make them fall out. But it was big. Denise left home over it. Jean was in tears when I mentioned I'd not seen her about. Told me she'd fallen out with Karen and gone to live with her aunt. Then Karen had a falling out with her mother and she left. Jean was on her own for a while, but then Denise came back. Karen never did though. Don't know where she went, but I've heard she lives up in Greater Compton now."

"What a shame for their mother. When was all this?"

"I don't know, twenty-odd years ago I suppose. Must have been because Denise was back for the Millennium party. I remember she helped me set up the buffet."

"And what about boyfriends, did Denise and Karen fall out over a boy, perhaps?"

"I doubt it. You've met Karen, can't see a bloke being interested in her when Denise was about. Karen also had a nasty mouth on her. I do remember Jean being worried about Denise back then. Said she'd become secretive, and she was worried Karen was dragging her into trouble, but that passed. When Denise came home, she just settled down. Not sure if she had a boyfriend until she took up with Knight. I don't like him much, wasn't good enough for her in my opinion. Her mother's too. She told me he was a gambler, and that not many marriages survived when a gambler was involved. I always thought it was a shame she'd never had children. Denise would have made a lovely mother, but probably for the best, what with her dying like that. Anyway, what do you want to know?"

"Nothing specific. I didn't like Karen, she was a bully and chalk and cheese with Denise. Wasn't she, Mr Large?"

Tom nodded. "Horrible rude woman. If I hadn't been told, I'd never have believed the two of them were sisters. Did Denise have any boyfriends before she went to live with her aunt? I doubt she would have liked leaving them because of her sister."

"Probably, I didn't keep track. Oh, she was walking out with young Jim for a while, but he went off to university. His family lived in the big house top of Hawthorne Lane. I thought he would go back there, but when his mother died his father had to go into a nursing home because he kept wandering off." Alice tapped her temple. "His mind had gone. Don't know if he's still alive. Jim sold the big house to a family from Cirencester and built that modern thing down by the estuary. Don't tell him I said so, but I reckon it looks like a warehouse with windows. Him and his wife must like it though, they're still there."

"Who's Jim?" Tom asked. "I've not been here long, but I can see Liz knows."

"Ha. That's because Denise went to work for him. Whatever happened, it was water under the bridge between them two. Jim is the Amery of Amery and Cheriton." Alice emptied her cup. "I love a good chat, but I'd better get off to church. That'll be two pounds please. You don't have to return the jar, but it would be appreciated. You might want to save any you get for me too."

Liz helped Alice up while Tom fetched the money. "I'm looking forward to those. How long before I can make a start, I'm going to the cheese shop tomorrow."

"Give it at least a fortnight. I might pop up again, I enjoyed that. So many memories, and you don't get fed up with them as you've not heard them before."

"I'll look forward to it, Alice. Do you want me to see you across the road?"

"I'm not that useless, lad. I can see a car coming. I only asked you to carry my bag because I hadn't met you yet. Didn't know if I liked you."

"Oh, I see. And there was me thinking I was being a gentleman. How did I do?"

"You're alright, I wouldn't have drunk tea with you if not. I'm fussy." Alice winked at him and went to stand at the edge of the road. She waved her free hand both ways. "Nothing coming," she called as she walked across. "'Bye."

Tom laughed as he closed the door. "What a game old girl. I like her too." He turned to Liz. "What do you think? Is Jim Amery Alana's father? It's obvious Denise went to stay with her aunt to have the baby. If there was an aunt of course."

"I don't know. Add Amery to the list of to-dos. I really must go. Might just get home before I get a clip around the ear."

Opening the door he'd just closed, Liz stepped past him. "I'll see you tomorrow. Think it all through, what else do we need to do? I'll write down a list of suspects."

"We can't just..." Tom shook his head as Liz raised her hand, waving away whatever he was about to say. "'Bye, Liz."

Tom went back to the notes he'd started making with Liz and spent an hour typing them up and adding theories in red. He printed a copy and read through it. He was glad Denise had found her daughter, he'd be lost without Emily, even though she lived so far away. He wondered what her surprise might be and smiled. He'd give her a surprise too. Amazing even himself, Tom went into the hall, grabbed his coat and set off before he could change his mind. He was going to buy butter.

Hands in pockets and head down he walked briskly. His fists were clenched, and his heart was beating fast, but he felt in control. It took him three minutes to reach the express supermarket, and he stepped over the threshold with a triumphant smile. He called good morning to the chap at the cash register. Having never been in the shop before he had no idea where the butter was. Picking up a basket he wandered up and down the aisles. By the time he reached the checkout, his basket was bulging.

Tom was still smiling when he exited the shop. That had been easy. No more home deliveries for him. Next outing he might brave a quick half of Strangled Badger. He looked across at the pub knowing it wouldn't be today. His eyes widened. Standing outside smoking were Andy Knight and Karen's son, Craig.

When Tom arrived home, he found his excursion had taken twenty minutes. He would definitely be going out tomorrow. He stored his groceries, and updated the notes he'd prepared, printing the updated copy. Having already decided not to update Liz until the next day, he popped his ready meal into the oven, and settled down to the England v New Zealand rugby match. He couldn't wait for Emily's call. They'd be surprising each other.

Emily texted him at nine thirty when he was in the shower, he didn't pick it up until he'd settled himself in front of the television at ten. His heart fell as he read it, she'd been up most of the night with a dicky tummy and was going back to bed in the hope of grabbing some sleep. She loved him and she would call the next day. He sent her a reply telling her he hoped she felt better soon, and that he had a surprise for her too.

Getting to his feet he went through the nightly ritual of switching everything off and trudged up the stairs. He looked at the bedside cabinet. Not tonight. He went back down to the bookcase and collected the Val McDermid he had yet to start. He'd see if Emily's suggestion worked. At the end of chapter five he was engrossed but still wide awake. Opening the drawer he poured a small measure, popped two pills, and settled back down to chapter six. When he awoke the next morning the light was still on, and the book lay on the floor next to the bed.

THE HAIRDRESSER

L iz arrived at nine thirty, he'd hoped she would be longer as the account he was trying to bring into some sort of order was proving particularly irritating. The proprietor of All Things Bright was either a little dim, or had totally ignored his instructions when he'd sent the spreadsheet last year. If anything, this year's attempt seemed to be even more chaotic.

"Liz, I'm sorry, but I do have to work. It's too early to go dashing off anywhere."

"I know that. I've got to do two clients first, I just popped in to ask if twelve thirty would suit you? Look, I've not even taken my coat off."

"Perfect. Here, take this. Check if I've missed anything, but not here, not now. I must get this done."

Taking the neatly typed up log of events, Liz nodded as she read through it.

"I said not now."

"And you knew that wouldn't happen, because... what were they doing?"

Tom closed the lid of his laptop, a smile threatened. "Who?"

"Don't give me that. You know exactly who I mean. Andy Knight and the Arsenal cap."

"Just smoking. It was probably totally innocent. A chance encounter perhaps."

"Don't be ridiculous. Andy Knight knew where they lived. Mr Burnham told us Karen and son had been sitting at the bar talking to him while the football was on, and on Sunday lunchtime he's back again. I wonder if Karen was in there. Even if she wasn't, why our pub? They've got three in Greater Compton."

"Have they? I've never been, I might take a trip there one day. Is there anything else there?"

"Not really. The little industrial estate has a discount store there. That's useful if you want curtains, rugs or cushions. But not anything else we haven't got here. Oh, the doctors are there of course. And the sports centre. Anyway, listen to you planning trips out. Where did you go yesterday?"

"So, quite a bit in Greater Compton then. I'd run out of butter and didn't have anything in I fancied. Ended up with a chicken korma."

"A curry on a Sunday, how cosmopolitan. Look at the time, I'd better dash. See you at twelve thirty. I expect he's been barred." Liz was in the hall with her hand on the door.

"Who has?"

"Craig. Karen's son. If he's got a temper and a gambling habit, he might have been barred from the pubs in Greater Compton."

"That's a big jump."

"It's a theory. That's what we need, theories to prove or disprove. Come on, Tom. Keep up." With a flash of a smile she was gone.

Tom smiled as he went back to his laptop. She'd called him Tom. He wondered how long that would last. She was funny, suggesting that the pubs in... Tom slammed the laptop shut and picked up his phone. His face fell as he scrolled through his photos. It was the first time he'd looked at them. There were eight in total. Three of Denise, two of the surrounding area, a gum wrapper, a crumpled packet of cigarettes, and yes, half a betting slip.

Opening the laptop, Tom updated Denise's log with the new heading: Evidence. Craig was a gambler? Both Andy Knight and Craig smoked? He didn't bother printing it off, he'd wait until Liz came back. He was sure there'd be plenty to add by the end of the day.

By the time Liz arrived, Tom was ready to leave. He'd been pacing up and down the hall for ten minutes. His eagerness to carry on had raised his blood pressure, now despite being ready to leave, he wasn't sure that he could. Oh boy. In through the nose, out through the mouth. He was becoming breathless, probably shouldn't be marching at the same time. When Liz knocked and opened the door, he was sitting on the bottom of the stairs, his head between his legs. He looked up.

"I'm not sure I can come, I feel weird." He snorted a laugh. "No change there then."

Walking up to him, Liz put her hand on his forehead. "Your temperature feels normal. Even though you're inside with your coat on. What sort of weird?"

Tom didn't know how to explain the feeling of heat that started in his feet and worked its way up through his body. His heart would pound, his head would spin, and his mind would scream NO. Not in a way that Liz would understand, anyway. So he compromised.

"I came over all dizzy. I don't think I should stand up. Certainly not walk."

"Then it's just as well I brought the car. Here let me help you." Grabbing him by the elbow, Liz hauled him to his feet. Tom drew in a deep breath and nodded. "And walk." Liz took his keys from the table as they passed it. As he pulled the door shut, Tom nudged her.

"You'd better be a good driver because Amy always said I was an awful passenger.

"I'm brilliant. Who's Amy?"

"My wife? Surely you know that. I mention her all the time."

"You do. But never by name. Always my wife."

"Do you know I didn't know that? Progress do you think?"

"Absolutely. Jump in."

Liz had indicated the car parked where Sally's would normally be. Tom did a double take, it was a shiny dark blue Alpha Romeo. It was a few years old, but even so Tom was shocked.

"This isn't what I was expecting. I thought more a Micra or perhaps a Mini. I like these."

"Me too. Get in." Liz smiled as she fastened her seat belt.

He'd forgotten he didn't want to leave his house.

"Where first, hair salon or nail bar?"

"The closest."

"Hair salon it is. It's on the row of shops at the top of the estate. I doubt you know they exist."

"I do as it happens, have you not heard of Google? I'll let you do the talking because I don't do ladies' hair."

"You don't do your own very well either."

Liz was a very skilled driver, and by the time they arrived at Blow Your Top, Tom was totally relaxed and enjoying the feeling of freedom. They went into the salon. One old lady sat with her head buried under a huge dryer, a young woman was sweeping up hair, and a girl in her late twenties was putting the finishing touches to an elderly man. She brushed the back of his neck, swept off the cape, and lifted the hand mirror to show him her handiwork. He nodded his thanks.

"Perfect, Toni. I'm going next door for a cup of tea while she bakes." He jerked his thumb to the woman under the dryer.

"You can have a cup of tea here, you know that. Tell the truth, you're after a bun, aren't you? Don't worry I won't tell Doreen." Still smiling she walked over to them. "Hello, Liz, it can't be for you because you were only in a couple of weeks ago, you on the other hand... do you want doing now? I can squeeze you in."

"It's not that... Go on then. Don't go mad, I don't like it too short."

"Over here, end basin."

"You're going to wash it? My old barber used to just squirt water on it."

"And well he might have, but I'm not old, and not a barber. End basin." As Tom walked away, Toni turned back to Liz. "You are together, aren't you? I just assumed."

"Yes, he's a client, I gave him a lift."

"Ah. Okay, well it shouldn't take long. Have a seat." Toni walked over to Tom, and as she showered his hair with warm water, she began to make small talk. "Do you live close by? Only Liz said she'd given you a lift."

"Not far. But she was coming this way. I live on Lower High Street. One of the bungalows."

"Ah, I know. You must know Sally. She lives there."

"I do. Nice girl." From the limited vision allowed him, with his head tilted back at an angle, Tom could see Liz had picked up a magazine.

That wouldn't get answers to their questions. "She's just started dating the officer investigating the murder of Denise. Poor old Denise, I liked her. Oh, I'm assuming you knew her, did you?"

Toni squirted shampoo into the palm of her hand and paused. "Murdered? I did know her, yes. Lovely lady. I didn't realise it was murder though. That's bloody awful, excusing my French. Jeepers. You're not safe anywhere these days. I don't think we've even had a burglary here before. I wonder why they haven't made more of fuss on the local news. Poor old Denise."

"She was burgled too. After she died, so she didn't know about it. Liz found the back door smashed in when she went to get rid of the perishables in the fridge. No family I understand, just the ex-husband."

"She did have family. A sister and a nephew, she hated them she told me. She was in here, last Tuesday, having her roots done. Very chatty, it's horrible that someone that happy was murdered hours later."

"Happy you say, do you know why? Ooh, that's nice." Tom closed his eyes as Toni massaged the shampoo into his head. He opened them when Liz spoke.

"Why was she happy, had something happened?"

"What hadn't happened would be quicker. I asked, as you do in the trade, 'How's your week been, Denise? Anything exciting going on?' Well, she started talking and I don't think she stopped till I put the dryer on. That's a long time when you're having a colour."

"What did she say?"

Toni rattled off what Denise had told her. Apparently, her sister, Karen, had turned up out of the blue. She'd heard of Denise's divorce, although that had been ages ago, and wanted half of the house. Denise told her no, and then her nephew, the one who she'd never met, turned up. Told Denise she'd upset his mum, and she had to do the right thing. He got a bit aggravated, but nothing Denise couldn't handle. But as if that wasn't enough, she thought she was being followed, and had found someone looking in through her window. And the same person, probably, maybe, had destroyed her garden and scratched her car. She'd said it had been an awful time and that she was looking forward to seeing the back of it. That was until Monday lunchtime. She'd taken a call that had made all her dreams come true, although she wouldn't share what, then she went into work and got even more good news. It was why she was having her hair done, she was going out that night, totally unexpectedly.

Liz was listening avidly.

Toni continued, "She wouldn't tell me who with, but as she was going on to have her nails done, I can only guess it was a man. Oh my God, do you think it was him who killed her?" Toni tapped Tom on the head. "That'll do, I'll wash it all away otherwise. Middle chair."

"I don't know, Toni, I really don't but I think you should tell the police all that. It's important. Call them once you've finished with Tom."

Tom smiled, she'd used his name again, and it had been well worth coming out. More clues, and a haircut. When Toni had finished and done the trick with the cape and the mirror, he was more than pleased. For some reason he couldn't fathom, a decent trim made him look a little younger and a little cleaner. He washed his hair every day. He commented on the latter as Liz started the engine.

"And it makes you look younger. I thought that was why you gave her such a generous tip. That or you fancied her."

"I did not. She's far too young. What is it with you thinking I'm after every woman I see, including yourself? Behave now. I tipped her well because I liked the cut, I will be going back, and because she's given us enough information that the police can't pretend nothing suspicious was happening. Where are you going?"

Liz had turned away from their village.

"Greater Compton. I'll point out all the attractions."

By the time they pulled up in the layby by a row of dubious looking shops, Tom had seen three pubs, the sign to the small industrial estate where the bargain home store could be found, and a ruined church taken out by German bombs during the war, although no one knew exactly why, they guessed Avonmouth, a few miles up the coast, had been the intended target. Tom looked at the row of shops.

"I can't see a nail salon. There's a betting shop, a café, newsagent, and dry cleaners. Where's the nail salon?"

Liz pointed to a swing sign outside the newsagents. It had an arrow pointing down, with Nifty Nails hand-painted on it. "Underneath the newsagents. I've never been. I do my own, but I know where it is."

Liz led the way and opened the door which led along a dark corridor.

"Why have they painted the walls black? It's gloomy, although there's a lot of light down there." Liz stepped onto the first stair.

Tom looked down over her shoulder. His knees wobbled, his chest constricted preventing him from drawing in breath, and his vision blurred. Throwing himself backwards, he pressed his body against the wall. Unable to work his lungs, panic took over and he fell to his knees clasping his chest. Liz was halfway down the stairs before she realised he wasn't following her. When he didn't answer her, she turned around and saw him crouched on the floor, hands clutched to his chest, moaning incoherently. She ran back up the stairs and fell to her knees next to him.

"Tom, Tom. What is it? Is it your heart? I'll call an ambulance."

Before she had time to hit the final digit, Tom grasped her hand. "No. Just get me out." He held out a hand.

Liz led him back to the car, and he dropped into the seat, his legs hanging out of the car, and forced in one breath after the other until he felt his body was doing it automatically. He looked up at Liz. "Thank you. I'm fine now. I'll stay here though. You go and speak to them."

"I will not. What just happened? I thought you were having a heart attack. I'm not leaving you."

"Please, just do as I say, we have to do this for Denise."

"Not until you tell me." Liz's arms were akimbo. She wasn't going anywhere.

"I will tell you, but not here, not now. I want you to get as far as we can. I've got something else to add, but I'm not telling you until you've dealt with them." He jerked his head towards the nail salon.

"Promise you'll tell me everything, not just what you'd forgotten to tell me. Because I know you're a gentleman of your word and you wouldn't lie to me." Liz's eyes narrowed while she waited for a response.

"Promise."

Liz was back ten minutes later. She slammed the car door and looked at Tom. "How are you?"

"Fine. What happened?"

"Five minutes trying to convince me I needed false nails, and five telling me how lovely Denise was and how shocked they were that she had died. They're foreign. Their English was limited and even if I could have made them understand what I was asking, I'm pretty sure Denise wouldn't have shared anything with them. There would have been little point. So are you going to tell me now?"

"This morning, you mentioned Craig Parker being barred from the pubs here because he was a violent gambler, or words to that effect. I saw both him and Andy Knight outside The Swan, smoking. When I found Denise, I made sure to look for any possible evidence on the way home, guess what I saw?"

"Just tell me. I'm not doing guessing games. Mainly because I'm rubbish at them." Liz started the car and drove off, Tom didn't notice immediately, but she wasn't heading back to Little Compton.

"A gum wrapper, which for the time being has no consequence. A screwed-up packet of cigarettes, Marlboro, I think. And half a betting slip."

Liz gasped as she turned to look at Tom.

"Eyes on the road woman, there's a bend coming up. Is this a different way back?"

"No, I'll show you in a minute. Back to the cigarettes and betting slip. When we were in the pub, I'm sure there were Marlboro cigarettes on the bar. We'll have to go back in. I wonder what Craig smokes? Again, we'll have to find out. But a betting slip. That's serious. But it's probably not there now. We've had loads of rain since then, and the friends of Compton do litter picking every weekend, whatever you saw will probably have been cleared away. No point in even going to the police with that. But for us, it helps."

"I have a photograph."

"You do? Why? Not that I'm complaining. Here's why I came this way." Slowing down she pointed towards the estuary. "That's the house. Amery's house. The warehouse with windows."

"Accurate description, but what a fabulous view. I wouldn't mind waking up to that. You can probably see the bridge." Tom looked at the boxy, flat-roofed building, clad in dark wood, and dotted with uneven sized windows. "Odd setting on the windows. I wonder if there was a reason for that? If it's structural, sort of understandable, but if it was for aesthetic value, it failed. Might work inside though." As Liz pulled into a layby, he turned in his seat to look at her. "I am not going in there."

"I know that. Do you think I'm stupid? Show me the photo."

"I'd rather not, the others are on there. They'll upset you." "I won't look at the others." Liz held out her hand.

Tom found the photo and handed her his phone. "Not much to see. Standard Coral betting slip. I'm guessing, Mummy's Boy didn't win the race."

"Probably not. But would be worth finding out when he was racing. Shame we can't see the date properly. Do you know anything about horse racing?"

"No. I've had the odd bet on the Derby or Grand National, horses all chosen by a draw or the name. No interest in it."

"Nor me. We'll have to leave that for now. Let's move onto the other thing."

"What other thing?"

"Ah, come on. You promised, don't make me mad. My driving goes to pot when I'm mad." "Let's do this over a cup of tea. I've had a funny turn you know."

"Hmm."

Tom looked at Liz from the corner of his eye. She was smiling.

Once they were back at Tom's, Liz pointed at the clock. "I've got an hour before I need to pick Gemma up from school, no mucking about or you'll be doing your own cleaning tomorrow. I know it might be hard, so I'm going to make the tea while you talk."

"It won't take that long." With a sad smile and a deep sigh, Tom spoke, for the first time ever, about how he'd lost his wife. He'd spoken to grief counsellors, doctors, sleep technicians, at one stage he was so desperate to move on, more for Emily than himself, he'd have spoken to anyone. Then he'd just accepted it, not given up, but accepted he was... weird.

It had been a normal Saturday afternoon, Emily was out doing whatever teenagers did, and Amy had convinced Tom to go shopping. They'd had lunch in a favourite bistro and bought all the bits and pieces Amy wanted for the newly decorated bathroom. After a couple of hours, they'd decided it was time to call it a day. They were on the second floor of a shopping mall. Amy had a thing about heights, and sometimes a downward-moving escalator made her dizzy. She always clung on to Tom's hand just in case. This day had been no different, they'd stepped on, and Tom held his hand out. Seconds later the escalator stopped. The old lady behind them lost her balance at the jolt and hit Amy in the back. Amy had been thrown forward. There was no one in front of them to break her fall and her hand was torn from Tom's. As Amy's head collided with the one of steps, the escalator started again. He could see Amy's hair was going to get sucked into the machinery and he screamed for someone to hit the stop button. Luckily, a woman who had seen what happened ran and hit the button again. Amy's beautiful hair was saved. Amy on the other hand remained motionless. While the old woman cried out in agony, Amy just lay there. The blood from her unseen wound trickled along the grooves of the step below. There was silence for a few seconds, and then all hell broke loose.

Those able to leave the escalator did so by walking back up the stairs. While they waited for the paramedics, Tom knelt beside Amy, holding her hand and speaking to her quietly, telling her she'd be okay but would need to get her hair done. A helpless first-aider sat comforting the old lady who yelped in agony every few moments. They'd used Amy's super thick, soft cotton bathmats to support the old woman's head. They'd been too worried to move Amy's in case her neck was damaged. While they waited and waited, a crowd built up. A big crowd. Even those who wanted to go about their business, couldn't get past them. The crowd held their ground, concerned they might miss something if they stepped aside, their ghoulish fascination causing them to wince every time the old lady cried out in pain. After what seemed like hours, security guards forcibly cleared the crowd to let the paramedics through. They came along the first floor intending to attend to Amy first. Tom had to move back to allow the young woman room to do so. She spoke to Amy in a kind voice, lifting her wrist to take her pulse. That was the first time Tom realised how critical Amy's condition was. His chest began to tighten. The paramedic beckoned her colleague, whispering something to him. Tom's heart thundered. The second paramedic knelt and pressed his fingers to Amy's neck then lifted her eyelid. He shook his head at Tom as he spoke quietly into the walkie talkie pinned to his pocket.

Tom tried to gasp in air, the pain in his chest was incredible. Amy couldn't be dead, she couldn't. She had a new bathroom to accessorise. If she was dead, then he was too. He stopped trying to breathe as a voice came over the speakers, and the security guards began to push the crowds the other way. The female paramedic came to stand in front of Tom and tried to prise his hand off the rail. She pointed up to the floor above. He couldn't hear her words, but he looked. More faces, all of them looking at him. When they gasped, he looked around to see why. Amy was now covered in a red blanket, and the man who had done that was coming towards him.

The next thing Tom remembered was being strapped to a trolley, the bright lights of the shops flashing past, and the faces. All those faces looking at him.

Amy's funeral took place on a bright, warm, spring morning. He wore a floral tie with his black suit, and Emily a pretty floral dress. They'd asked everyone else to do the same, but most there, and there were a lot because Amy was a popular woman, were decked in black. They all watched as he and Emily, their hands gripped together, followed Amy down the aisle. All those faces watching them.

They spent a miserable couple of months comforting each other. Neither wanting to see anyone, neither listening to the 'it will do you good' advice. Eventually Emily's friends had arrived to sort her out. They'd even brought a tent. When Emily said thanks but no thanks, they'd set up camp in the back garden, coming in and out of the house to use the toilet, and shower. Eventually, short of cash for takeaways, they'd said they needed to use the cooker. Tom had laughed and told them to come in. He'd laughed. That was the beginning of getting Emily better. Tom too, to a degree. But he wouldn't go out, too many faces. And he had to drink himself to sleep.

While Emily got back to some kind of normal, Tom closed his office, halved his clients, and ran his business from home. They'd tried everything to get him back to a regular routine, none of it worked, and a frustrated and concerned Emily went off to university.

Tom held his hands up. "Turns out you can't mend this broken heart." He thumped his chest. "Emily went to Australia to see the country, but met some chap, Jason, and as all she had to come home to was me, stuck behind four walls, she stayed. She's visited, of course, although it took her five years to do that. I encouraged her. None of it was her fault, she was young, her whole life ahead of her, and she seems happy. But I'm getting there, I truly believe that, but earlier, when we went into that corridor, looking down those stairs it all came flooding back. What I was having was a panic attack. It's happened several times now. The first when they wouldn't let me go in the ambulance with Amy, the last this morning. It's frightening, and it's humiliating. It's the not knowing what will bring it on that's the worst. Thank you for looking after me."

Liz's mouth had drooped at the corners, she swallowed and blinked rapidly before she spoke. "How did you end up here?"

"A conspiracy. Emily and my sister. Emily says she won't come home unless I'm trying, my sister told me it would be easier to try in a new place. No memories. And I want to, I truly do. That's why this lot" he swung his arm around "is all new. Other than her wedding ring, and loads of photos, everything around me is new. We settled on Little Compton because of the layout. Everything I needed in a straight line, nothing crucial more than a couple of minutes' walk away, but mainly because it was new."

"That coat isn't new." Liz twitched a smile and Tom roared with laughter.

"No. It's possibly an antique. Right. Bargain kept. What next with Denise?"

"I'll have a think about it. I can't believe I made you tell me that and now I've got to go. I'm sorry I'll try to come back later."

"You will not, not unless something crucial turns up. I do have work to do, and dinner to cook."

"In which case, I'll stop bothering you. Have you got something in for your tea?" Liz's smile was kind.

"Yes, I have *dinner* in the fridge. I went shopping. I'm trying to get better. Now go and get Gemma before I have to kick you out. I've got to get to the library."

When Emily called that night, Tom couldn't wait to tell her about his outings. Omitting the panic attack of course.

"My fridge is full of all the stuff I fancied, and I have butter for my bacon sandwiches. What have you got to say about that?"

Emily laughed. "First, your hair looks good. You should go there again. Second, I'm so chuffed and excited I really can't begin to tell you. I miss you so much Dad. This last week it's been like getting my real dad back." Emily choked up and looked away.

"Ah love. Don't get upset, I'm happy you are too."

"Happy tears, Dad. Happy tears."

"Glad to hear it. Now, what's my surprise." He didn't miss the hesitation or the frown which made a brief appearance. He also saw the deep breath she drew in. He loved seeing her, and he'd have known none of that if they weren't on a video call. "Emily?"

"I got the job. They want me to start asap."

"That's brilliant. Isn't it? I hope you've got a posh title. But why the hesitation?"

"Because I wasn't sure if I was going to take it. It ticks all the boxes except one. Location. And you know what they say location, location, location."

"I thought you'd worked all that out. Surely you took everything into consideration before applying. Is there anything I can do? Do you need money to help you move back to the city? Is it financial?" He watched Emily's eyes well with tears.

"That's so kind Dad, but no it's not that, it's... complicated. When Jason and I split up, I kept this place because... it was mine. It is—"

"Wait one moment, back up a little there. When did you and Jason split up? You haven't mentioned it. Are you okay?"

"I didn't mention it because, well because of you. I didn't want to give you something else that you really don't need to worry about. It was my decision in the end. There was no showdown, he knew his days were numbered. He'd had more than one chance."

"Chance to what?"

"You know, the usual. Get a job he keeps for more than a week, stop drinking away money we didn't have, but most importantly to stop sleeping with the baker's wife. He's moved into the city with her now and good riddance. Means we don't have to see him."

"We? Have you got a new bloke?"

"What? Um no. Me and the baker. He took it harder than me because he didn't have a clue. I feel guilty I hadn't told him the first time."

"How long has all this been going on?"

"I don't know, does it matter, eighteen months maybe, more than a year. He's been gone six months. I think I'll be moving too if I take this new job. I need a better job."

"That's what I said. I can help you with that, can't I? I've got money, Emily, you know that."

"I do. Who paid for my university, who paid for my ticket here, and who paid for the very large deposit on this house having never even met Jason? You. You've done enough and I love you for it. But I need to stand on my own two feet. Just like you, I need to pull my shoulders back, and as Tina, she's my neighbour, says, strap a pair on." Emily delivered the last few words in a strong Australian accent.

Tom laughed despite his concern. "I'll bear that in mind. Now, if you change your mind, or if you struggle, don't you hesitate, the offer will remain open. For ever."

"Thanks, Dad. I know you're weird, but you're getting there. I do love you. I can't wait for a big daddy hug. I'll let you get off to bed now, happy sleuthing."

"I thought that was interfering?"

"Oh, it is, but you've been shopping and had a haircut in a salon. I almost hope it's a serial killer." Emily's hand appeared as she waved the comment away. "That was a joke. Poor taste, but a joke none the less. I'd better go before I get myself into trouble. Speak tomorrow. Love you."

"You too, love. Night."

Tom put the phone on the arm of his chair. Eighteen months, and he never knew. Never had an inkling because he was bloody weird. The guilt was so overwhelming he almost went upstairs and got the bottle. But that was part of the problem. He needed something to keep him occupied. Putting thoughts of the bottle to the back of his mind, he decided to update the murder log, and then read a bit more of that book.

He finished the book, but it was still another hour before he got to sleep. He woke later than usual the next morning, and not at all refreshed. Cursing, he hurried into the shower, he had work to do and very little enthusiasm to do it. Still, he told himself, no pills, no booze, despite having a lot on his mind.

THE EVIDENCE

A s Tom came downstairs, he sniffed. Lemon and coffee. Liz was here.

"Liz?" he called as he entered the kitchen. "It's not your day today."

"In here. I know that, but I've been a bit slap dash what with our investigation. Thought I'd have an early start, Mum's dropping Gemma to school. I didn't realise you only got up early on my days, thank goodness you've decided to wake up. I put on a pot of coffee hoping the smell would rouse you. It worked. I've done downstairs, you go and get your breakfast while I vacuum. Then I'll give the bathroom a quick once-over and we can decide what we're doing about Denise."

"I must work. The bills don't pay themselves you know. I can't tell my housekeeper her wages will be short because I've been busy solving a murder instead of working."

"Well, if you did tell her that, your housekeeper would say, same here, and she has a child to care for, ferry about and feed. So fit work in around it, that's what she'd say."

"And as always, I'd probably concur because I'm frightened of her. She's got an awful face on her when she's mad."

Grinning while rolling her eyes, Liz switched on the vacuum, and Tom went back into the kitchen.

Vacuuming done, Liz looked at the amended log of events. "Did you find out when Mummy's Boy last ran?"

"No. Didn't get a chance to. I work, remember?"

"Then let's start now. Laptop at the ready."

They discovered that the last time Mummy's Boy had run was Wednesday, the day after Denise had been murdered. It had won.

"How odd," Tom commented. "The race before that was over a month ago. Let me look at that picture again." Tom emailed the photograph to himself and opened it on the laptop, he enlarged it as much as he could without the purple print applied when the slip was run through the printer blurring too much. Some of the print had washed off. "I have no idea what any of that means." Tom looked up as Liz pulled her coat off the back of the chair. "Where are you going?"

"To see if it's still there."

"Take your coat off. What's the chance of it being there? Even if it is, we've had rain since. It will be ruined." He smiled as she paused with only one arm in her coat. "You're right. We'll have to go to the betting shop. Get your coat. You can stay in the car if you want."

"You have the car again?"

"Thought it might be safer, you know, just in case." Embarrassed, Liz turned away. "I didn't know where we were going, if anywhere, either."

"But we don't know which shop the bet was placed in. It's a chain, it could be in town." Despite his words he was on his feet.

"I'm going to bet it's the one in Greater Compton, or GC as the kids call it. Our Gemma said 'we're going to GC today, Mum. On a coach.' I asked where's GC and she looked at me as though I were stupid. Six years old going on sixteen. Print that. It will be easier than using your phone. I'll get your coat." Before they'd even come up with a story to tell, they were in the betting shop standing behind a young woman dressed only in jeans and a T-shirt despite the bitter wind. She was placing a bet on a complicated accumulator. The cashier winked at Tom.

"Won't be long, sir, Jack's about to become a millionaire again, aren't you, Jack?"

"Got to be in it to win it, Mags."

Bet placed, he kissed the slip and tucked it in his wallet. "I'd better get back to work."

Mags smiled as he left. "Bless him, I don't know what he'll do if he ever wins. The money would ruin him. What can I do for you?"

Liz handed over the printout. "I think I'm in trouble, Mags. My friend placed this bet, and thinking I was helping, I washed her jeans. When I got them out of the machine, I found that. I've photographed it and enlarged it, because at the end of the day it might not be worth anything, can you help me?"

If Mags was surprised, she didn't show it. Tipping her head to allow her glasses to fall from her forehead onto her nose, she inspected the printout. Holding the printout in one hand, she tapped her keyboard with the other. Glancing from one to the other she frowned.

"I know who placed this bet. She's dead. Want to start again?"

"Denise Knight placed that bet?" Tom couldn't stop himself. Although he told himself silently, that could have been a statement not a question.

"Of course." Liz hoped her irritation with Tom didn't show. "We knew that didn't we? That's why we're here. Her daughter is about to inherit everything, and if that won, I washed it. I used to help Denise out a couple of hours a week, things she wouldn't do because of her nails." Liz wiggled her fingers. "We'll come clean with you. Denise was murdered. Whoever killed her ripped this up. It's clear the race hadn't been run yet, so when did she place the bet, and why was the slip ripped up? Weird don't you think?"

Mags looked at Tom. "Why didn't you just say you were a copper? I remember Denise came in last Tuesday, see here." Mags tapped some of the digits still visible. "She'd just had her nails done and I had to get her card out of her purse for her so she didn't damage them. When I saw her picture in the paper, it didn't say she'd been murdered. I recognised her and thought how sad it was. She seemed so happy. Thirty-eight pounds fifty. That's how much she won. Do I give it to you?"

Tom's voice dropped several octaves. "No, no. Wouldn't be right, we'll let the daughter know. Thanks for your help. We might be back if we need more information." Saluting, Tom turned away. "Come on, Ms Thorne. Let's be off."

Liz could barely contain herself and made it to the door before Tom. Once outside, she turned to him, her eyes sparkling with amusement. "What just happened to your voice?" She hooted out a laugh and was still giggling when she got in the car and started the engine. "I wish I had recorded that."

Tom closed his door. "I was trying to sound official. Stop laughing and tell me what you make of that. I reckon it's another clue. The questions are, and hear me out because I'm thinking aloud. When, and I suppose more importantly, why, was the slip there? Did she drop it on the way to where she met her end? If so, how? And, and this could be important, what happened to the other half? She doesn't strike me as a litterbug, why not shove it in your pocket? Was it in her pocket and it fell out? Or did the killer take it, think it was worthless, and drop it? That means it could have been a simple robbery gone wrong, but we know from the heels, Denise hadn't gone for a walk. So, not a robbery as such. Because if it was, what else was taken? I know the police didn't get off to a very good start, but there has never been any indication it was a robbery, because had they thought that, they'd have known it was murder, or manslaughter at the very least."

Tom was drumming his fingers on his knee, Liz glanced at him.

"Have you finished? I know you didn't expect any answers to that lot, but I think first we need to go and speak to whoever else works at Amery and Cheriton, because other than the vicar's wife, they saw her last. And then we need an update from Patrick."

"Amery and Cheriton? Who would we speak to, and what are we going to say?" Tom was shaking his head. "I don't think that's a good idea, not until we have a plan anyway. Speaking to Patrick, that's a different kettle of fish. Let's go back to mine and I'll give him a ring."

"You might be right, I'll just drop you off though, we'll have to catch up later, I must get to my next client. I don't know what people must think, I've been all over the place the last week, you can usually set your clock by me."

"And I must also work, although as you kindly pointed out I could work until midnight. But I do have to work this afternoon. I'll try to get hold of DC Connor though."

"Call him Patrick. He's you know *whating* with our friend. That means first name terms, and it makes him more obliged to share."

"He might well be, but I don't think he'll see it like that. You can stop by the deli if you wouldn't mind, or should I call it the cheese shop like

Alice? I'm going to get some of her recommended extra mature. Do you know, when Emily was younger we went to America, Disney for most of it, but we did a bit of sightseeing, which as always involved going into the biggest shop Amy could find. This store was huge. Sold everything. Anyway, we just wandered along the aisles comparing prices and buying bits and bobs, when Amy says, 'Look, the cheese cabinet. I could fancy a bit of cheese after all the meat we've been eating.' Talk about trade descriptions. Ninety percent of it was packets of orange and yellow plastic sliced stuff. There were also tubes of gloop or bags of shredded plastic, not grated, shredded. Finally, there was the European section. Bags of mozzarella, shredded mozzarella, and packets of sliced gouda, or similar. Amy was very disappointed. That said, their meat is so cheap. You could feed a family of ten for a week on the pieces of beef they'd packaged up, and for a fraction of the cost. Me and Amy agreed we'd rather have a decent bit of cheese than half a cow. Oh, we're here. I'll catch you later."

"Blimey, I don't know what happened to you last night, but you've not stopped talking today. Are you sure you'll be okay, do you want me to wait, just in case?" Liz nodded at the delicatessen.

"I'll be fine, thanks for the consideration. As long as it's not too crowded or at the bottom of a steep staircase. Just kidding, Liz. I've got to get on with it," he added quickly as Liz leaned across him for a closer look into the shop.

"Go on then. We'll speak later. And don't eat those onions with it. They're not ready."

Smiling, Tom went into the deli. He ended up with far more than the cheese, even risking a variety of the disgusting stuffed olives. When he got home, it took only moments to centre himself, and then he was torn. As he unpacked his purchases, he couldn't decide whether to get on with some work or call Patrick Connor. Solving what happened to Denise, he decided, was more important. Updating Denise's log with the latest findings, he made the call.

"Mr Large, I'm on my way to see you. Shall we speak then?"

Having agreed, Tom realised he'd have to show Connor the photographs of the evidence. He emailed all three to himself and had them ready to view on the laptop. He studied Denise's murder log again. The police must take it seriously now, surely?

When Tom opened the door, DC Connor nodded a greeting and walked straight through to the kitchen and took a seat at the table. He looked around. "She's not here?"

"Who Liz? No, she had to work." Tom watched as Connor's shoulders relaxed, and a smile almost appeared. "Tea? I've boiled the kettle."

"Go on then, but I haven't got long. What did you want to tell me?"

"You first. There's so much, I'll show you Denise's log in a moment. Why were you coming here?" Tom poured the boiling water on the teabags. "It wasn't to ask what progress we'd made."

"No. One sugar. Thanks." Connor sipped his tea. "I'm back on the case. The driver of the hit-and-run came forward. So here I am." Connor held out his arms. "Do your worst. What have you got?"

"No, no, no. You didn't come here to tell me that. You wouldn't bother. What else?"

"We found Alana. Actually, that's not true. We found out where she should be, but she's not."

"Oh dear. That doesn't sound good. Go on." Tom joined Connor at the table.

"She's at UWE. That's the University of the West of England. Lives in a shared house in Bristol. But she's not been there since last Friday. Was reported as missing by her housemates yesterday afternoon. I've been to the house, all her stuff appears to be there, no phone, purse, or keys though. She had a car and we're searching for it. I've gone through all the stuff we discussed with my governor, and I'll be honest, I didn't tell him it was you who did most of the legwork. He was impressed. More inclined to believe it was murder and told me to take the morning briefing. I've never taken the briefing before. I reckon I did okay." Connor looked pleased with himself.

"Congratulations. So, you came here to get more information and make yourself look even better, am I right?"

Connor looked shamefaced. "Bit transparent? And I thought it would be easier without Liz here." He winked at Tom.

Tom thought back to what Liz had said about using first names. "Patrick, I am more than a pretty face you know, as I shall demonstrate in a moment, but what else?"

"Else?"

"Yes, about Alana, what else? Or have you spoken to the hairdresser?"

"The hairdresser? Blimey, you're in the wrong profession. No, I've not as yet. Alana told her housemates about finding her birth mother. It's why she chose UWE, so it was only a bus ride away. They met at least once a week, and Alana was happy. She told them she was going to move in with her mother, and that her mother had left her everything in her will. She knew about that, so she had a motive. It's possible she did kill Denise for the money. And perhaps she's gone to ground."

Tom had left the table and was rummaging in the fridge. "If she's at university, Alana is not stupid. She'd know you'd find out about the payments and about the will. Do you want some cheese and biscuits? I'm starving. Unless it was an unplanned attack, she wouldn't go to ground, which is why you found her room as you would expect to."

"No food for me, and yes, that's what I told my gov. He wasn't convinced."

"So here you are after our evidence. I need to eat, so I'll just give you this." Tom collected the updated log from the printer. "Although we didn't necessarily find out the information in that order, that's when we believe things occurred. The notes in red are supposition."

Connor took the sheet. "Denise – The Murder." Tom sliced some cheese and popped it on a cracker. "Monday am. Denise tells Liz about a stalker. Monday pm—"

"You don't need to do that, I wrote it, I know what it says." Tom smiled before cutting more cheese. "The cheese shop really does do a good extra mature. Shame I can't have a pickled onion yet."

"Oh, go on then. Grab me a plate, I'll join you."

Ten minutes later, Connor placed the murder log to one side, and held up his finger while he finished his mouthful.

"So, Toni, the hairdresser, can confirm that Denise believed there was a stalker, that she didn't get on with her sister and nephew, and Denise had had good news. First call on Monday, I'll have a look at her phone records and check that out, and then something also happened at work. Possibly another call. Toni also thinks she had a date. Years ago, Denise left home under a cloud, probably to have Alana, but came back. Before she went, she was in a relationship with James Amery, so he's the possible father of Alana? That was a surprise, I didn't know Denise, but I've got a feel for what she was like, I can't see her with Amery. He's very straightlaced. I've met him a few times."

"Doesn't mean he wasn't fun when he was young though," Tom observed. "I used to have fun once."

Connor pushed his plate away, and hands clasped on the table his face became serious. "Which brings us to your evidence. Evidence you withheld from the police. That's serious trouble."

Tom looked incredulous. "Withheld? Behave yourself. If you're going to be ridiculous because you've been allowed to do the morning briefing, you can get out. Go on. Take a hike." Tom jerked his thumb at the door. "We told you this was murder on day one. Wednesday. Go on look at the murder log. It's all written down. You – weren't – interested." He enunciated slowly. "How can you withhold something from someone who doesn't want to listen? What would your inspector say about that? Go on, tell me that."

"Look, Mr Large, Tom, I —"

"Let's stick to Mr Large now you're throwing accusations about."

"I'm not. What I'm saying is you should have told me."

"Why? Would you have listened? No. Anyway it slipped my mind. I only took them because I didn't know how long it would take you to get there. If it had been hours, like the burglar in the garage, it might have been lost. In the event, you were twenty minutes. Unless, of course, you're telling me you didn't take photographs of *all* the evidence. Did you?"

Connor was looking shamefaced again. "I don't know. I came back down to see you."

"But you haven't looked, despite being told Denise was murdered. You haven't bloody looked, so don't come into my house telling me I've withheld evidence. Apologise."

"I'm sorry, I didn't mean to offend. Now—"

"Good. Do you want to look at the photographs? I'm guessing only the evidence, because one has to believe someone with competence took photographs of poor old Denise."

Connor's eyes widened. The man had taken photographs of the victim. Why? He didn't ask though, as that would probably gain him another earful. Instead, he nodded. "If I may."

Having looked at Tom's photographs, Connor asked for copies, and Tom emailed them across to him.

"Thank you. I really should be telling you to step away from all this now. With this last lot of information, I've no doubt my inspector will officially upgrade this to murder, but—"

"But you won't do that, because then you'd never find out anything. Liz was right."

"I wish you'd let me get to the end of a sentence, it's quite frustrating you know. I—" This time it was Connor's phone that interrupted him. He mumbled a few words, thanked the caller, and grimaced as he looked at Tom. "We've found Alana, she's—"

"Dead! Oh my god, we've got a serial killer. Is it serial if it's two people, I—"

"NO!" Connor immediately muttered apologies and lowered his voice. "She's in Southmead hospital. Her mobile had run out of battery so she couldn't call her housemates."

"Oh dear. That's not nice. Someone is going to have to tell her about her mother. What's wrong with her?"

"Car accident. It looks like someone had been messing with her brakes."

Tom banged the table and pointed at Connor. "Ha! Supposed to be dead then. Same thing." He grinned, then realising what he was grinning at, his face fell. "That's very worrying, will you give her protection, if someone has tried once, you never know, they might try again."

"I doubt it. We'd have to know first that it was done with malice aforethought." His face serious, Connor got to his feet. "The someone who has to tell her is me."

Tom walked him to the door. "Three things before you go, Patrick. First, if you tamper with someone's brakes, the outcome isn't hard to work out.

There was malice. Second, good luck. It's not going to be easy to tell a young girl that." He patted Connor's shoulder. "Be gentle with her."

"I will. I'm meeting Tiffney, our FLO there, she'll help."

"FLO? What on earth is a FLO?"

"Family liaison officer. You said there was a third thing." Patrick paused on the other side of the door. "And sorry, you know I didn't mean to cause offence."

"None taken. All forgotten." Tom flipped the comment away. "The third thing? Oh yes. Don't forget to come back and update us. We investigators must share and share alike." Tom winked.

"We would have got there, you know, in the end, just not as quickly as you did."

"Rubbish. You don't have Liz and her local knowledge working for you. Think about that for a second."

"I'll try to pop in later. Might have to be a call though."

"Perfect. Bye, Patrick. I'll see you later."

Closing the door, Tom almost tripped over his own feet trying to get to his phone. Liz needed to know this. He tutted in frustration as her voicemail picked up his call.

"It's me. Tom. I've updated Patrick, calling him by his first name worked by the way. Anyway, he tried to reprimand... I won't bother you with that, that's sorted. To the point. He's found Alana, a student at UWE who was going to move in with her mother. Alana is in Southmead Hospital. Someone tampered with her brakes. Patrick is on his way to see her and tell her about her mother now. I don't envy him that job. He's back on the case by the way. His hit-and-run driver did the right thing, and his inspector is starting to believe Denise was murdered. No need to call in or phone. Patrick said he'd update me, but I'm guessing he'll need to be chased tomorrow. I'll call you if there's anything else."

Tom went to clear the table, after all, he did have his day job to do. Liz was on the phone before his cheese was back in the fridge.

"Tom this is terrible news. That poor girl. She'll be devastated. I think we can rule her out as a suspect though, don't you?"

"I do indeed. Emily was much the same age when we lost Amy. It's hard for a girl to lose her mother, and poor old Alana had only had her for a little while. Lost her adoptive parents, lost her birth mother, doesn't know who her father is. It's a crying shame is what it is."

"You're right, we have to go and see her."

"What? I never said that. When did I say that? Liz, under no circumstances, unless I'm strapped to a stretcher again, am I going to a hospital. I couldn't cope. Quite apart from anything else, it's... inappropriate, ghoulish, invasive. Think of a horrible word, and that's what it would be."

"Have you finished?" Liz demanded, clearly irritated.

"Good. I meant to go because she had no one. No one to visit her, Tom. What if that were Emily? Wouldn't you want some caring people who knew her mother to comfort her? Yes, you would. Don't be telling me it's inappropriate. I'll buy some grapes. I doubt she's up to reading the gossip magazines."

"I can't come. I won't come."

"But—"

"What if I have a panic attack? Either she'll be even more traumatised, or you'll be sorting me out when you should be with her. Tell her I'd like to meet her once she gets out. And, Liz, I'm not going to argue about this, I'll just hang up."

There was silence for a moment before Liz spoke. "Agreed, you'd be a liability. Question is, should I go this evening, or tomorrow? I'm supposed to be doing you in the morning."

"I'd say tomorrow. Don't worry about me, I barely crease the sheets. Let her have tonight to accept this."

"Will do. I'll go straight there once I've dropped Gemma off and let you know how it goes."

"Thank you. Take a phone charger. Don't know who she'll want to call, but her phone was dead. And chocolate. Women, particularly young girls, like chocolate. I'll give you the money tomorrow."

"Will do."

Tom updated the murder log, and then choosing the worst account he had outstanding, lost himself in the numbers. He wouldn't have gone even if he were capable. He didn't want to see the pain he knew he'd find in her eyes. He was a coward. A weird coward, and Liz was really quite a remarkable human being.

It was nearly eleven when Emily called and putting the day's events to one side, he smiled at her. She looked tired, dark rings were just visible below the makeup she'd applied.

"Hello, Emily love, how are you? You look tired, did you not sleep well? Have you decided what to do about the job?"

"Blimey. In order:" Emily closed her eyes and nodded as she spoke. "I'm okay. Ish. I am, because no I didn't, not yet." Her eyes opened and there was a twinkle there. "Let's not talk about me. When I've decided I'll let you know. How goes the investigation, and where have you been today?"

"It progresses, we may have a serial killer as you thought. And the betting shop followed by the cheese shop."

"Oh. My. God. I was joking. Tell me all." Tom brought Emily up to date.

"I've not heard back from Patrick, and Liz is going to see her tomorrow. That would be a step too far for me. It's all very sad, Em. Very sad."

"That poor girl, I know what it's like to lose... well you know."

"Is exactly what I said to Liz. Told her to take chocolate."

"Good shout. To take the positives, the police are now taking this seriously, although I'm amazed they seem to be working with you on this, not telling you to back off." Emily missed the slight rise in her father's eyebrows. "And you've been into a betting shop impersonating a police officer, and have a fridge full of deliciousness from the deli. Or cheese shop as it shall forever be known. That's great, Dad. Really great."

"I know. Not bad given this time last week I was only sneaking out late at night for a brisk walk. Poor old Denise, she'll never know what she's done for me. Before you know it, I will be on that plane."

"Seriously, Dad? Would you come, I could do with seeing you properly, there's so much I need to tell you, I can't do it over the phone. It's too... You know." Emily fell silent.

"What? What do you need to tell me? Why can't you tell me on the phone? Emily, raise those eyes and look at me."

"Stuff. Loads of stuff. Stuff that takes too much time. Stuff to be batted back-and-forth."

"But unimportant stuff?" Tom wasn't convinced.

"Mostly. Sometimes it's more important than others, but I forget to mention it. Anyway, that doesn't matter. What matters is if you keep going out to bigger and more exciting places then one day you will get on a plane and come to visit us."

"Are you back with Jason?"

"Never. I have a sensible head on my shoulders, I'll have you know. I meant Australia and me."

"Glad to hear it." A phone rang in the background and Emily turned to look. "Do you have to go?"

"I do. Sorry, Dad. I'll call you tomorrow. Love you. 'Bye."

Tom didn't believe a word of it. He was letting her down, just as surely as if he were ignoring her. There were important things she needed to speak to him about face-to-face. Maybe just so he could console her with a hug – who knew what? He hadn't known about Jason. He'd never even met the man she'd lived with all those years. He was ridiculous. He was weird, a coward and a failure. He needed to pull himself together and fast. That girl needed him.

Lights off, he took the stairs two at a time. Two pills washed down with a large swig straight from the bottle, he'd never sleep tonight worrying about what she wasn't telling him, and he needed to sleep. He then went to the bathroom and poured the remainder down the sink.

HOMEMADE CAKES

The next morning, Tom decided that today would be the first day of the rest of his life. He was going to change, and he was going to get better. He was going to stop being such an inadequate father and a burden to his daughter. Once breakfast was out of the way he got a notebook and went through the cupboards. He was going shopping. As he'd already been once, and then hit the delicatessen, he didn't need that much, but it was the action that was required, not the necessity. Before he managed to leave, Kathy Lambert, the vicar's wife called. With no Denise she was having trouble juggling cover for the library. Could he do a couple of hours for her? He agreed to do four to six that afternoon as a one-off.

Before he donned his coat, he went to the gate and looked down the street. There weren't that many people about. He'd do it now. Collecting his coat and shoving a carrier in his pocket, he set off at his usual brisk pace. On reaching the mini-market he was pleased to note that his heart was almost normal. He felt a little nervous, but nothing that he couldn't cope with.

When he saw Alice perusing the cake display, he smiled, and called a greeting as he entered, "Hello, Alice. Are you treating yourself?"

"No, I am not. Look at the price of them. I could make half a dozen for the cost of one. And they probably come from a factory and aren't baked on the premises like they do at the bakers. Do you bake?"

"Now come on, Alice. We've had this out before." Derek Vaswani stepped out from behind the till. "It's the convenience. You can't buy cakes at the bakers on a Sunday, nor can you any other day after five at night. I've got overheads, keeping this shop open for your convenience doesn't come cheap. You weren't complaining last week when you came in at half six for some butter, were you?"

"No, I wasn't. But that's different. These things are all preservatives. I'll tell you what, Derek, I'll bake a couple of batches fresh for you, display them all pretty and you can flog them at that price. We'll split the profit."

"I'd love to, Alice, but what about additives, allergy warnings, and health and safety? Can't be done I'm afraid."

"Rubbish. The vicar sells my cakes at all the church dos, and for your information ASDA in town don't have a list of ingredients on their fresh cake display, and nor does the baker, and they're not all boxed up. If I didn't know better, I'd say you were looking for an excuse. But also there are no additives, not numbered ones anyway, but I'll get Tom here to print off a list of ingredients for those with allergies." She looked at Tom. "You could probably make up a sign for them too, couldn't you? He's got one of those printer things in his dining room. I saw it," she told Derek.

"Um, well, yes. A basic one."

Tom looked over Alice's head and mouthed apologies to the shopkeeper. The shopkeeper brushed it aside and stooped to look Alice in the eye. "And when was the last time you got a hygiene certificate?"

Alice's hand flew to her chest. "Are you suggesting my kitchen is less than hygienic? What do you think Liz would say about that? I'll be having words with your mother. Is Grace working today?" Alice looked around as though Grace Vaswani might have sneaked in. "She's been in my kitchen many a time for a cup of tea. She'll tell you."

Derek held his hands up. "Okay, okay. If you're going to fight dirty, I'll give in before I get hurt. You get it sorted with this gentleman, bring the cakes and the info and we'll do a display."

"Splendid. I'll be needing a few more things now. More money in your pocket, but you get half of the profit, so I'll keep the receipt..." Alice's elbow poked Tom in the stomach. "You're an accountant, aren't you? You can do the numbers too, then."

Tom was dumbfounded. He'd only come in for a half a dozen items, yet here he was being roped into Alice's entrepreneurial endeavours without so much as a by-your-leave. But Alice's triumphant smile was enough to convince him.

"Let me know what you want me to do, Alice, and I'll do my best. I'd better get on. I'm supposed to be working."

"Don't get leaving without me, I might need help with the carrying again."

"Alice, you live two doors up. I can do that." Derek rolled his eyes at Tom. "Sorry, she gets a bit carried away, don't you, Alice?"

"Don't you patronise me! What are you apologising for? He's a grown man, he can say no if he wants to. Can't you?" Alice's expression challenged Tom.

"I could, but I won't. You get your stuff, I'll grab mine, and we'll meet at the checkout. How does that sound?"

"Acceptable. But before you do, you tell me what you'd like, because I know you'll want to buy some. Fairy cakes, cherry slices, rock cakes, or scones. They'll be the quickest, so chose two."

"Buy? I thought I'd get one of each as payment for the paper and ink I've got to use. Overheads, Alice."

Alice pondered this for a moment before sticking out her hand. "Done. But what two?"

"Cherry slices and fairy cakes I reckon."

Nodding, Alice wandered off, and Tom pulled his list from his pocket. This going out lark kept eating into his time, not that he minded, but what an earth had he done with his time before discovering a murder and meeting Alice?

Tom got to the checkout way ahead of Alice, and having paid for his groceries, he asked, "Does she need the money? She sold me a jar of onions walking across the crossing the other day."

"No, I don't think so. She just gets bored. Likes to be busy, likes to be needed. We all need to be needed, don't we? I've worked out who you are now. She said she'd met Pendry's owner, and that you were talking about poor old Denise. I understand you found Denise. That must have been a shock."

"Just a bit. Did you know Denise well?"

"My wife, Nadine, did. They were at school together. She was so upset when we got the news. She'd had a coffee with her in the café on Tuesday afternoon, and just hours later, gone." Derek clicked his fingers. "Not right, is it?"

"No, it's not. I don't suppose I could speak to your wife, could I? I'm sort of investigating what happened, the police are being a bit slow. Although I am liaising with DC Connor. It's all above board. Between you and me, Denise was scared on Monday morning when she saw Liz, do you know... yes, everyone knows Liz, daft question. Anyway, Denise thought she had a stalker, and Liz was worried about her as she was so scared. Then something happened and by Monday afternoon she was her usual happy self. I worked with her in the library on Monday. It would be useful if I, or the police if you prefer, could ask Nadine what Denise had to say. Up to this point, we had no idea what Denise did between going to work on Tuesday and seeing the vicar's wife."

"I'm not sure I understand all that. But I'm sure Nadine will do whatever she can to help. She's at her mother's today. Monday, Wednesday, Friday afternoons, always the mother-in-law, but I'll certainly get her to give you a knock tomorrow. No problem." Derek looked to their right. "Oh no, here she comes. Two batches you said. The bakery would be jealous of that stock."

"Get on with you. You know this is going to be a success. You won't be moaning when that till keeps dinging, will you?"

Derek scanned Alice's shopping. "I'll tell you what, to save Tom a bit of work I'll pay for half, that way it'll be a straight fifty-fifty split."

"Suits me. Bag it up. My bag for life isn't big enough."

On the short walk to her flat, Alice gave Tom strict instructions on what she expected him to produce. She patted his hand. "Thank you for doing this. When I saw you clinging on to the lamppost, I thought... Well, I won't tell you what I thought, but I knew you were a kind man. I'm never wrong. If I can ever return the favour, I will, you only need to ask."

"Thank you, Alice. I will certainly do that. I'll drop the printing down later before I go to the library and pick up my payment, if they're ready of course."

"They'll be ready. I'm starting as soon as I get in. Hope I've not made a rod for my own back. They'll fly out and Derek will be nagging me for more. Have you got my number? You'd better check you've got the ingredients right before you think your job is done. Easy to remember, are you ready? Two-seven-two-six-two-five. I don't use the mobile thing. I like a proper button to press. I kept getting the wrong person. Oh no. Here comes the rain again. 'Bye, Tom, see you later."

Tom sprinted the rest of the way, but the shower was fierce, and he was soaked by the time he stepped into the hall. His grocery bag left a wet patch on the carpet. Hanging his coat on the hook, he ran his fingers through his hair. Wouldn't take long to dry now he'd had it cut. Once the shopping had been put away, he opened his laptop, and before starting work, updated the murder log. He hoped Nadine did come to him and not the police. Apart from anything else it would be nice to get to know another member of the community.

In a moment of clarity, he realised why the detection rate was so low in the UK these days. No more community police officers. That was why not. If there were, they weren't very visible. When he'd been young, a bobby was always around. One had been very tall, and the kids had nicknamed him Lurch, but he was good natured about it and used to come and watch them play football in the Sunday league when they were playing at home. Another, Bob the bobby, used to regularly pop into the youth club. If community police officers existed these days, they would know all the locals, like Liz did. Know who to ask what. Perhaps then they'd be able to run a more effective investigation and not have someone like Liz running circles around them. He couldn't wait to share this insight with Liz. But then she'd probably point out that he hadn't been very visible in the community either, so how could he know?

Opening the first set of accounts which needed his attention, he sighed. He'd keep that nugget of observation until he spoke to Patrick. He'd be more sympathetic than Liz.

With two sets of accounts done and ready for the clients' self-assessments to be completed, Tom heated a tin of soup and sketched out what Alice had requested. Pushing the bowl to one side, he pulled his laptop over and typed up the contents. Then he started playing with the layout, fonts, and colours. In less than ten minutes he was satisfied. What he had was colourful if basic, but it certainly did the job. The rain had stopped, so he'd take them down now, it would only take five minutes. Then he could get some more work done before he had to set off for the library. He was disappointed not to have heard from Liz, but she had other clients as well as a mercy dash to undertake. She'd be in touch soon enough.

Alice was delighted with the outcome and asked him why he didn't have one of those things that covered them in plastic.

"Never had need for a laminator, Alice. Doubt I ever will. Don't worry I've saved that on the computer, I can always produce more if necessary. I have to say your cakes smell delicious. I can't wait to be paid," he told her as she shuffled back along her hall.

"And you will as soon as the job is done. Don't just stand there, come and get them. It might rain again any minute."

So much for five minutes, he thought as he followed her to the kitchen. Alice had lined two trays with greaseproof paper and laid out the two types of cake on them. Covering each with a tea-towel, she lifted one and passed it to him.

"They aren't heavy, stick your thumbs up, we can balance the other one on top. I'll carry the paperwork and open the doors."

Ten minutes later, the factory boxed cakes had been reorganised and Alice's creations took centre stage. The paperwork had been attached to a nearby pillar. A florescent piece of card declared they were fifty pence each, and a stack of paper bags were removed from the box of apples and placed next to the trays.

"One moment." Derek ran behind the counter. "I got my mother to bring these in. She's coming back later to sample them." Returning with a set of tongs, he placed them carefully on Alice's display. "We don't want people using their fingers, do we? Are you happy with that, Alice? I think they look a treat."

"I am."

Smiling, Derek went to serve a customer at the till. Alice lifted a bag, and taking the tongs dropped two of each cake into it. "Payment. I wasn't expecting such a good job." She handed the bag to Tom as the door opened. They both looked up as Craig, complete with his Arsenal cap, walked in.

Alice called to him. "Over here young man. Freshly baked and still warm. Sniff."

Craig looked at her as though she were mad, but used to doing as he was told, he approached with a frown. Tom noticed Craig's nose twitch. The frown fell away, and Craig lifted a bag and went to reach for a cherry slice.

"Hang on. You've got to use these. Health and safety." Alice passed him the tongs she was still holding. "How many are you having?"

"One. I ain't made of money."

"You'll be back for more."

Craig merely raised his eyebrows and headed for the checkout.

"Come on. I want to see Derek's face when he sees we've already sold one." Alice tugged Tom's sleeve, and they followed Craig to the checkout. He dropped the bag on the counter.

"And a packet of Marlboro."

"Are you old enough to buy cigarettes? I've not seen you in here before."

Craig pulled his shoulders back, clearly insulted. "Yeah! I'm nineteen."

"ID please." Derek tapped the sign stuck to the till.

Proof of ID may be requested. Do not to be offended if you look young for your age but rejoice in the compliment.

Alice had a little smile as Craig fumbled with his wallet trying to extract his driver's licence. Tom was fixated by the packet of cigarettes in Derek's hand. Identity proven, Craig snatched the cigarettes and his cake, and left muttering to himself.

Alice stepped forward. "First sale of many, Derek. That will be ten pounds please. I made twenty of each."

"I beg your pardon! I've got to sell them first."

Alice opened her mouth to respond, but Tom jumped in.

"I'm going to let you two battle this out. I also need to earn some money today, so I need to get back to work, I'm on at the library at four." He held up his own bag of cakes. "Thanks, Alice, I'm looking forward to these."

As he left the shop, he heard Alice telling Derek to get an extra pound out. She'd forgotten to add Tom's wages. He smiled all the way home. Another clue, and some cakes he couldn't wait to sample. When he got home, coat on the hook, slippers on his feet, he paused as he entered the kitchen, cake bag in hand. He'd not needed to centre himself. He'd not even needed to breathe. Progress.

He still hadn't heard from Liz, perhaps a text would prompt her. He sent a short message saying he'd agreed the extra hours at the library if she needed him. Content he'd done all he could without calling her, he fiddled about with his accounts while eating a cherry slice, before heading off to the library.

Tom's stint at the library was boring. A total of five customers and two of those were only returning books. Liz had still not been in touch, and he decided to call her as soon as he got home. He'd forgotten to sort anything out for dinner, so his meal would be either another frozen offering, which he didn't much fancy, or bacon and eggs, or an omelette. He was lost in this conundrum as he strolled home. It took a while to register that the light was on in his sitting room. Frowning, he pushed open the door. The scent of lemon reached him. Liz was here.

"Hi, Liz. Are you doing nights now?" he asked as he removed his coat.

"Case of needs must at the moment. I watched you come back." Liz came to join him in the hall. "You were strolling."

"Were you expecting a tango? I didn't know you were waiting."

Liz laughed. "Can you even do a tango? You've been watching too much *Strictly*. I meant you were strolling home, all casual, like you had all the time in the world."

Tom moved her out of the way and went into the kitchen. "I did have all the time I wanted because I didn't know you were waiting. I was wondering what to do for dinner. I forgot to get something ready."

"When was the last time you strolled anywhere?" Liz pointed at the look of surprise on his face. "You see. Strolling not rushing. Now, sit down. There's a pot of tea made, and a shepherd's pie in the oven. One of Mum's, she did me a favour, and I'll tell you how I got on."

"I was going to call you. I assumed you'd been too busy to call."

"I have! Hospital, Mr Burnham, quick visit to Mum, Bristol again, hospital again, pick up Gemma, back to Mum's, and here. I'll be glad to put my feet up."

"The hospital twice? That doesn't sound good." Tom pulled out a chair.

"It was okay. She's a lovely girl. Absolutely devastated, because now she has no one, and someone tried to kill her. We had a good cry together. She told me Patrick was very nice to her. His colleague was coming back to get a list, but I said I'd do it. She liked the chocolates by the way. Sent her thanks."

"A list for what? I know you need to get home, but slow down and explain."

Alana had needed some personal things from home. She'd been in a hospital gown since her arrival. Liz had volunteered to get them and had gone to Alana's student house to collect them. Alana's room had been on the top floor of a four-storey building. Liz had collected what was needed and taken them back to the hospital. The doctor had been with Alana when she got back, and assuming Liz was a relative, included her in the conversation. Most of Alana's wounds were minor and would heal over the coming weeks, and she could go to her own doctor's surgery to have the stitches on her head removed. Her wrist would be as good as new in a couple of days, but the knee needed to be rested, might take up to six weeks, but if Alana followed instructions, as little as three.

"And therein lies the problem." Liz held up her hands. "She can't go back to her student place. Even if one of them agrees to swap rooms or she camps in the tacky living room, which I don't think it's ever seen as much as a duster, the bathrooms are on the third floor. She asked if she could move into her mum's. There's a downstairs toilet, and she said she'd wash in the kitchen sink. But that's not ideal, not for up to six weeks, is it? What with the back door being boarded up, and Denise didn't have curtains at the back of the house. I'd also be worried about her until someone finds out who tampered with her brakes, and I told her that. Poor girl hasn't got anywhere else she can go."

"What's the damage to her knee? Sounds bad."

"I think it is. I didn't get the details, I'm a bit squeamish with stuff like that. But she's got this booty case thing on, and there are pins going into her knee to right the damage done by the impact. Looks like a robotic contraption. They adjust them over the weeks of healing or something like that. Anyway, I thought of you."

"What about me? I'm an accountant, not medical."

"You live in a bungalow, you have two spare bedrooms, and a shower room downstairs. Problem solved. I won't charge extra for the extra cleaning, and I can run her to the doctor's or hospital appointments. She's got her own laptop, and about a hundred books so she can continue with her studies. She's still saying she'd like to live here in Little Compton, even without Denise, and despite the fact there are only a handful of people her age. Do you see?"

"No."

"No, you don't see, or no she can't?"

"Both."

"You don't want her here?"

"No."

"Why?"

"I don't have to give you a reason, Liz. You have her."

"I can't, no spare room, and my flat is tiny. I couldn't see that poor girl stuck in the hospital for the next six weeks. Well, that or apparently they might be able to get her into a nursing home. A nursing home! People dying around you every day. That's no place for a young girl. And she's so nice. Really nice. But orphaned twice in four years, or as good as, and just when she was planning on moving in with her real mum. We've been saying poor old Denise, but she is in a better place, or so they say. No, it's poor old Alana." Liz sniffed and zipped up her coat. "I'll leave you to it. She can't leave hospital for three or four days anyway, so you've got time to think about it. I've done you for today, perhaps I'll see you tomorrow." Despite her words, Liz remained seated.

"Have you told her she's coming here? I hope not, because that will be a disappointment on top of everything else she's had to deal with. That would have been stupid."

"Which I'm not. I told her I'd talk to someone who might be able to help. I thought you might need convincing."

"I don't. I've already made up my mind. I can't investigate her mother's murder, which you've not asked about, look after her, and deal with my own issues. This answer is, and will remain, no."

"We'll see. She doesn't need looking after, and I'll do any—"

"No."

The timer in the kitchen pinged, and Liz got to her feet. "I'll get that shepherd's pie Mum made you out. You can have it when you're ready."

"Give her my sincere thanks. There really was no need, but it's much appreciated. Are you off, or do you want me to tell you what I found out today?" Tom called as Liz got the pie out.

"No thanks. I'm going to leave you in peace. We'll catch up tomorrow perhaps. I need to go and see my daughter, if she isn't already in bed, and put my feet up." Liz put her coat on. "Have a lovely evening, Mr Large. Enjoy your... dinner."

"Thank you. You too. And Liz?"

Liz turned back, hoping her expectation didn't show.

"Don't sulk. It doesn't suit you."

Liz's eyebrows rose, for a moment Tom thought she was going to retaliate. She didn't. She turned on her heel and left, slamming the door behind her. And just like that Tom deflated. All the good things that he'd achieved wiped out in a couple of minutes. Stomping up the stairs, he showered and got ready for bed. He had no appetite for anything. Not for eating, not for television, not for speaking to Emily. With that thought he went down and texted her.

Long day, can't keep eyes open. I'm going to bed. Hope all is well with you, have a good day. We'll catch up tomorrow. Love you. Dad

The pie was covered, the lights switched off and the doors locked. Once in the bedroom he fell flat onto the bed, his feet dangling off the side, and he groaned. What was the woman thinking about? She said he'd strolled home, he doubted he would tomorrow. Not after this. After a few moments, he pulled himself to a sitting position and looked at the drawer.

"Rome wasn't built in a day," he mumbled as he opened it.

With a growl, Tom allowed his head to fall on his chest. It was empty, he'd poured it away. Staring at the empty glass for a while, he snatched it up, and went into the ensuite. He filled it with water and then popped three pills on to his palm. Tonight he must get oblivion. He'd deal with whatever tomorrow had in store tomorrow. There would be no lying awake half the night churning through the possibilities.

LITTLE COMPTON MYSTERIES

THE PUB QUIZ

The next morning, Tom woke from his oblivion with a thumping headache. As the water pounded on his head in the shower, he wished he'd at least had a drink to warrant the pain and wondered if he should restock on alcohol. Having taken some painkillers for breakfast, he got straight on with some work.

After an hour or so, the doorbell rang. He checked the time. It was nine thirty. Who would be ringing his doorbell at this time? He knew who. Liz. Liz showing him he'd upset her so much that she wasn't going to use her key. Resisting the urge to look out of the window first, he flipped the switch on the kettle. Walking down the hall, Tom checked out the distorted reflection behind the opaque glazing in the front door. Right height, right coloured hair, bright clothes. He was right. He yanked open the door.

"I knew it was you. Have we become formal all of... h-hello. It appears I was wrong. Apologies." His smile was weak. "Can I help you?"

"Are you Tom? Derek said Pendry's but he might have got that wrong." Nadine Vaswani pointed at the engraving in the stone above the door. "I'm Nadine."

"Nadine? Oh, Nadine. Come on in. I'm sorry I was expecting my cleaner. I thought she'd forgotten her key." Tom swept his hand into the hall. "Go through, I've put the kettle on. Tea?"

Nadine was an attractive forty-something woman of slight build. She had dark flowing hair which framed a pretty face. Like Liz, she clearly liked bright colours as she was wearing red jeans and a pink fluffy jumper. In her hand she carried a daisy patterned umbrella which she held up. "Just in case. It's milder today, too warm for a coat, but that rain comes from nowhere. Tea would be lovely. I'm spitting feathers."

"Yes, I got soaked myself yesterday coming back from your shop. Amazing how wet you can get in such a short space of time. Have a seat."

"Thanks for helping Alice with the cakes. Derek doesn't want to admit it, but they were a hit. The cherry slices have already gone and there's only a few of the others left. I don't know what Fred thought when he came in to get his papers this morning. Mind you, he might not have noticed them, Fred's not usually shy in voicing his opinion."

"Fred? Who's Fred? I don't think I've met him." Tom put the tray on the table. "Help yourself to sugar."

"The baker." Nadine looked shocked. "Everyone knows Fred, mainly because he's quite nosey so speaks to everyone, and is very opinionated. If you'd met him, you'd know you had."

"Ah, not been to the bakers yet."

"I thought you'd lived here a year." Nadine spooned sugar into her mug and stirred, her eyes never leaving Tom.

"Almost. I get most of my shopping delivered. But I pop down to you for stuff too," he added quickly.

"Oh." Nadine knew very well that Tom had only been into the shop a couple of times. Derek was nosey too. He was just a little more discreet than Fred. "We could deliver for you if you needed us to. You know, if you can't get out."

"Thank you, I'll bear that in mind. Bad habit I've not got out of, you know, ordering online after the lockdown. Trying to break it now though." Tom smiled, the habit had formed well before lockdown, but the rest was the truth. He needed to move this conversation on before it got awkward, so he pulled his notepad forward. "So, I understand you went to the café with Denise on the Tuesday before she was murdered. How did she seem to you?"

Nadine's face fell. "Murdered. Yes, I'd heard that rumour, is it true? You'd have thought the police would have made more of a deal about it, wouldn't you? Until I heard on Saturday, I'd been carrying on as normal.

Now I'm looking over my shoulder every five minutes. Do you mind me asking why you're asking the questions, and not the police?"

"Because it took them nearly a week to recognise that there had indeed been a murder. It was Liz, my cleaner, who realised. So we started our own investigation and give what we find to the police to follow up." Tom felt guilty calling Liz his cleaner, but he didn't want new acquaintances to think that it was he who had elevated her position. "Cuts," he announced to explain why they were doing the police's job for them.

"Ah. Okay. Denise was happy. She'd been irritated over the weekend, she'd had vandals, or a stalker, damaging her things and looking through her window, but on Monday she had spoken to Alana and they'd agreed she should move to Little Compton to live with Denise. She was so happy, she was... I can't believe that hours later she was dead." Nadine dabbed her eyes. "She was too young, and finally getting her daughter back. Poor old Denise, poor Alana." Nadine blew her nose. "You do know about Alana, don't you?"

"We do, yes. We were with the police officer, DC Connor when he found Denise's will and Alana's birth certificate. Oh, I've just had a thought, you probably don't know, do you?"

"Know what?"

"Alana was in a car accident and is in hospital. It looks like her brakes had been tampered with. Liz had to tell her about her mother yesterday. They had a good cry apparently."

Nadine jumped to her feet. "Tampered with? Oh my God. Is someone out to kill her too? What in the world is going on?" Now pacing up and down, Nadine's heels were clicking on Tom's kitchen floor. "Why? That's what you must find out, why would anyone want them dead?" Marching back to the table she dropped down on to the chair and pointed at Tom. "That's what you have to find out. Because it's not money. The house is worth something, I suppose, but do people get murdered for a couple of hundred grand? Oh, I suppose they do. Blimey, Tom, this is like something you watch on the telly, not real life. Not our lives. How is your investigation going? Tell me what you've found out, and I'll see if I can help."

Tom considered this for a moment, it wasn't the way he thought this meeting would go, but if Nadine was Denise's best friend, then she was best placed to fill in any gaps. He collected his copy of the murder log and held it against his chest. "I'm going to show you all the details we've found out so far, but, and this is important, I need you to keep them to yourself. If the murderer gets wind of what we know, who knows what repercussions that might have. He might do a runner, or he might try to silence someone else."

"Of course." Nadine held out her hand and Tom passed her the document.

"Don't say anything until you've read it all, then we'll go through it step by step." Tom's pulse had quickened, and for once it was because he was excited, and not because he feared something he couldn't name. He sighed. By rights, Liz should be here, she was missing out. If it weren't for her, then they wouldn't even be investigating. His thoughts were disturbed by his phone. He picked it up. "Oh, that's a surprise. It's my daughter. I'll take it in the other room."

Closing the door behind him, he went and sat at the far end of the living room.

"Emily, love, what's wrong?"

"Nothing. I was calling to see how you were. You said you didn't feel right yesterday. I was worried. I won't stop long, just didn't want to go to bed without checking on you."

"Oh, you lovely girl. I'm fine. I wasn't ill, just miffed and upset I suppose. I'd had such a good day, what with the clues and the cakes, and then I fell out with Liz. Stupid really, but I didn't want to moan at you."

"Well, that's a relief. You'll have to tell me about the clues and cakes, but it's not good you've fallen out with Liz. Seems to me that she's the one that's pulling you back into the real world. Tell all. I'm not that tired."

Tom started with his trip to the shop and ended with Liz slamming the door.

"I felt guilty. But why should I? I felt upset because Liz had taken it personally, it wasn't personal, not to her anyway, to me. Certainly not Alana, I've never even met the girl. It was the principle. You see?"

"Sort of yes. I can see it from all sides. Perhaps you should meet Alana, maybe then you'll see why Liz thought it was the perfect solution. How do you feel now?"

"You agree with Liz, don't you? I should have known. Why am I, a grown man, not allowed to make my own decisions, or have my own opinions? And why is it when I do, I'm always wrong? In answer to your question. I'm bloody dandy. Liz isn't speaking to me, and you think I'm mean spirited. Will that do you?"

"Dad, you're making stuff up now. I never said or intimated any of that. Calm down."

"I will. Now, if you don't mind, I have a guest." Tom's eyes shot to the door. He wondered if Nadine had heard his little outburst.

"A guest? Who?"

"I'll tell you later. I must go. Will you be calling later, or will you be disappearing like Liz?"

"I'll call later, and, Dad, I really do have a surprise for you this time."

"Oh. Did you take the job?"

"Better than that, I hope."

"Go on then, tell me now." Tom smiled for the first time. "I like a surprise."

"No, I must go to bed, I've got to be up in a couple of hours. It will take too long. 'Night, Dad. Love you."

Tom stared at his phone. She'd hung up on him. A smile brightened his face. He had something to look forward to though. A chink of china from the next room reminded him he really did have a guest, and he hurried back to Nadine.

"Sorry about that, Emily, my daughter, is in Australia, so she'd normally be in bed now. I had to take it in case anything was wrong."

"No problem." Nadine blew her nose, it was clear she'd been crying again. "I made some notes and helped myself to more tea. Hope that's okay."

"Perfect."

Tom had thought she meant she'd written in his notebook, but she handed him back the murder log. He looked at it. Nadine had drawn lines from his notes, and in a neat script had added her own comments. "Perfect indeed. Do you mind if I run through them with you?"

"That's why I'm here. Fire away."

Tom went back to the Monday before Denise's murder. "So she'd mentioned the stalker to you, I should add that Denise may not have called him a stalker, Liz could have enhanced that, but Denise didn't seem worried about it to you?" Using his notepad, Tom jotted down his own notes as Nadine answered his questions.

Denise had been happy when she'd met Nadine. Although finding someone looking in her window the day before had spooked her, and she was going to go to the discount shop in Greater Compton to get some blinds. Despite having the feeling someone had been watching her, she'd forgotten all about it the minute Alana had agreed to go and live with her. She had been on cloud nine. She'd never wanted to give her baby up. But they'd struggled to pay the bills at home as it was. Karen was, and had always been, a nightmare to live with and adding a baby they couldn't really afford into the mix might have broken her mother. She hadn't been forced to give up the baby. Her mother had allowed her to make her own decision. The father's only input was to tell her to terminate the pregnancy, which she couldn't do, so she did the next best thing to keeping it, and put the child up for adoption. She'd regretted that before she'd even left the hospital. But Denise had been told everything she needed to know about the adoptive parents to know it was the best for her child.

When she'd got home, she was different. Denise was still cheerful and up for a laugh, but she had an edge to her that hadn't been there previously. You wouldn't have known that if you hadn't known Denise before, but it was there. Nadine used Denise's marriage breakup as an example. Old Denise would have forgiven Andy his indiscretion and given him a second chance, but new Denise put their little flat on the market, packed his bags, and had the locks changed before she'd even confronted him. She told Nadine she would never be used again. Andy had been through all the usual ploys, upset, angry, suicidal, made up his own version of events, but Denise had stuck to her guns. They'd not spoken for a couple of years but had recently got back to being civil to each other. Neither had found another partner.

Denise had gone out with Jim Amery a few times, Karen had hated it because she had a soft spot for him, but Nadine didn't think he was the father. Denise never told anyone who the father was. Denise appeared to be on good terms with Amery, and Nadine didn't think that would be the case if he'd been the reason Denise had to give up her baby. But it had been a long time ago, and Denise may have forgiven him. They didn't speak about it. Denise was all for looking forward. Living in the moment, not in the past. You couldn't change the past.

Karen and her son had first reappeared a few months after Mrs Mills died. Karen had demanded half the house, said Denise had talked their mother into making her the sole heir. Denise was having none of it, and when they moved to Greater Compton, and employed a solicitor, Denise had taken them on. She'd won, because Karen hadn't seen their mother since the day she left, and their mother had kept the note Karen had left for her on the table. Denise had found it while going through her mother's things. Nadine hadn't been told what was said in the note, but it had been enough to make Karen back off. Nadine had no idea if Karen knew about Alana.

When Nadine had met with Denise in the hours before her murder, she was happy. Alana was coming home, and having had the afternoon off, she looked fabulous too. Denise had not mentioned a date, though she had said she was going out. Nadine assumed it was to the pub with the girls from work, they did that quite regularly, and suggested that Tom check out what night they did the quiz. The staff from Amery's often went to the quiz night together.

By the list of evidence Tom had created, Nadine had made more notes. A question mark had been written against the gum wrapper, but all the suspects' names had been written against the cigarettes and the betting slip.

Tom shook his head. "What are the chances they would all like to gamble, and all of them would smoke the same brand of cigarettes?"

"Weird isn't it? I didn't know Craig gambled until I read your notes, but all of them have bought cigarettes in the shop at one time or another. Jim Amery has always gambled. Goes into town to the casino. Denise used to tell me that on the days he had a face like a smacked arse they knew he's lost the night before. But does it matter? If you've found out Denise made the bet, I mean. Never knew she liked to gamble, must have been a reason, I'm sure it wasn't a regular thing." Nadine grimaced. "I've not been much use, have I?"

"I don't know. You've certainly filled in a lot of gaps, so that helps." Tom fell silent as he reread the murder log.

Nadine got to her feet. "I'm going to have to go. Let me know if you need any more information, and good luck. Denise needs someone like you working on this. Can't believe the police thought it was an accident. Surely there were signs of a struggle. They must have missed them. Do you know where Alana is? I must go and visit her. She doesn't know me, but she soon will."

Tom jumped to his feet. There it was. It wasn't the hair and the nails that meant she was dating. It was the heels. He said none of this, instead he smiled. "Only that it's Southmead Hospital. I'll get more details from Liz for you. I'll see you out. Thanks, Nadine, you have been an enormous help. I promise you that."

Tom waved to Nadine through the window of the sitting room and picked up his phone. He still had no idea who killed Denise, but the others had to be updated now. He called DC Connor first, after all it was possible he was barking up the wrong tree, but he didn't think so. It went to answerphone, and Tom left a message for an urgent return call. He then dialled Liz and tutted when that also asked him to leave a message.

"Liz, it's Tom. If it's any consolation Emily is also miffed with me. I'm probably wrong, but there you are. I'll have to accept that. You said you'd be in touch today, and you really do need to speak to me. I've got more information that neither you nor the police know about, and I know... it's too complicated. Come round, I've already called DC Connor."

Hanging up, he went back to his laptop. Opening the murder log, he updated it with all the new information he had, including his own observation at the end. This he typed in capitals. He printed three copies. One for him, one for Liz, and one for the police. He left them neatly squared in the centre of the table.

His stomach rumbled, he'd had no breakfast so lunch would be early. The way his luck went, neither Liz nor Connor would be rushing around to see him. He settled on cold shepherd's pie with pickled onions on the side. He didn't care whether they were ready or not.

Over the next hour, Tom got three texts.

Mr Large, I am tied up all day, but I'll be in the area early evening, I'll pop in and see you. DC Connor

Mr Large, I'm not sulking, nor am I avoiding you, but I've got a lot on today. Mum has a hospital appointment so I'm going to see Alana while we're there. Gemma's class have a production, which I can't miss or she'll never forgive me, then I need to catch up on clients I've missed. I'll pop in once Gemma's had tea and settled, if Mum can watch her. Liz

I won't be able to call you tonight. I'll explain all tomorrow. Sorry if I upset you. Love you, Dad. Emily x

After the third one, Tom closed his laptop. Everyone was so busy. Everyone had more important things to do than speak to him. He knew he was being ridiculous and feeling sorry for himself, but it didn't stop him feeling slighted. He had clues galore and a theory of sorts that he knew could be the key to finding Denise's killer. Trying to concentrate on Mr Hardy's accounts had been hard enough before, now it would be pointless. Walking into the sitting room he dropped into his chair and switched on the television. He had hours to kill before anyone would see fit to contact him. He'd find a good film. After flipping through the channels, he settled on *Clue*. He'd seen it before, but Tim Curry had brilliant comic timing, and those facial expressions were enough to cheer anyone up. And of course, it seemed rather apt.

When it finished, Tom was still smirking as he looked in the fridge for inspiration. He'd had brunch today, and not knowing what time he might see someone, he decided something quick for dinner was in order. If he got it ready before he did his stint at the library, he might get to eat it before the others turned up. Nothing seemed quite quick enough, so he left a saucepan and a tin of beans ready for his return.

Tom's library duty was uneventful in that no more witnesses were found, and nothing out of the ordinary happened. It was relatively busy though, and his hours passed quickly. Kathy Lambert told him to go at around six as she was happy to lock up. He took little persuading.

Neither Liz nor Connor had contacted him, so he went straight to the kitchen. As he opened the tin, he realised that his life was punctuated by three things: Emily's calls, Liz, and eating. The latter he could never do without, the other two he could but certainly didn't want to. He needed to sort himself out, or he'd have no choice. He'd almost finished his beans on toast when he received a text from Patrick Connor.

I'm on my way, can I meet you at Sally's at 6.30 please?

Tom responded in the affirmative and texted Liz to update her. At six twenty-nine, armed with the updated murder logs, he lifted his coat from the hook, just in case, and walked up the road. There was a chill in the air, the sky was clear, and he could see the plough quite clearly. There might be a frost tonight. He knocked on Sally's door and was surprised when Liz opened it.

"I was outside when I got your text. Patrick has jumped in the shower. Sally is pouring wine. They're doing the quiz tonight. Come in, you're letting the heat out."

Tom accepted a small glass of red, and sat himself at the table. He passed no comment when Liz said she needed a large one. Patrick joined them, his hair still wet. He checked his watch.

"Perfect timing, Mr Large. We need to leave at seven forty-five. What do you have for us?"

"Ah, so you're not going to update us first. Surely, you've made some progress too, haven't you?" Tom hoped his tone wasn't too accusatory, he could do without further upset today.

"A little. We know the vicar's wife saw Denise at around five thirty pm, and prior to that she'd been picked up on a home security camera at the other end of Church Road. She was already wearing the outfit she died in. We're trying to work out where she was before that. We've also asked Bristol to keep us up-to-date on developments regarding their investigation into what happened to Alana's car."

"Shouldn't that be undertaken by the same team? The two events must be connected." Liz willed her hands not to hit her hips. She'd decided she wasn't going to be confrontational.

"Not necessarily. Anyway, our team haven't got the manpower, but rest assured we won't miss any connection should one be there."

Tom rolled his eyes at Liz. "Like the two victims being related? I'd have thought that was a connection that smacked you in the face."

Liz winked at him, and his shoulders relaxed. Things were getting back to normal.

"Other than that." Connor drummed his fingers on the table. "So while I've been watching hours of cars coming and going, oh, and a couple of fox cubs upending a bin, what have you been up to?" He looked at Tom's folder. "Your message seemed quite urgent."

"I'll get to that in a moment, but can you tell us who Denise's estate would go to if Alana wasn't the sole heir?"

"Her sister. She's the only other blood relative we can find."

"What? You know that would probably be the last thing that Denise would want." Liz shook her head. "Karen doesn't deserve it. I don't know who does, but not her."

"Unfortunate, I agree, but Denise should have specified what was to happen if Alana didn't succeed her if she didn't want the law to make that decision for her." Connor shrugged. "Don't shoot the messenger."

"How's your investigation into Karen and her son going? Is there a Mr Karen around?" Tom asked.

Connor made a point of checking the time again. "No offence, Mr Large, but you know I shouldn't be discussing this with you. Shall we move on to what you wanted to share, or we might not be able to do it tonight."

Tom gave a curt nod, his expression told Connor he was not impressed. He opened his folder and passed a copy of the murder log to Liz. He held back the one he'd printed for Connor. If he wanted one, he could ask for it.

"First, I know where Denise was immediately before she met Kathy, and therefore why she was at the other end of Church Road. It's all here." He waved the murder log with a smile. "I also know that Karen was sweet on Jim Amery, and as Denise went to work for him, he's not a dead cert to be Alana's father. I think a DNA test is required. Denise never told anyone who the father was, only that he'd suggested a termination which she wouldn't have. I know that Jim Amery, Craig Parker, and Andy Knight all smoke Marlboros, and all of them gamble. Although we now know that it was Denise herself who placed the bet."

Tom took great satisfaction in watching Connor's eyebrows raise. Clearing his throat, he continued, "You need to speak to Nadine Vaswani, as Denise also told her she was being stalked. She told her that Alana was coming to live with her although... while I think about it, Liz, could you contact Nadine, she would like to go and see Alana. How was she today?"

Tom watched Liz consider her response. Eventually she gave a little nod.

"She was better than yesterday, not so many bouts of tears. One of the girls from her house had managed to get in to see her with some of her books, but she's been moved out of the room she was in onto a ward of geriatrics who do nothing but snore, cry or wander off immediately there's no staff there. Said she'd spent the night calling for the nurse. She looked exhausted. She's still determined to come and live in Denise's when they release her. I told her it wasn't safe, not until the police have got their fingers out and found out exactly what happened to her car, and that she shouldn't be alone. But she won't listen. I think if Nadine agrees, the three of us need to set up some sort of rota to keep an eye on her. It will only be for a month or so before she can get about. But I'll need to ask around for someone who can make the place more secure and get some blinds up on those back windows."

"Why doesn't she go back to her student house?" Sally asked. "Patrick said there were eight of them there, they could look out for her, surely?"

"Top floor room. Not suitable," Patrick replied. "I never thought of that. Poor girl. Still, her mother's house is in good condition and sitting empty, she will be more comfortable there. The house she lives in is disgusting."

"How long is she going to need somewhere else? Because if she wants to she can come here. I've got the spare bedrooms downstairs, they'll need a spruce up, they're very old fashioned, I've not touched them since I moved in. And there's a downstairs bathroom. Do you think she'd want to? I mean, she's never met me. She might think it's weird. But there's only me, and I am out at work most days."

Liz thought Connor looked put out, but she clapped her hands in delight.

"Sally. You are a star. I'm sure she would be delighted. Tom's two seconds away, he could pop in or pick stuff up if she needed anything, and with a copper in and out, hopefully whoever tried to kill her the first time, might think twice. I can get on to the stuff needed doing at Denise's, and if Patrick's lot do their job properly, by the time she's fit enough to move in, they'll have him locked up. Sorted. Tom, we got side-tracked. Tell us the rest and I'll give Alana a ring and see what she thinks."

Tom smiled. A perfect solution, so why did he feel miffed again? Had he been intending on being the hero and taking the girl in? He had no idea, he'd simply have to put it down to his weirdness. Realising they were all waiting for him, he cleared his throat.

"We need your team to investigate all the things I've already mentioned, but first and foremost we need to establish where Denise was killed. Because unless you produce some evidence to prove otherwise, it wasn't where she was found."

"And you know that how?" Connor didn't look as upset at this revelation as Tom had hoped.

"Back to the heels. We know Denise was not out for an evening stroll in that get-up. If she were, she wouldn't have been wearing the heels. Had she been cajoled into going then those heels would have left their mark. There was none. I had my torch switched on all the way back looking for the clues I've already revealed. There were no marks left from stiletto heels. Even if she'd walked on the grass verge, which she wouldn't have because the grass would have been over her ankles, her heels would have left their mark. And she certainly didn't get there from the other direction under her own steam. That would have been a good half-a-mile walk, with a stile to negotiate. I checked the Ordnance Survey map. No. Denise was killed elsewhere, and her body carried to that spot and rolled or thrown into the stream." Tom triumphantly crossed his hands over his chest.

"Agreed." Connor nodded and winked at Tom. "You are good at this."

"Agreed, what do you mean agreed? Do you know where she was killed?" Liz demanded.

"Probably. Awaiting forensic results, but odds on it was the churchyard. The old boy who cleans up the gravestones found blood on one of them. He thought initially it might have been a prank left over from Halloween but told the vicar just in case. Mrs Lambert had a look and she saw the heel marks and called us."

"Kathy? But I was with her this afternoon, she didn't say a thing."

"Because she was asked not to. No point in frightening half the village."

"Definitely a man then. There's no way Karen could have carried a body from the graveyard to the stream. Could have got Craig to help though," Tom mused. "Denise was not a huge woman, but nor was she slight. I don't think I could have managed that. Perhaps there were two of them."

"Or perhaps they used the gardener's wheelbarrow," Connor announced. "Bit of blood on there too."

Liz's hands flew to her mouth. "They killed her, stuck her in a wheelbarrow and pushed her up to the stream! Poor old Denise. How did no one notice them?"

Tom rapped the table. "I think you're right. There were tyre tracks on the path in some areas. I thought someone had been up there on a motorbike, you know one of those cross country or trail bikes. The tread was quite wide. I didn't for one second consider it might be a wheelbarrow. But you wouldn't, would you? I need to update the murder log."

"If she saw the vicar's wife at around six by the church, what time did she die? Tom didn't find her until midnight. That's six hours! How did they push a dead body around in a wheelbarrow without anyone seeing them? Although murderer or no murderer on the loose, I don't think I'd use the lane behind the church late at night unless I had to."

"Time of death is difficult to pinpoint. It was cold that night, we'd had a frost and the pathologist guessed she'd been half in the water for at least an hour. Her body would have cooled quickly. But there was lividity, that's pooling—"

"Of the blood, yes we all watch the telly, Patrick, cut to the chase," Liz demanded.

Tom laughed. "It's amazing what you pick up. Your lot must get sick to death of people like us."

"We do, yes. Although to be fair you two have been useful. It's more likely than not she was killed within an hour of seeing the vicar's wife, she then lay on her left side for two to four hours before she was put in the stream. I told you we would get there, but these things take time. We can't go off firing on all cylinders on a hunch like you do, we must have evidence. But, yes, it was murder. Yes, it is being treated as such. And yes, my governor is co-ordinating the two cases, albeit they're not being run by the same team. Now, I've told you far more than I should have. You're going to have to keep it to yourselves, but I know that I can trust you. If I could have a copy of your notes that would be great, but now I'm going to love you and leave you, as I promised the lovely Sally here that I would take her to the quiz night at the pub."

"I love a pub quiz," Sally told them. "Although I'm also loving this in a morbid way, and with no disrespect to Denise, of course. It's so intriguing. I can see why you two have got carried away. I know, why don't you come? To the quiz, I mean. That would be good, wouldn't it, Patrick? Four heads will be better than two. I can't tell you how many times I wished I knew someone who could make up a team with me here, and there you all are. Please say yes."

Patrick's smile was merely a twitch of his lips, but he nodded. Liz looked at Tom and shrugged.

"I'll have to warn Mum I'll be late home. But I'm guessing Gemma is already in bed. What time do you think it will finish? What about you, Tom? Do you have anything better on?" She walked into the hall to make her call.

Tom's instinct had been to agree, Emily wasn't going to call, and as Liz pointed out in her own inimitable way, he didn't have anything on. Ever. But he'd not been to a quiz night before, how many people would be there? Would it get rowdy? He chewed his lip until Connor broke into his thoughts.

"Come on, Mr Large, I need you to balance the team. I've yet to be convinced, but it might be fun. We'll get a pint out of it, whatever happens."

"Okay. You're on. But I might have to leave before the end to speak to my daughter Emily."

"You're coming? Me too." Liz picked up her glass of wine. "Do we need a team name? I suggest the searchers, or perhaps the seekers. What do you reckon?"

"Weren't they sixties pop act?" Tom asked.

"Probably, but I was thinking it's more about us all seeking the truth. We don't need to explain it, it's just a name."

"Sounds perfect. Shall we make a move?" Connor had had to be convinced to go with Sally, and now he knew he should have stuck to his guns. He needed a drink.

The pub was busy when they got there. Tom could feel his chest tightening as he looked at the people squashed at the bar. But Liz grabbed a table near the door and offered to buy the first round.

"You lot sit here, I'll get them in. It'll quieten down when the quiz starts in a moment."

Tom was relieved to find that Liz was right. The scramble at the bar had been to get drinks in before the quiz started. The quizmaster was none other than Derek from the supermarket, and when he tapped the microphone and asked everyone to get their pens ready, a hush fell over the room.

Derek took the names of the teams, there were ten in all. The entry fee was five pounds per team member. Fifty percent of the takings would go to a charity of the winning team's choice. First prize was a free meal at the pub for the team, with the runners up getting a free drink.

"And the good thing is, that I, as quizmaster get free drinks all night. Cheers." Derek took a swig from his glass. "Let me know if I start slurring. There will be six rounds, and a short break for you to refresh your glasses after round three. Now, thinking caps on, it's time for round one. Geography."

At the end of the second round, Connor asked if it was the same again as he'd get a sneaky round in before the break. Tom got to his feet. "I'll do it. I might not be around for the later rounds."

But by the end of round four, Tom was thoroughly enjoying himself and had decided to see it through to the end. Although some of the teams were taking it very seriously, for most it was an excuse to get out, socialise, and have fun. Tom had laughed till he cried at one of the answers Sally had suggested which had set the rest of his team mates off, and they'd been told to get a grip by Derek.

In the end they lost by three points to the Grey Geriatrics, a team of four widows, who when not taking part in quizzes, watched them on TV.

"And in second place, a new team to The Swan, The Seekers. You can collect your voucher at the bar. I hope you'll be back next week... A & C's team aren't in tonight, I reckon you'll give them a run for their money. That's it, folks, safe journey home. Keep the noise down, think about the neighbours. See you next week if not before in the shop. Got some lovely Christmas goodies coming in at my usual bargain prices."

It was almost ten o'clock, and half the teams were pulling their coats on, and preparing to leave.

"Are we going to cash in our winnings, or can we use them another time? I'm up for another one if you lot are?" asked a happy Sally.

"We could always use them next week. I'm up for it, if any of you are? But I'm off now, need to be in for Emily," Tom lied.

"Me too. I've got to let Mum get to bed, and I've got stuff I need to catch up on, my feet haven't touched the ground today. This was just the tonic I needed. Happy to use mine next week too, if Mum will babysit."

Connor emptied his glass. "That's that sorted then. Come on, Sally, I could do with an early night." He winked and Sally's neck flushed. "You three can do next week, and I'll make it if I'm free."

When they reached the turning for Liz's street, the other three insisted on walking her home.

"There is a murderer on the loose, Liz, and if they can cart dead bodies around in wheelbarrows, well, let's just err on the side of caution," Tom said when she objected.

Liz dug him in the ribs with her elbow. "Thanks for that. I'd managed to forget about poor old Denise for a while."

Liz's home was the ground-floor flat of two in a converted 1930s house. Her car sat proudly on one half of the drive.

"I'm the garden flat, lovely big garden, too big for me really, it's a pain keeping it tidy. Mum lives over there." She pointed to a row of little bungalows. "Handy for babysitting."

They said their goodnights and walked back to the High Street. When they reached Tom's, Connor promised to keep Tom informed of any progress, and suggested he could take his foot off the pedal now the police had a launched a full murder investigation. Tom merely nodded and waved them off.

"As if," he muttered, and smiled to himself as he went through his nightly ritual of making sure everything was switched off. When he got upstairs, he readied himself for bed and sat looking at the drawer. He'd forgotten to buy more alcohol, perhaps he'd see if he could sleep without the pills.

Duvet up around his chin he lay staring at the ceiling as he considered the day's events. A solution had been found for Alana, Liz was talking to him normally again, and the police had got their fingers out. The key thing now was not to lose momentum. They could do little to find out who had killed and moved Denise. But they could look at the suspects a little closer.

"Jim Amery. We need to speak to you. If you weren't Alana's father, you might know who was," he murmured then dismissed the thought. Alana's father was unlikely to have a motive to kill his own daughter. He needed to talk this through with Liz, perhaps they had reached the end of their usefulness.

LITTLE COMPTON MYSTERIES

The Secret

Sleep had come quickly to Tom once he'd stopped thinking about Denise. He slept soundly for five hours, and then tossed and turned for another hour, refusing to get up at four am. At five o'clock he'd given up and was sitting drinking tea and running through his ledger of outstanding accounts.

It was a busy time of year. The end of January was the deadline for self-assessment tax returns, and despite his constant nagging, too many of his clients still left it until the last minute. Apart from the five larger business accounts he had to do, he had nine self-assessments sitting on his laptop, and a further five still to come in. He'd chase them, then with a fair wind, they'd all be done by mid-December. He'd be free for Christmas. Emily said she'd be home for Christmas.

Smiling, he opened his laptop, and sent an email to the five errant clients. He warned them they had two weeks to get their accounts to him or he couldn't guarantee they'd be completed by the deadline. Once that was done, and still in his pyjamas, he started on the others.

He completed the first one quickly and went for a shower before hitting the second. The reward for completing two would be breakfast. Liz should arrive just after nine, and if he cracked on he should get it done before she arrived. When the doorbell rang at eight thirty, he hoped whoever it was wouldn't keep him long, he was nearly there, and his stomach was urging him to give in.

A windswept Kathy Lambert smiled at him. "Tom, sorry to bother you so early, but I could see you were up."

"You could? How?"

"Bedroom light's on. I'm not stopping, I just came to drop this off." Kathy held up a carrier bag bulging with papers. "All the bits and bobs on the church hall accounts. I'm reliably informed we only need a spreadsheet for income and expenditure, then the church accountants will slot it into whatever they do."

"Ah okay. Thank you. Is there a timescale?"

Kathy grimaced. "End of the month. But don't panic, we're always late."

It had been a long time since Tom had dealt with sorting through paperwork. He'd trained his clients to complete the spreadsheets he prepared for them, and had the appropriate disclaimers signed that he'd been given accurate information. That way he didn't need to go anywhere, and it kept his prices down. His smile was a little forced, but he nodded.

"I'll do my best to get them to you on time. At least I haven't got to balance the bank. Shouldn't be that bad."

"Don't you? Why are there bank statements in there then? Oh well, I'm sure you know better than me. If you need more info, the vicar's your man. He's a Tom too. You have our number. I'll leave you to it."

"This sounds very messy, and not at all what I was expecting." Tom watched Kathy's face fall and prepared to pounce. "I'll have a look, but... like the church, it is my busiest time of year."

"Please don't abandon me, Tom. I'm not cut out for numbers. I promised Tom, that is the vicar, that I could take over the hall. I'm determined to make it work. We had words when he told me I wouldn't be able to keep it up." She flapped her hand at the bag. "I kept all the paperwork. How was I to know Mrs James would pull out on me? Not that it's her fault of course." Kathy was speaking very quickly, Tom could see the panic kicking in.

"I'll be honest with you. Would you like to come in? No, okay. Well Liz and I are still working with the police on Denise's murder and it's taking up a lot of time. Denise has a daughter. Did you know? I can see you didn't. Alana. Lovely girl, I'm told. I'll bring her over to meet you once she... I'll cut to the chase. It's taking up a lot of time, if I could cut that down in any way, I should be able to squeeze this in. If you could tell me what you know about the investigation over at the graveyard, that would mean I could crack on, and not have another couple of hours taken up meeting with DC Connor. He's told us that was where Denise probably died, and that she was moved in the wheelbarrow. He didn't have time for more, so if you could fill in the detail, this," he held up the bag "might get done a lot quicker."

"Oh well, in which case put the kettle on."

Kathy told him how Gerald, the chap who looked after the church grounds, had found blood on a gravestone, told the vicar, and she'd gone out to see if it was anything to worry about. It wasn't much blood, but enough to make it look sinister, particularly given the location. The stone in question was on the end of a rank, and a small path next to it led through to the other ranks, and a gap in the wall to the alley behind. Like Gerald, she initially thought it was local youths sneaking in and playing a prank. But something told her they'd have been more exuberant in the daubing, so she looked around.

In between the cobbles that made up the path, many of which were missing, were holes. There was a particularly large concentration of them next to the blood-stained gravestone, and when she stepped forward to look closer, her own heels, although stouter than the ones which had made the holes she was inspecting, sank into the ground. Kathy had remembered that Tom had asked her about Denise's attire when she'd seen her that day, and two and two had made four. The police arrived within the hour, and further blood had been found on the wheelbarrow. The forensic chap, who arrived first, had photographed the wheelbarrow from every conceivable angle, and announced it was the same as the one that had been used by the stream. The whole graveyard had been taped off, and men in forensic boiler suits had covered every inch of it. Kathy had watched from the window in the vestry. When they took the tape down, she asked what they'd found. She knew they'd found something because one of them was carrying a box containing evidence bags.

"But," she concluded, "nothing very exciting. A few cigarette butts, a piece of red fabric, which could have been caught on the bush by the gate years ago, and a very soggy handkerchief. Does that help get the accounts done?"

"It will certainly help. I didn't make you tea. Do you still want one?"

"No. I should be somewhere else. Nothing changes. I'll see myself out, but, Tom, you really must come to the Christmas fete. The Compton Women's Institute has made some marvellous cushion covers and throws. Very colourful. Just what this room needs to give it a lift."

Tom looked around, but before he had time to answer, Kathy was calling goodbye and the front door banged shut. His stomach rumbled, and he decided breakfast would now have to come before he'd finished what he was working on. Leaving the carrier containing the hall's accounts by the armchair, he headed for the kitchen. He'd not even opened the fridge when Liz called out from the hallway.

"Only me, Mr Large. I'm going to flit around upstairs, do the lounge, and then we can talk." She put her head through the kitchen door. "Did I just see the vicar's wife leaving?"

"You did. She pressurised me into doing the accounts for the church hall. I agreed when I was vulnerable, I'd found Denise only the day before."

"Talking of which, did you ask her about the graveyard?"

Tom smiled as he lifted the frying pan out of the cupboard. "I thought you were flitting somewhere. I've been working since five, I'm getting my breakfast."

"A fry-up? You usually have cereal. What did she have to say?"

"Not much. Go and flit and then we can catch up. But before you go up, stick your head in the living room and tell me if it needs a lift."

"A what?" Liz disappeared. "Oh, yes. Well I've told you before that it needs a splash of colour. All those browns and creams need something."

"She suggested I go to the fete. The women's something or other have made cushion covers and throws. I've still to work out what a throw is."

"Or you could go to the discount store and get it for half the price. So are we talking now or am I going upstairs?"

Tom merely pointed at the ceiling with a smile.

Breakfast cooked and eaten, Tom even managed to do another ten minutes on his accounts before Liz hung up her duster. She flipped the switch on the kettle.

"That's you done for the week. I wasn't expecting to get that much done. I deserve a cup of tea."

"You do. Let me just save this and I'm all yours. If you get the cake tin down from the top cupboard, you'll find one of Alice's cherry slices."

"Which reminds me, I saw her on the way up. She said to tell you she needed another poster. One for idiots who don't realise that almond slices have nuts in. Did you do the others for her?"

"I did, I'm sure I told you. Now stop talking and sit down."

Tom told Liz what had been found at the graveyard. "There may be more of course, but that's all Kathy managed to find out. I'm just glad I asked her about what Denise was wearing so it struck a chord when she saw all the punctures in the soil."

"Who else was about?"

"When?"

"When the vicar's wife saw Denise. Keep up, Tom." Now we know that Denise went for coffee with Nadine, and then up to the church. In the six hours between seeing Kathy and you finding her she probably met whoever it was she was meeting, there. At the church. Perhaps not in the graveyard, but certainly in the vicinity of the church. Because if not, what was she doing there? When you come out at the end of Church Road, you turn left for the church, and right for where Denise lives. Turning left gives you two possible meeting locations, the church, or the bowling club. The bowling club is all shut up for winter. My guess is she was meeting someone at six, six thirty at the church. She was probably killed soon after meeting them, left in the graveyard for at least two hours and then transported up to the stream. How long do you reckon it would take to push a body up there?"

"No idea. I've never walked it, let alone had to steer a heavily laden wheelbarrow."

"Then let's go and find out."

"No. Because one, we don't have a heavily laden wheelbarrow, and two, what would it prove?"

"It would give us some idea of when she was moved. You didn't see anyone coming back down with the wheelbarrow, so that will help, you see?"

"No. Let's move on for a moment. Have a read through this, I've updated it, and see if you can work out what else we need to do." Tom handed Liz the updated murder log. "I'm going to have to order more paper for the printer."

"You could just write on the original. Hush, let me concentrate."

When Liz had considered what they had, and what they were missing, she tapped Alana's name. "We must go and see Jim Amery. We have two reasons, first and foremost is to find out what happened while Denise was at work to make her happy. The second, is there is a chance, even if he isn't Alana's father, that he might know who is? And before you say it, I know her father is unlikely to have tried to kill her, but having lost Denise she will probably want to find out who he is. Which reminds me, I should phone Alana about Sally's offer, you can phone Amery's and make an appointment. Or do you think we should just walk in off the street?"

Tom didn't need to think about it. He didn't particularly want to go wandering around by the church for no purpose, so he said simply. "Walk in."

"Get your shoes on then. I'll just make this call."

Amery & Cheriton's office had a large plate-glass window with vertical slat blinds. The blinds were open, the light was on, but the front office was empty. Liz shrugged and pushed open the door. Immediately they entered, they could hear a female shouting.

"You always take her side. It's pathetic. Well, when she gets back, I'm telling her I'm going, and I expect you to back me up."

A quieter male voice replied, although they couldn't hear what was said. Seconds later a young girl came storming out of the rear office. Tom held his hand up and tried a smile. The young girl paused, rolled her eyes, huffed, and headed for the door.

A tall, slender man with a mop of dirty brown hair, followed her more slowly. He looked harassed. By the time he'd greeted his unexpected visitors, the girl had left. Jim Amery smiled.

"Teenagers," he said by way of explanation. "She's had a row with her mother. How can I help?"

"Two things," Liz jumped in before Tom had a chance to speak. "The first is a bit delicate. The short version is that Tom here found Denise's body, and as a result we've sort of got tied up helping the police with their inquiries. Would you mind us asking you a few questions?"

"Really? Um... No. But we've already spoken to the police. Not sure how speaking to you will help, we didn't know anything. Come through. I haven't got long."

Taking them through to the rear office, Jim offered them a seat in front of a small desk off to one side. Most of the room had been taken up with a huge drawing board.

"What did you want to know?"

"I saw Denise on the Monday morning before she died, and she was frightened. She'd had vandalism to her property, and she believed she was being stalked. But by the time she went into the library mid-afternoon, she was happy. She'd been working here that morning. We know two things happened to make her happy, one we know about, the other we've yet to find out. Can you tell me if she took any calls, or perhaps mentioned what was making her happy?"

"No. The police asked a similar question. I didn't see her much. I was tied up with work." He looked at the drawing board. "My wife Becky was here, as was Damien, our apprentice, he's at college most of the time, but happened to be in. The police spoke to them too. Neither of them were able to help. I'm sorry, I did say I doubted I could help. You said two things, what was the second?"

"Denise has a daughter, Alana. No one is sure who the father is. We understand that you and Denise had a relationship in the months leading up to Denise leaving Little Compton."

"I am not the girl's father. Sorry."

"Can you be sure of that?" Tom smiled. "We haven't got the dates straight yet. But is there any chance that Denise could have been pregnant when you split up and she didn't tell you?"

"No. I left for university in late September, Denise's daughter was born in September the following year. We didn't continue our relationship when I came home in the holidays, I met Becky, my wife during my first year."

"Denise didn't confide in you?" Tom had the niggle at the back of his mind again and needed to keep Amery talking while his thoughts formed.

"No, she didn't. Why on earth would you think that?" Amery glanced at the clock.

"Because in all the people we've spoken to, you're the only one who even had an inkling that Alana existed. So, she must have told you something." Liz leaned forward, her eyes trained on Amery's face. "What did she tell you? Because Alana is now alone in the world, she's going to want to find her father. One of the two things that had cheered Denise up was Alana coming to live with her, here in Little Compton. It also gave Alana hope too. Now that's been snatched from her. You never know, her father may have gone on to marry and have other children, Alana may have a family somewhere. She won't have her mother, but she might have someone. Please, Mr Amery, if you know anything you must tell us."

Liz had overdone it. Amery was shaking his head before she'd finished.

"When I said I didn't know, I meant I didn't know. Not that I did, but you'd have to prise it out of me. Now, I really must get on. I'm sorry but I can't help you."

"I'm sorry about that. When will your wife and your apprentice next be in? Perhaps we could have a word with them?"

"I've told you, they know nothing. You're welcome to try with Damien, he's in on Monday, but Becky won't speak to you. She's already spoken to the police. She wouldn't speak to... I don't know what to call you." He did, but not wanting to cause any upset he got to his feet and held out his hand. "I'm sorry I couldn't be of more help."

Liz clasped the outstretched hand in her own. "Thanks for listening. There is one thing you could do, you know, to put paid to any rumours that start once Alana moves here, did I tell you she was moving into Denise's house? I didn't, did I? She is. And as if she hasn't got enough on her plate, someone is trying to kill her too. Poor girl."

"Kill Alana? Why? How?" Amery was clearly shocked, and he left his hand encased in Liz's.

"We don't know yet. But we're getting there. Someone tampered with her brakes, luckily the crash didn't kill her, but she is in hospital. She'll be coming to Little Compton as soon as she's fit enough."

"Oh, my goodness, that's terrible. Isn't she too frightened to come here, you know with her mother being killed? I would have thought she'd go

as far away as possible. I would. Perhaps you shouldn't encourage her."
Amery's brow had furrowed, and he looked genuinely concerned.

"We didn't. She'd already made her mind up when I met her. I'm just helping the poor thing. She has no one else." Liz released Amery's hand and looked at Tom. "Did you want to ask anything?"

Tom nodded. He'd barely been able to get a word in. "Only one thing. Would you take a DNA test, Mr Amery? To rule you out as Alana's father, once and for all?"

"I would not. I am not her father. I feel sorry for the girl, and I wish her all the best, but no. Now, if you wouldn't mind, I really must get on." Now free of Liz, Amery walked to the open door and indicated they should leave. The door from the street was closing and he frowned. "Abi, is that you?" he called as the others filed past him.

"No one out here," Tom told him. "Must have been the wind, it's blustery out there today. If you change your mind, Mr Amery, please let us know. I live in Pendry's bungalow. It's—"

"I know where it is. Goodbye." Pulling open the door to the street, Amery grimaced. "Once again, sorry I couldn't be of more help."

"But you could. We'll leave that to you and your conscience. Have a good afternoon." With her nose in the air, and shoulders back, Liz marched back towards Pendry's.

Tom trotted to catch her. "Do you always have to run? One minute you're there, the next, gone. It's like being with that cartoon thing, the Road Runner. That's it. Do you beep beep too?"

"I don't like dawdlers, I told you that. It'll do you good to get that heart working a bit harder. It's good for you. What did you think of that?"

"Can we get inside, and have the kettle on first?"

Settled back at Tom's table, they discussed Jim Amery's response. They decided he was hiding something, otherwise why not agree to the DNA test. Tom wondered if it could be because Amery truly didn't know and didn't want to risk finding out. Liz was of the opinion that if he truly didn't know, he certainly thought he was. Liz also didn't like the fact that he said his wife wouldn't speak to them and wondered whether that was because he controlled her. Tom was in the middle of saying he thought

Amery seemed like a decent chap, but even decent men had guilty secrets, when the doorbell rang.

When Tom opened the door Abi Amery pushed past him. "Sorry, but I can't talk on the doorstep. I might be seen."

"No problem. Is it Abi?"

"Yes." Now in the hall, Abi blushed. "Can I speak to you about why you came to see my dad?"

Liz appeared in the doorway. "Why don't you ask your dad? I'm not sure your parents would want us discussing this with you."

"Because he's a parent. He'll tell me it doesn't concern me. Only it might. I'm right, aren't I? I might have a half-sister, and if that's the case it is to do with me."

Liz ushered the girl through to the dining room. "Take a seat. How do you know that?"

"Because I'd forgotten my phone. I came back in to get it and heard you mention Denise, the dead woman who used to do the typing. I wanted to know what it had to do with my dad. If he is my dad."

"Why would you think he's not your dad?"

"Because they hate me. Well, Dad's not too bad, but Mum has no interest in me whatsoever. The only time she speaks to me is to criticise or stop me doing what I want to do." Abi scowled and her cheeks coloured. "Don't smirk. It's true. I'm a virtual prisoner, not allowed to do anything except study. She's even cancelled my gym membership. But we'll soon see."

"Why aren't you allowed to go to the gym? What did you do?" Liz asked. "Don't get me wrong, I won't judge, but I was a teenager myself, and there was always a reason for a punishment, to my parents that is. What I thought didn't come into it. So, I know enough to know there was something."

"That doesn't matter. What matters is whether we can help each other."

Despite her petulance, Abi was a confident, well-spoken young lady. There was a spark about her that Tom liked, he smiled. "Let's hope we can. You tell us what you think we can do for each other, and we'll tell you if that's possible."

"Dad refused to take a DNA test. Don't you think that's suspicious? Because I do. I'm an only child, a miserable, lonely, only child. If I've got a half-sister, I want to know about it. Know her. If me and Dad are all she's got, she should know about it, and so should I. I'd love a sister, half or not. Although it is a relief, it would be Dad's half not Mum's."

"Okay, how do you propose we do that? How old are you?" Tom asked.

"Seventeen. Why do you ask? Because I'm not old enough? There are ways and means you know."

"Are you suggesting we encourage a minor to break the law? I don't think that's going to happen, Abi. We have the full co-operation of the police as things stand. We wouldn't want to compromise that."

"You wouldn't be. Has this Alana had her DNA tested?"

"We don't know because we haven't asked yet. She's been in a serious car accident and—"

"I know, I heard that. How awful must it be to know someone wanted you dead? All the more reason to find whatever family you have. How old is she by the way?"

"Twenty. She's a nice girl. Seems kind, is pretty, slim, blonde..." Liz let the sentence drift away as Abi repeatedly pointed at herself as Liz uttered each element of the description.

"Does she have blue eyes?" Abi was grinning. "I bet she does. Can I meet her?"

"Whoa! We need to discuss this with her before you start getting carried away, and of course, whatever your opinion, we do have to consider your parents."

"No, you don't. If we were ten months down the line, I'd be eighteen and free. I can't wait. And anyway, it's too late."

"What do you mean too late?"

Convinced that she must be adopted, which is why her mother hated her, Abi's friend, Bella, had agreed to let Abi use her name and date of birth to send off a DNA sample to *WhoAreYou?*, a family tracing site. The results were due in the next week or so. Abi had also heard Liz tell her father that Alana was coming to live in Little Compton, and she'd decided she would contact Alana as soon as that happened.

"But now I know about Alana, perhaps that's why my mother hates me. Perhaps I was a revenge child because he already had one. You know something to keep him tied to her, because any sane man would have left her by now. She tries to control him too, you know. I have no idea why he puts up with it. I don't know, I haven't thought this through because I've only just found out, but the DNA will tell us. You must ask Alana to get her DNA tested."

Liz and Tom exchanged glances, but it was Tom who spoke. "That's all very well, Abi, and if you don't mind me saying, it's pretty daft. Have you put either of your parent's DNA on there? If you haven't, what did you expect to find? I doubt very much your mother knows about Alana, even if you share the same father. The father of Denise's baby wanted her to terminate her pregnancy. I doubt that was something he would have shared with future partners. He may even have believed that's what Denise did, because she went away to have the baby. Adult relationships are complicated. You're assuming that because you have an issue with your mother, your father does too. Have you ever considered he might be perfectly happy? Other than the conflict you seem to have with her of course. I'm guessing the need to play peacekeeper probably upsets him."

Abi shrugged. "That was patronising. This isn't teenage angst, you know. The woman is mad, something is wrong with my family, and I intend to find out what, if I'm able. Now I know about Alana, the best result for me would be that she is my sister. If she wanted me to, I could go and live with her. That would solve everyone's problems."

Liz blew a breath through pursed lips. "Let me speak to Alana and see what she wants to do. Even if she's not related to you, she might like you as a friend. That's not patronising you, but a statement of fact. In the meantime, go home and keep your head down. Your father could be telling the truth, and your mother might not know about his relationship with Denise. After all, it was before they met. But you saying anything could make matters worse. From what you tell me things don't need to be made worse. Will you do that for me?"

"When are you going to speak to Alana?"

"I'm going to see her later if I can't get her by phone. I've already tried once, she didn't pick up, but she could have been otherwise engaged."

"Will you tell her about me? Please. Just let her know that I'm here for her whatever."

Liz nodded and convinced Abi she should go back to her father and keep her thoughts to herself until they knew more. Abi agreed and smiled for the first time since she'd arrived. Tom saw her out and found Liz was already speaking to Alana when he returned. Alana readily agreed to staying with Sally and confirmed she had already sent her DNA off to *WhoAreYou?* She'd decided to do that and see what turned up when Denise had told her it didn't matter who her biological father was.

"Wow." Tom raised his eyebrows as Liz relayed the conversation. "So, we'll know soon if the two girls are related."

"We will indeed. I still want to do that walk and was trying to avoid doing it in the dark but needs must. Will you come with me this evening?"

"As long as I'm in by ten. I should be here for Emily's call. We didn't speak yesterday."

"Oh dear, was that our fault for dragging you to the quiz night? I really enjoyed it, I'd like to do it again."

"I did too. No, it wasn't the quiz, she got tied up and texted to say she wouldn't call."

"I should have her number you know. Just in case."

"In case of what?"

"In case anything happens to you. In fact, anyone's number would do."

"Nothing is going to happen to me. But if it makes you happy, her number is in the phone book."

"Fabulous. If only I knew where that was."

"Top drawer in the sideboard. I'd better get on with some work. I'll update the murder log. If you change your mind about creeping around a graveyard at night, just call."

"That's me dismissed. See you later."

Liz didn't return until seven thirty, by which time Tom had done another two self-assessments and sorted the paperwork Kathy had dropped off into some sort of order. They started at the gate where Denise had bumped into Kathy, walked past the entrance to the church, and through the gap in the stone wall that led into the churchyard. They walked along the path at the side of the church, then up through the gravestones along the cobbled path which led to the lane beyond. Tom shone his torch back and forth and although they thought they'd found the location of Denise's murder, any blood which had been there had been cleaned away. Wherever the wheelbarrow had been, it was now absent from the scene. They entered the lane. Liz led the way, walking slowly, her yellow wellies squelching on the leaves underfoot. At the top of the lane, she stopped.

"You wouldn't know this if you haven't been here, but if you go along this way, it comes out where you would have joined the path along the stream. It's an unofficial route, quicker if you're trying to get back to Lower High Street. But this way, and this is the way I think they would have come, leads to... it's easier to show you. Come on."

They walked side by side, the going underfoot became very claggy in patches. Liz maintained the pace she thought the murderer would have been able to travel with a body in a wheelbarrow. Tom's torch revealed little other than footprints from boots like their own, and dog prints. After a few minutes, the path narrowed, and falling in behind Liz, Tom handed her the torch. She swung it back and forth too quickly for his liking, but he kept that to himself. Until something caught his eye on a bend in the path.

"Stop. Back up a minute. Give me the torch."

Now in control of the light, Tom shone it along the bank on the right-hand side of the path. The earth had been scored by something a foot or so above ground level.

"You see that?" He followed the line in the bank again. "This is the way they came. I reckon that's where the wheelbarrow listed to the right as they tried to guide it around the bend. How much further now?"

"Not far. Keep walking."

With Tom now leading the way, they walked another hundred yards or so. The path widened up to a clearing Tom was familiar with. On the other side of it the stream emerged from the rear of the village. He walked to the centre of the clearing and then followed the narrow path that ran alongside the stream. At this stage you couldn't see the stream, only hear its progress as it flowed towards the river and the estuary beyond. Immediately the bank lowered, and the dark stream came into sight, he slowed, and shone his torch towards the water.

"There. That's where they left her."

Liz shivered and grabbed the sleeve of his coat. "Are you sure?"

"Of course I am. Look over there. No grass left, worn smooth from all the emergency service chaps doing their job."

Liz checked the time. "Twenty minutes. Although I think possibly half an hour. I don't think they would have been able to travel that quickly with the wheelbarrow. Come on. Let's get home. It's almost eight. See how long it took you."

Tom turned away, and walked at a brisk pace, shining the torch back and forth as he had done his phone. Past the clearing, through the gap in the hedges, and they were at the end of Lower High Street. Tom stopped walking.

"It's seconds down to my place now. How long was that?"

"Two minutes, tops."

"As I thought. Now take me from here back to the lane and explain why they wouldn't have come that way. It seems to me it would have been quicker."

"Don't need to. There are two sets of steps. Only two steps a piece, but would you try to get a wheelbarrow with a body up them? And look how bright it is here. Think the steps are lit too."

"Show me."

Tom decided Liz was correct in her assumptions. Although the route was probably half the distance they'd travelled to the stream, and cobbled underfoot, most of the path was encased by walls, and at the two sets of steps there were wall lights to illuminate the steps.

"You were correct, I believe, Liz. Even if they didn't allow for the steps, over half of that journey left them exposed to being seen. If someone had chanced upon them, there was nowhere to hide. Going the other way, although it might have been difficult, what with the body, they would have had a chance to leave the path. Whoever moved her knew this. Interesting."

"Not really. Most people who live here will know about it. If we think about our main suspects, Andy, Jim, and Karen, they would have all known. In the summer when the fair is on, following this path along to the other end is the easiest route. But I'm exhausted, it's been a long day, I'm not showing you now."

"Nor would I want you to. Come on."

As they approached Pendry's, Patrick Connor pulled up outside Sally's, and Sally jumped out of the car.

"Hello. Glad we bumped into you two. We've just been to see Alana. Thought I'd better meet her. You were right, she is a lovely girl. It's such a sad situation. Looks like she can come home on Sunday, so I've roped Patrick into getting her room ready with me tomorrow. If you fancy popping up and lending a hand, feel free. Where have you been?"

"Just for a walk. I'll pop up after swimming. Tom might be earlier. Have a nice evening."

Connor opened the boot and lifted out a tin of paint. "As long as you didn't find any more bodies. Apparently, I'll get the first coat on tonight. I don't need to be called out. And before you ask, nothing new, yet. See you tomorrow." Connor ushered Sally up the path to avoid further conversation.

"You didn't want to chat then." Tom grinned as he pushed open his gate.

"Not tonight. Don't want to take advantage. See you tomorrow. 'Night."

"Goodnight, Liz."

As suggested by Liz, Tom made a few notes on the printout of the murder log and got ready for bed. He'd recorded the new series of *Vera*, and decided he'd watch that until Emily called.

"Hi, Dad, sorry about yesterday. Unavoidable. How are you? You look well. You've got rosy cheeks."

"That's because I had a bracing walk, and the heating is on. It's miserable here. Had a busy couple of days. You'll never guess what I did last night. How are you by the way? You look a bit worried."

"Not worried, not really. What did you do? I'm intrigued."

"A pub quiz. We came second. Won a round of drinks, we're going next week to cash in. What does 'not really' mean?"

"Dad, that's fabulous. Who's we? Liz I'm guessing, I can't wait to meet her."

"You will if you come over at Christmas. But back to you, what's happening with the job, and what does 'not really' mean?"

"Would you say you are in a good mood?"

"I was. Now I'm getting nervous. Why?"

"Oh, no. You don't need to be nervous. Shit. I'll just say it."

But she didn't. Tom gave her a moment before prompting.

"Go on then. Say it. It can't be that bad."

Emily blew out a breath. "Here goes. I'm coming home."

"Yes, you said... Oh... Do you mean *coming* home? Home to live?"

"I do."

"That's bloody marvellous. When? Oh, hang on there's a catch. When you say home, you do mean near me, don't you? Not Scotland or somewhere else miles away?"

"Near, as with you... initially anyway. Would that be okay?"

"This is getting better and better. Of course, you daft girl. That's perfect. When?"

"By Christmas, next few weeks. That job I told you about, it wasn't here. It's in Bristol. I'm renting my place out here, can't bring myself to sell it yet. I can't find any properties I like. Or if I do, they are as far as you are from where I'll be working. I thought if I could come and live with you while I look for something suitable?"

"Which sounds imminently more sensible than going for something you've not seen. Estate agents are very good at taking misleading photographs. For instance, I hope you don't expect the sitting room here to be huge. It's not. No point in rushing into anything. You are welcome to stay here as long as you want. You never know, you might decide Bristol is too pricey. Because it is, you know. When do you start? Oh, I haven't got a car yet, how will you get back and forth, public transport is awful I'm told."

"I get a car with the job, and I start on the fourth of January."

"This all sounds splendid. If I had anything in the house, I'd raise a glass in celebration. The best news. Just the best." Tom's smile faded as he saw Emily didn't share his enthusiasm. "What? I can see there's something else. Is there a but?" He watched Emily draw in a breath and crossed his fingers and curled his toes as his heart rate increased. "Spit it out, Em, there's not much you can tell me that will take the edge of this."

"I think there might be. It's all my fault, I kept waiting and waiting. You know, for the right time, and it just never... then it seemed... you know."

"No. No idea." He watched her chest expand again, and she closed her eyes.

Without opening them she said. "I won't be coming alone." Opening one eye she grimaced.

"You're back with Jason. I'm sure—"

"No not Jason. Eddie."

"Who's Eddie, a new boyfr... Not... but why?" Tom frowned and pulled the phone closer to watch Emily's changing expressions.

"Eddie who you spoke to the other night. He's your grandson." Emily blinked and her eyes welled with unshed tears.

"But how? I mean I know how, but why don't I know about... Oh, I see. You've adopted him. For one moment there..." Tom watched his daughter's face crumple and her shoulders bounce. "You're his mother? His proper birth mother? He's how old? Four? Five?"

"Four in January. He's quite big for—"

"I'll tell you what he's quite big for. He's quite big for me only to be finding out about him when he is so big. I can't speak to you." Tom's shaking finger managed to disconnect the call on the third jab.

Emily tried to call back four times. Tom ignored her calls. He was pacing up and down cursing his stupidity at having thrown away his alcohol. He didn't go to bed, there was no point. He simply could not comprehend why she hadn't told him. Had he known all along, how might that have changed things? He didn't know, but now, despite having his immediate family double in size, he felt as alone as he had the day Amy died. He couldn't sit and relax, nor would his body function properly. His attempts at making a sandwich at three am lay scattered on the breakfast bar. He didn't even read the end of the text Emily sent him.

Dad, I know sorry isn't good enough. But when I fell pregnant, you were in a really bad place. I was so excited and so thrilled, that I couldn't tell you. I didn't want you to bring me down. To take that excitement and joy away from me. It had been a long time since I felt that good. Eddie was born two days after Aunt Jane had to have you taken to the hospital. We didn't speak for a week if you remember. That wasn't because I was avoiding you, it was because I was in hospital too. The birth hadn't been straight forward. When you were allowed home, I didn't know how to tell you what you'd missed. Then you seemed to get better, and I thought...

Tom stopped reading. Four years ago, on what would have been their twenty-fifth wedding anniversary, he'd had a full-blown breakdown. He didn't have any memory of what happened, or the treatment he'd received, his mind had locked itself. He was in hospital for over a month. He couldn't remember much, only how much he hated it, and the relief at getting home. Once there, he'd redecorated the living room and moved what he needed in there. And there he'd lived like a hermit for over a year. It was only when his sister, Jane, and Emily, had told him they would break off all contact unless he did something about it, that he'd started trying. He'd seen doctors, therapists, even a hypnotist at one stage, but none of them understood. Eventually when he'd not spoken to Emily for over a month, and the neighbours had complained to the council about the state of the garden, he realised that he had to do it for himself. He still lived in the one room. Couldn't bear to be reminded of what he'd lost. Even using the bathroom without Amy's carefully chosen accessories was a challenge. But he started looking for somewhere else to live.

It took three years, but with the help of the internet he'd settled on Little Compton. Everything was close enough for him to dash to, once he'd managed to get out of the house, that was. The main setback had been Covid. But in between lockdowns they'd got there. He attacked the garden himself but had employed a company to come in and clear the house of everything but the personal items. Jane had sorted through those, decided what he wouldn't want to keep, and she liaised with Emily to find out what she wanted. That was boxed up and remained so in the cupboard in one of the spare bedrooms. He'd never looked.

Falling to his knees, Tom wept. He wept for Amy, for Emily and for Eddie. A boy he didn't know. But he never wept for himself. Self-pity was something he'd given up on years ago. He didn't deserve pity. He'd let them all down. If he'd held Amy's hand tighter they might never have been in this situation, but he hadn't. Even in moments of clarity, when he realised it wasn't his fault, it wasn't even the fault of the child who'd pushed the button to stop the escalator, he couldn't pity himself. He had a child. A child that needed him more then than she ever had, but he'd wallowed in his own self-pity. He'd failed her, and eventually he'd lost her. How could he blame her now? This was another loss he'd brought upon himself. Emily had protected herself and her child from him. On realising this, he wept for the man he should have been.

When his legs began to cramp, Tom wiped his nose on the back of his sleeve and using the chair as an anchor pulled himself to his feet. He hobbled to the bathroom and ran a bath. He had to clear his head. He had to think. He had to phone Emily and apologise.

THE DNA TEST

T he bath water was hot, his mind and body exhausted, and Tom slipped into sleep. He awoke only when he heard Liz calling. The bath water was cold, and his body covered in goosebumps. Teeth chattering, he put his head around the bathroom door.

"Liz, I'm in the bath. You go on, I'll catch you up."

"I'll put the kettle on. They're not up yet, all the curtains are still closed. Probably painting until the early hours. That's nice isn't it?"

Tom wanted to argue, but what could he say. He shivered and closed the bathroom door. Turning the shower on, he stayed under the hot water for as long as it took for his body to feel normal again. His mind wouldn't rest. Wouldn't stop reminding him. He took his time dressing too, he didn't want to face Liz. He didn't want her to know that man. Eventually he had to go downstairs.

Liz was sitting at the table, her back to him. His eyes darted around the kitchen. She'd cleaned up what should have been a sandwich.

"Do you want to tell me about it?" she asked without turning to look at him. "I can't find the bottle, but something went wrong in here last night."

"Wrong?" Walking to the kettle, Tom flipped the switch. "Do you want another one?"

"No thanks, this is my second. Yes, wrong. What happened? Don't say nothing because you're a neat freak. This kitchen looked like a bomb had hit it. There was a smashed jar of pickle on the floor, the fridge was open, and the butter knife, complete with melted butter was on the sofa.

Your phone was in the middle of the carpet, dead. I put it on charge. The temperature must have been nearing one hundred as the heating was on all night, and don't try to tell me all that happened this morning, because I was here for ten minutes before I shouted for you. Although it's almost eleven, I thought you might be having a late lie in too, like those two up the road. I was going to leave a note. So, no lying. You don't have to tell me, but don't lie to me."

"I have a grandson. Eddie. He's four years old in January." Tom's voice broke as he ended the sentence.

Liz spun to face him. "You didn't know?"

Tom swallowed the lump in his throat, coughed, and shook his head.

"And Emily told you last night?"

Tom nodded.

"Ah. In which case you're forgiven. I thought you'd hit the bottle. You didn't, did you?"

Tom shook his head.

"Why did she choose yesterday to tell you?"

Tom's shoulders twitched.

"Tom, I'm a nosey cow, if you want me to go just point at the door, but if you want me to stay, you're going to have to speak to me. I won't be able not to ask questions and that will annoy both of us."

Tom nodded and Liz rolled her eyes and grinned at him.

"Well at least you don't want me to go. Sit down. I'll make your tea. Did you want something to eat?"

Tom shook his head, but he sat at the table as she busied herself. He mustn't cry. All this was his fault, he didn't deserve sympathy. If he cried, she'd be sympathetic.

Placing the tea in front of him, Liz took hold of his hand, and he closed his eyes as he snatched it back. The first tear appeared. Liz pulled a tissue from her pocket and shoved it in his hand.

"When you're ready."

Tom reached across to his phone and found the message from Emily. He passed it to Liz. "I hung up on her, she sent me that. I didn't get to the end." He shredded Liz's tissue while she read the message.

Liz knew nothing about Tom's history, only that his wife had died and more recently, how. She knew his daughter was in Australia, and that he was doing his best to conquer his fears. The message didn't go into detail, but it said enough for her to know how low Tom had been, and the impact that had had on Tom and his family. When she finished reading, she put the phone on the table and cleared her throat.

"I don't want you to talk to me. But you must talk to Emily. Now. She says you can call at any time, even if it's the middle of the night there. She's still coming to England with Eddie, and she'll let you know where she'll be if you don't speak before. That's ridiculous. That's absolutely crackers. You could have your family here with you, and all it will take is one phone call. I'll tell you something else too, you're going to have to brave the discount store. You'll need bedding and stuff for them, and you said yourself you needed to brighten up that living room. We'd better check your crockery and that kind of stuff too. You're a bit needy in that department as well."

Tom just looked at her. He wanted to smile his thanks, but his lips just wouldn't work. His eyes filled with tears again.

"Don't start that, you'll set me off and you've just ruined my only tiss..." Liz jumped to her feet and grabbed the kitchen roll. Tearing off two sheets, she gave one to Tom as she dabbed her own eyes with the other. "I'm not leaving until you call her. I don't know how it will go, but good or bad you can't lose that girl. Them. Once she's answered, I'll leave you to it and call you later."

Tom didn't respond. He was folding the sheet of kitchen roll into neat squares. Liz waved her hand in front of his face.

"Did you hear me? You're not even nodding at me now."

Tom got to his feet and went to the sink. He splashed cold water on his face which he dried with a tea-towel before walking over to his phone. He picked it up.

"And you're going to go as soon as you hear her voice. You're not going to hang around being nosey. Because that would be your preferred position." He almost managed a smile.

"Well, now you mention it, I can if you'd like me to." Liz winked at him. "Make the call."

Tom turned his back on her and opened WhatsApp. He pushed the video button with a nod. Emily answered almost immediately.

"Emily, I'm sorry. I'm a poor excuse of a man, and I should never have created the situation where you had to put yourself in that position. I'm sorry, sorrier than you'll ever know. I think you need to get on that plane and get over here as soon as possible. I'm going to the discount store with Liz, and we'll get bedding and everything else she seems to think I need. But that will only take a couple of hours. I'm sure it will take longer for you to get back. But when you do, and it had better be soon, everything will be ready for you. Now, what time is it there? I'd like to speak to Eddie."

"Dad, I'm so—"

"Don't you dare apologise to me. None of this is your fault. None of it. We won't mention how we got here ever again. We're going to move forward. This family is going forward. Now Eddie." Tom turned around, to smile at Liz. But true to her word, when Emily had spoken, she'd left. He heard the front door click shut.

It was midnight in Australia, and Eddie was in bed. Emily crept into his bedroom and turned the phone so that Tom could see him.

"You can speak to him tonight when I call. I don't want to wake him, he won't be very happy about that."

"And nor would I." Tom brushed the tear from his cheek. "I love you, Emily, Eddie too, even though I don't know him yet. Go to bed, get some sleep, and we'll speak later."

"You haven't told me the latest on your investigation yet. I love you too, Dad. 'Night."

"Goodnight, Em. Don't let the bedbugs bite."

"Thank you. Eddie will be so excited when I tell him he's going to speak to you. He already thinks you're nice because you didn't tell him off for answering my phone."

"He knows about me?"

"He does. I told him all about you once you'd spoken to him. He's very excited about coming to England, he'll be more so now that he's going to live with you. You might have a bit of trouble from him at Christmas though."

"Why?"

"He's never seen snow. He thinks it always snows in England at Christmas. I haven't got the heart to explain what grey, damp drizzle is like."

"If Eddie wants snow, I'll have to see what I can do."

"Dad, don't go saying stuff like that to him. He thinks that adults aren't allowed to lie. I only tell him the truth... most of the time."

"Then I will surprise him. Somehow. I don't know how, but I'll sort something out. I thought you were going to bed?"

"That's what you said, but I'm too excited, too happy."

"Then rest your eyes with a smile on your face."

"Are you trying to get rid of me?"

"Never. Never ever believe that, Em. I will never stand in the way of things you need to do, but I'll never want to lose you again either."

"Now you're going to make me cry again, so I am going. I'll speak to you later. Oh, hang on. Hello, sleepy head."

"You woke me up. Why are you talking?"

Tom smiled at Eddie's voice. "Let me say hello. Then I'll let you get him back to bed."

"Come here, Eddie. Grandad wants to say hello.

"Grandad!"

The phone blurred for a moment and then Eddie's eyebrows appeared. His mother lowered the phone and he smiled at Tom.

"Mummy told me we were going on a plane and coming to see you. She said we could have a sleepover in your house." His head nodded as he spoke.

"And she was right. I'm going to buy you some new sheets and stuff for your bed. What's your favourite colour?"

"Blue. But I want jungle ones. Like they had in the shop. I'm not a baby."

"Then jungle ones it will be. What's your favourite animal?"

"All of them. But I like lions the best. In Lion King, Simba's my favourite. Scar was a baddie."

"Oh, I haven't seen that. I'll have to watch it before you come, or perhaps I'll get it for you so we can watch it together."

"Okay, but Pumbaa farts all the time. He's funny."

"Does he now? I'll forgive him if he's funny."

"Can we come tomorrow?" Eddie's face turned away, and Tom looked at his perfect ear as he asked his mother the same question.

"Not tomorrow, Grandad is busy. Next week. Don't forget you've got to say goodbye to everyone. That might take some time."

"Oh, okay." Eddie looked back at Tom and yawned. "It's not till next week. I'll bring you my Lion King book. Then you'll know everyone." Eddie yawned again.

"That sounds like a brilliant idea. Now I need you to go back to bed, and tomorrow and next week be very good for Mummy. That way the time will fly by, and you'll be here before you know it."

"I will. Ni-night, Grandad. Love you."

The phone blurred again before Emily's face appeared.

"He's in my bed now, but I'm going to leave him. Today was huge. Momentous. I will go now, or he'll be up again. 'Night, Dad. Love you."

"Goodnight, Em, from the happiest man in the world."

They spent another few minutes saying goodnight, but eventually hung up.

Tom messaged Liz a simple 'Thank You', he had a lot more he wanted to say, but she would know from that the conversation went well. He hoped her smile was as wide as his own. Message sent, he opened his laptop. The first thing he searched was Lion King, he ordered numerous plush animals from the film, the film itself on DVD, although he was sure he should be able to find it on one of the endless television channels he now had access to. He also ordered Lion King Lego, and a jungle with over forty rubber animals. That done, he found a flower shop who would deliver the same day, and closing his eyes tried to remember Liz's address. He knew the road was Hyacinth Close, but the number was evading him. Running their first conversation with Patrick Connor on a loop, he remembered and felt very smug as he typed it in. The message to be written on the card was the same as the text, although he added his name.

Satisfied, he picked up a notepad, went into the hall and opened the doors to both bedrooms. Both had been freshly decorated when he moved in, they didn't need attention in that area, and of course, Eddie would have the smaller room. He needed to get him a bed. That was the first item on his list. There was already a bed in Emily's room because his sister had threatened to come and stay, but so far had only visited once. But she worked full time, had a family, and who would want to give up their spare time to stay with the old Tom? The new Tom would be quite a different kettle of fish. Now though she'd have to have Tom's room, and Tom would make do with the couch. Both rooms had built-in wardrobes, so only drawers and bedside cabinets were needed. The bedding and the curtains in Eddie's room were suitable for an old lady, not a young boy. The list grew as did Tom's excitement. When he'd exhausted all possibilities, he went to put the kettle on.

He'd left his phone on the table and hadn't heard Liz's message come in. It was also simple. A smiling emoji and see you after two. That gave him another hour. He was starving, and in the absence of anything more exciting, he got a ready meal out of the freezer and put it in the oven. He thought about taking a stroll down to the shop to treat himself to something sweet, but seeing it had started raining, he decided against it. His mind wasn't in any condition to work on the accounts, or concentrate on reading a book, so he decided to put the television on. As he went into the sitting room, he saw someone hurrying up his path, seconds before the doorbell rang. It wasn't Liz, but other than that he had no idea who it could be as their umbrella shielded their face. He opened the door as they rang the bell and was surprised to find a young woman standing there. She looked irritated.

"Are you Tom?"

"I am. How can I help you?"

"My nan told me to come up and get the poster."

"The what? Who's your nan? Do you want to step in, you're getting soaked there?"

The girl stepped over the threshold and turning, opened and shut the umbrella to dispel the rain. "Thanks. I told her I'd get soaked but she wouldn't listen. Thinks the feds will get her because she's selling cakes with nuts on."

"Oh, Alice. Okay, I understand that bit, but feds?" Tom frowned and then laughed. "You mean the police. Apologies... sorry, don't know your name. It's been a long time since I've encountered youngsters."

"Bella. And I'm not a youngster, I look younger than my age."

163

"Everyone under forty is a youngster to me. No offence intended. Come on in. I've not done it yet, but it won't take a second, I saved the other one." Tom walked into the dining room and opened his laptop. "Bella, you say, do you know Abi Amery?"

"Yes. She said she'd spoken to you. What's the latest?"

"What did she tell you? I'd hate to break a confidence."

"Not much really, her mum arrived. Said she probably had a half-sister called Alana who was moving here, and if she could she'd go and live with her. She said you and Liz whatsit, the cleaner, were going to sort it all out. Have you?"

"Not yet, but Alana will get her DNA tested, I think she'd like a sister as much as Abi does."

"Probably won't when she gets one, mind you mine is younger and a pain in the ar... neck."

"I've got a younger sister, she was too, best of friends now though."

"I doubt that will ever happen. But as Nan says, stranger things have happened. When I was telling her about Abi, she said you were investigating Denise Knight's murder, and had interrogated her. She got quite offended when I laughed." Bella's face lit up when she smiled, she was a pretty girl, and if Tom squinted, he could see a likeness to her grandmother.

"We are helping the police, yes. Liz seems to know everyone, and everyone seems to know something, even if they don't realise they do."

"You're an Agatha Christie fan. My nan loves Poirot and the old girl, Miss Marple." Bella looked around. "Do you live here on your own? Nan said she thought you and Liz make a lovely couple."

Tom opened his mouth to deny any such thing but caught the devilment twinkling in Bella's eyes. He smiled at her. "I do at the moment, but my daughter and grandson, Eddie, he's almost four, will be moving in, in a couple of weeks. And as to Liz and I, as you well know, I'm far too old for Liz, she is my housekeeper, and yes, if you like, partner in investigating crime. So don't go starting rumours that aren't true. You'll get yourself a reputation."

"Fair enough." Bella grinned. "Can I take my coat off while you do it, it's boiling in here."

"Yes, I left the heating on all night. It's off now, but I can't bring myself to open a window in this weather."

"Has your grandson got his name down for preschool? If he has, I'll be helping teach him. Passed my final health and safety thing. The police have finally returned my DBS check. Also passed, 'cos I'm a good girl, I am."

"Two things, where is pre-school and how do I register him? I haven't discussed childcare with Emily. Should have though."

"Go onto the council website, go to the pre-school page, and put your postcode in. You should be fine. The nursery is allowed fifty pupils, it was only at forty-two last time I looked. What was the second thing?"

"Oh yes. You sounded just like Eliza Doolittle in *My Fair Lady* when you said that. That's a film by the way."

Bella's smile was back. "That's because I played her in the last am-dram production. I've seen the film three times. How beautiful was Audrey Hepburn?"

"Ah ha. You're a thespian. If you don't mind me asking, how do you know Abi? You seem a lot more mature than she is. Please don't tell her I said that, wouldn't want to offend. But she came across as a very angsty teenager, and you don't."

Bella explained that Abi had been in the year below her at school, and they caught the bus back and forth to town for years. Bella hadn't wanted to stay on, so went to college and studied nursery nursing, and Abi, who was heavily controlled by her mother, had stayed on. They were still friends, Abi was also in the am-dram group, and up until recently went to the spin and step class at the gym. Abi had been having a hard time lately, and Bella was her sounding board.

"You could get yourself into trouble, you know, falsifying DNA. But I understand why you did it."

"I doubt that. I'll just tell them our samples must have got mixed up. As soon as she can do it, we'll put it right. Don't panic. Are you going to do that?" Bella nodded at the screen. "Only Nan's waiting, and I'm going ice skating this afternoon."

"Yes, of course." Tom sat at his laptop and located the previous document. "Where do you go ice skating? It can't be in town."

"The Mall at Cribbs Causeway. They do an open air one, so it had better stop raining, but it's lovely. All Christmas trees and pretty lights, and they've got the German market selling all the Christmas bits. Can I make a suggestion?"

"Of course."

"Why don't you just do one list as a warning. All cakes might contain, or traces of: flour, sugar, eggs, nuts, fruit, and on and on. That way you won't have to do this each time she changes a recipe. She's never going to throw anything weird in there."

"Good idea, she'd better like it, or I'm grassing you up." Tom began amending the list. As he worked on it, Bella skimmed the murder log which was still on the table. Tom printed the amended sheet and held it out to Bella. "What's wrong? You look... perturbed."

"That's one word for it. I thought she was killed up by the stream late at night. Not by the church at half six."

"Well, the time is still open, but yes, we believe around then, I'm afraid she was killed in the graveyard and moved to the stream. Probably to put the police off their tracks."

"In a wheelbarrow. Denise's daughter must be gutted. I might have been able to stop it. God, how bad is that?"

Tom's heartbeat increased. "I'm not sure she knows that bit yet, so keep it to yourself. It wouldn't do for her to hear it from the wrong person. She's understandably quite delicate at the moment. Now, tell me how on earth you could have stopped Denise being murdered?"

Bella told Tom she'd taken her dog, Jasper, for a walk on Tuesday. They'd walked up Lower High Street, through the graveyard, along the lane a little way and then cut through to the stream and followed it as far as the stile. They'd gone further than Bella had intended and realising the time and that she'd be late for dinner, she retraced her steps. She'd checked the time at the stile, and it was six twenty pm. Her best guess was that it was about six forty when she heard the woman shouting in the graveyard. As her dog didn't like strangers and would freak out at one who was shouting, she'd taken the long route back, following the lane to the end, and coming out up the road from Tom's bungalow.

Tom asked her if she'd caught what was being shouted.

"Not really. The first thing I heard was 'I don't care'. I paused because I wasn't sure if that was it, but then she shouted something like 'it's not your business' and I went the other way. I didn't hear any more though, not when I was walking along the lane. Perhaps if I'd gone through the graveyard, she wouldn't have been killed." Bella looked devastated, and Tom sought to reassure her.

"We can't possibly know that. As someone has attempted to kill Alana too, even if you had, it probably would only have delayed the inevitable. Did you hear any response from whoever the woman was shouting at?"

"Nope. I assumed whoever it was simply wasn't as frustrated. Whoever was shouting sounded like my mum does when she's trying to get our Jill to do something You know, frustrated, not expecting to be killed.. Oh. That wasn't very tactful. I'd better get back to Nan. Should I tell the police?"

"Absolutely. Here, jot down your name and telephone number and I'll pass this onto DC Connor. He'll be in touch, probably tomorrow but we might get lucky, and they get their skates on."

While Bella jotted down the information, Tom slid Alice's list of ingredients into a plastic folder. "Here you go, I'll see you out. When you give it to Alice tell her not to forget my payment, and please keep all this to yourself. If the murderer is local, we don't want to alert them to the fact we're onto them."

Bella's expression changed a little, and she shook her head. "I won't. I can't believe you're charging an old lady for a sheet of paper and some ink."

Tom laughed. "She pays me in cake. I'll get one almond slice if I'm lucky."

Bella smiled. "I had one earlier. They're good. Thanks, Tom, see you around. If your grandson is here at Christmas, bring him to see the pantomime too. It's on at the village hall in Greater Compton, just down the road from the school, we're doing Snow White. It's quite good. You've got my number, let me know if you want tickets."

"I will. Thank you."

Smiling, Tom closed the door and went back to the living room. What a lovely young lady. Eddie could do worse than have someone like that helping him into the world of education. Although he himself had no intention of going into a crowded village hall, Emily might like to take him.

He'd have to ask. But first things first, he needed to call Patrick. Patrick answered almost immediately.

"Hello, Mr Large, all done bar the shouting, we're off out to get some lunch, so you're not needed. Did Liz not tell you?"

"Call me Tom. I haven't spoken to her since earlier, I was calling about the murder." Tom told him what Bella had heard and passed on her details.

"Hmm. I'll call it in now, get them to go and speak to her. We know the WI had been in the church planning the Christmas decorations. Mrs Lambert said there were a few of them about when she saw Denise, given what was said, and that it was said in frustration not anger, it could have been them arguing with each other. We'd better round them up next week and see."

"Bit of a stretch though, given what happened to Denise, don't you think?"

"Possibly. But elimination is necessary. Police work isn't all deduction like Sherlock Holmes would have you believe. To get to the truth you also need to eliminate."

"Yes, I can see that. Enjoy your lunch. My timer has just pinged I'd better rescue mine."

Tom added the notes to the murder log by hand as he ate his fish pie. It looked untidy, and he went to his laptop to update it, as much to while away the time until Liz came back as anything else.

When Liz arrived she had an odd way about her, and when she sat at the table, she kept her coat on rather than put it on the back of the chair as she usually would.

"Are you not stopping?" Tom was disappointed. He wanted to tell her all about Eddie, what he'd ordered, and ask advice on his bedroom. He didn't say this, he simply joined her and passed the updated log across the table.

"Not for long. Mum and Gemma were going into town, but Gemma's got a bit of a temperature. What's this for? Has something else happened? I came round to talk about your grandson." Liz smiled and looked more like her old self.

"Yes, I have news, but let me tell you about Eddie first." Tom retold his conversation with Emily, almost word for word. "So, immediately I got off the phone I got onto the internet and ordered loads of jungle related stuff, heavily weighted on the Lion King. Emily loved that film too, but I pretended I didn't know anything about it. Oh, and I ordered something for you, by way of a thank you. I regretted it after, but it seemed the right thing to do. It's good having a friend with a level head around."

"What did you regret? Why?"

"I'll ruin the surprise if I say."

"You won't, the flowers have been delivered."

"Oh, I hope they were okay. Don't like ordering things like that online. I regretted it because I didn't want them to be misconstrued. I don't want any more hand patting conversations. They weren't a romantic gesture, just a thank you because Eddie and Emily are coming here to live. On that note, Bella mentioned pre-school. She starts work there soon and asked if Eddie would be going, do you know anything about it? Did Gemma go there? I thought I'd register him, but not knowing anything about it, I wasn't sure whether I should wait for them to arrive."

Liz relaxed and her smile was wide even though she looked confused. The flowers really were only a thank-you. That was an awkward conversation dealt with. Instead of answering his question about the school, she asked, "Bella who? Alice's Bella? Must be, Alice was telling me about her job last week. Why have you been speaking to Bella?"

"Because she was at the graveyard around the time Denise was there. Possibly. Read it." Tom pointed at the murder log.

When Liz had finished, she shook her head. "That's crucial information, but as it stands it doesn't help much. The police need to start their alibi chasing all over again. They were asking people where they were late at night, what we need to know is where were Jim Amery, Craig, and Karen Parker, and to a lesser degree, Andy Knight in the early evening?"

"I agree we can almost rule out Andy Knight, because how does he benefit by the death of Denise and Alana? He doesn't. He might have had a row with Denise, after all she shouted 'it's none of your business' and perhaps he killed her in a crime of passion. But that would mean the attempted murder of Alana was for an unrelated motive. Too much of a coincidence for me."

"Exactly. The Parkers on the other hand have plenty of motive, with mother and daughter out of the picture, the house and anything else Denise owns might be theirs. On that point, what's happened on the burglary at Denise's, do we know?"

Tom admitted that element of the case had totally slipped his mind, and he made a note to chase Patrick Connor. He drew a circle around Amery. "Which leaves Jim Amery. If guilty his motive is what? Embarrassment, financial? Let's say it's one of those, would he kill his own daughter? I can see he might want the holder of his secret, Denise, out of the way. But why then kill Alana?"

"Perhaps he thought Denise might tell her, perhaps Denise threatened to if he didn't come clean. Belts and braces. Still not a nice thought though. We could find out if his father is still alive and try to speak to him."

"But Alice said he had dementia. Even if he didn't, would he know anything about it? It wasn't something a teenage boy would volunteer if the girl was going to keep her mouth shut."

"All the more reason, depending on what type of dementia he has. Some people live in the past you know. He might think Jim is still that teenager and have lots he could tell us."

"Or if he knows, he might protect his son. No, I think that's a long shot that would waste our time."

"Have you got anything better to do with your time?"

"As it happens, yes. I am awaiting the imminent arrival of my daughter and grandson, I do have to earn a living, I volunteer at the library... shall I go on?"

"We can get all that done, no problem. Let's start with the kids. Have you made a list?"

"I have." Tom flipped to the list in his notebook and handed it to Liz. "I'm going to have to go to that discount place for curtains, and I was wondering if I should get some wallpaper suitable for kids. Aren't blank white walls boring? I know Emily's used to be plastered with stuff."

Taking the list, Liz went through to the bedrooms, she made notes on the bottom of the list, and satisfied he had everything covered, she asked, "What are you doing this afternoon? If you can leave now, I can take you."

"I thought you had to get back?"

"I'll pick something up for Mum. She loves knickknacks, and our Gemma will be asleep or watching the television anyway. I shouldn't have taken her swimming really, I knew she had something about her."

Thoughts of large stores, crowded aisles, and panic attacks flitted through Tom's mind. But he ignored them and nodded. "I'd better get my coat on."

As they approached the industrial estate, Tom's heart started racing and he was blowing out breaths in short puffs. Liz looked at him out of the corner of her eye. "Are you going to be okay, because I can go in on my own and send you pictures of the stuff I think you'll like?"

"You will not. This is my grandson. Mine. How can I not do this? I know how, don't answer that, but I must give it a try. Onwards and upwards, at least I hope it is."

His heart sank as Liz pulled into the carpark. It was going to be busy. Liz crossed her fingers as she walked to collect a trolley. Tom didn't look well. The colour had drained from his face and his eyes were darting from side to side as though he were looking for someone. She decided being chirpy was the best way to handle it.

"Better have an extra-large trolley. We're going to need it. I like shopping. I hope you've got enough in your bank account. This way."

Liz walked quickly through the drizzle, Tom a little behind her, silently telling himself how to breathe, and focusing on Eddie's bedroom. As they approached the entrance, he grabbed her arm.

"Stop. Give me your keys."

"Why?" Liz handed them over.

"Because if I get overwhelmed, I'm simply going to leave, and we'll revert to the sending pictures plan. My heart feels like it's going to land in that trolley at any moment."

"Good plan."

As they entered the store, the chattering of others filled the air in competition with 'Let it Snow'. It wasn't quite December, but the Christmas songs had begun, and every display shouted they were wrong, it was Christmas.

It had been spring when Amy had died. He could cope with this. He grabbed Liz's arm again.

"Take this. My pin number is zero-four-zero-two. Just in case. I wasn't expecting Christmas to have arrived. That's another thing I need to think about. I'll have to buy for Eddie now too. He's expecting snow by the way. I told Emily I'd see what I could do. Bella mentioned an outdoor ice-skating rink, a Christmas one. That might go some way to sorting it. And as an added bonus it's outside. Although Bella might not be going, she was hoping this rain would stop."

Liz had already steered both Tom and the trolley into the bedding section. She kept him talking. "Can you ice-skate?"

"I could in my youth. I was quite good. I was rather hoping it would be like riding a bike. I used to do that too." He managed a smile, but his face contorted as his mouth fell open. "Will you look at that? It's a sign, Liz. A sign." Letting go of the corner of the trolley's handle he rushed forward.

Liz smiled. At the end of the aisle was a display of jungle themed bedroom items. Curtains, duvet set, lamp shade, and best of all a giraffe bedside lamp. The giraffe's head poked out of the top. Checking the measurement of the curtains, Tom loaded the items into the trolley. "Where's the wallpaper section? It says they have wallpaper too."

"We'll get there. Let's just follow these aisles, and get stuff as we come to it, otherwise we'll be running back and forth, and it will take ages. Now what sort of bedding did you want for Emily? You've got the embroidered white on there now, do you think a bit of colour would be nice?" Liz led him towards some abstract designs.

In less than thirty minutes, the trolley was almost full. The bedroom items had been chosen, and he'd taken a ticket so he could order a single bed for delivery. Throws and cushions had been purchased for the sitting room, together with a deep pile rug, which jutted out from the trolley, and which Tom wasn't convinced about.

"I'm making you bring it back if I don't like it in situ." He warned her with a grin.

"Then that won't be necessary. Now you go over there to the customer service desk and order the bed, they'll give you a docket to take to the checkout, and I'll pop up to the wallpaper section and see what I can find. If you're finished before me, I'll meet you by the Christmas trees. And no, we don't need to do that today, real ones are better anyway, and they sell them from the church carpark leading up to Christmas."

"That's good, I thought I could take Eddie to buy the tree and let Emily take care of the decorations. Are we running out of time?"

"No, why?"

"Because we're separating. Thought you were time saving."

"The wallpaper section is upstairs. You need to go up an escalator. It has no steps, it's flat and grabs the trolley's wheels, but it's an escalator. You've been here ages and not a sign of stress. Baby steps, Tom, I'm not risking you on an escalator or in a lift." Liz flapped her hand. "Close your mouth and go and get in the queue."

Tom merely nodded as his chest tightened. He had done well, he would see this through. "In through the nose, out through the mouth, think of snow and Christmas not escalators," he chanted silently as he joined the back of the queue. Someone came to stand behind him, then another and another. He grasped the keys in his pocket. "Breathe," he told himself. "Focus." Choosing to focus on the till, he couldn't help but count that there were five people in front of him. "Breathe." To his relief the first three in front had been together and left quickly. How had he not noticed that? He shuffled forward, his chest and lips doing their job. The man in front turned around and smiled at him.

"It's awful being stuck in these queues, isn't it? I can hear you breathing. Relaxation technique? I do that when I go to the dentist. Still shake like a leaf, even when it's only a check-up. Oops my turn. Nearly there. Hold that frustration, I won't be long."

Tom relaxed a little more. The man had thought he was frustrated not weird. That was a first. If he didn't have to concentrate on his breathing, he would have smiled. He managed one for the cashier. A few minutes later the bed and cabinets had been ordered. Clasping his ticket triumphantly he set off to meet Liz.

Next to the display of artificial Christmas trees was an aisle containing every shape, style, and colour of Christmas decoration you could imagine. His eyes found the red and gold box of baubles. They would go with the new soft furnishings nicely. Should he get them, or should he leave it to Emily? As he pondered this, Liz tapped his shoulder.

"I never said wander off, I said wait by the trees. You're worse than our Gemma. I decided against the wallpaper, I think it would be too much even on one wall. I got you this, what do you think?" Liz held up a roll. "It's a self-adhesive border. No paste or mess, and it's the same design. What do you think?"

"I think it's perfect. I've decided Emily can choose the decorations. Shall we pay? I think you're safe to hand back my card now. Erase that pin number from your mind."

Liz handed him the card. "I've already forgotten it."

Back at Tom's, they arranged the new cushions, throws, and laid the rug. Tom agreed it was perfect, the addition of the red had made his living room cosy. A very smug Liz left him surrounded by the packages. Tom decided to knuckle down and get Eddie's bedroom underway. He started with the fiddliest job which was the border. It took him far longer than it should have, but once he'd put the curtains up, you could barely see the crease he'd made, which was good because he was too frightened to peel it back and try again. He put the electric drill on charge. The flat pack furniture was promised the next day, he wasn't convinced it would arrive on a Sunday, but he was going to be prepared. Stacking the bedding in the corner, he went into Emily's room. He'd stripped one pillowcase when he changed his mind. Better to do it the day before she arrived, so it was nice and fresh. Leaving the unopened packets on the bed he decided he'd treat himself to a takeaway and a film, but not before he'd sent Liz a photo of Eddie's bedroom.

Might need to take the curtains down and iron them if the creases don't drop out, but what do you think?

Her answer was almost immediate.

Perfect, but will Eddie mind the animals being upside down?

Tom's heart stopped, and he ran to the bedroom. Laughing, he was glad Liz hadn't been there to see his unnecessary panic. He responded in kind.

He'll love it. A talking point.

When Tom sat to order his food, he found he was exhausted. After the night before and the trip out, he wasn't surprised. But he'd keep himself awake until Emily called. Then it would be straight to bed and no pills. He placed his order, and taking Denise's murder log, he started to think about it. What if Denise had been murdered by a stranger? They could find as many clues as they liked, they'd never work out who it was. Perhaps they should go and talk to Amery senior. Tom tutted. Now was not the time to become indecisive again.

He woke when someone rapped on the window. Bleary eyed, he went to the door.

"Evening, saw you were having a nap, hope I didn't scare you. No way to knock quietly." The delivery driver unzipped his bag. "Smells nice."

Tom collected some change from the hall table for a tip. "Chicken Chow Mein, and crispy shredded beef. Too much for one really, but I couldn't make up my mind."

He finished both and was showered and ready to give Emily the guided tour when she called. He never got round to the tour as Eddie commandeered the phone and asked him question after question. Some were quite sensible, others Eddie asked merely so he didn't have to give his mother the phone. Tom decided not to show him his bedroom until the bed was made up and the covers on. Eventually Emily had to prise the phone off Eddie as they were going into town with a neighbour.

"Booking the flights today, Dad. I'm just hoping I can find some jumpers and stuff, it's boiling here. I'm lucky if I can get him to keep a T-shirt on."

"I can get him those, send me his measurements or is age four internationally suitable? I'm guessing it is. Jumpers, long trousers, socks, ooh, he'll need a coat. Wellies. He needs a pair of wellies. What size feet has he got? Is shoe sizing the same as here?"

"Yes. He's a size ten, but you don't need to do this, Dad, I—"

"Let me do it. Think how much money I've saved over the last four years." Tom grimaced. "Sorry, that wasn't a dig. Just true. I didn't mean anything by it."

"I know. Look I really must go. Don't go mad, I think he grows an inch daily. Eddie say 'bye to Grandad."

Eddie appeared and grinned. "'Bye, Grandad, I love you."

Eddie's hand appeared and the screen went blank. He'd ended the call before Tom could return the sentiment. Tom didn't mind, he was so happy there was little that could upset him. Climbing into bed he switched off the light and stared at the ceiling. After an appalling start the day had turned into a good day. A very good day. He might not need oblivion tonight.

THE NEPHEW

After a good night's sleep, a refreshed Tom was up early, breakfasted and working on clearing the accounts due by the end of the year. He was making excellent progress, which was just as well as his experience of building flat packs told that him building all four items might take him longer than a day. He'd just taken a break for elevenses when the doorbell rang. He wondered if it might be Liz. It wasn't, it was Craig Parker.

"Yes?" Tom was surprised and his greeting was not as polite as he would have liked.

"Delivery for you. Big ones. I'm going to need a hand with two of them."

"Ah. Of course. Let me get my shoes on."

"Will do. I'll get the smaller ones."

Craig had clearly not recognised him as the man who had denied his mother access to Denise's house. He opened the door to Emily's bedroom.

"Pop them in there," he told Craig who had returned with the two bedside cabinets. He then followed Craig back to the van and helped him carry first the bed and then the mattress into Eddie's room.

"Two chests of drawers to go, I believe. Thirsty work this furniture lugging. Can I get you a drink? Tea, coffee, squash?"

"A cold drink would be great. I'm off for a pint after the next delivery."

"Can't be much fun working on a Sunday, I'd say you deserved it." Tom went to follow him again, but Craig held up his hand.

"I'll do them. You get that drink."

Tom made a pint of orange squash and seeing the murder log on the table, he buried it beneath his other paperwork. He stood glass in hand and watched as Craig deposited a box in each of the bedrooms. Craig ran his forearm across his brow as he accepted the drink. He emptied half in one go.

"Lovely. Not as good as a pint, but thanks, gov. Much appreciated. Hope you've got an electric drill for that lot. I can give you a price it you want."

"No, no. That's fine, I'm sure I'll manage. My daughter and her son are coming to stay, and they'll be arriving next week, so I need to get it done."

"Sixty quid, cash, and I'll do it for you now. Or after my last delivery anyway."

"I thought you were going to the pub."

"I am, but it's open all day. I don't think they'll run out. What's it to be?"

Tom chewed his lip. This was an opportunity too good to miss, and Craig seemed much nicer when his mother wasn't around. He knew he was supposed to haggle.

"Fifty-five and it's a deal, as long as it is this afternoon."

Craig emptied the glass and handed it back. "Give me twenty minutes. Last one is in Greater Compton. Fifty-five and a sandwich. I can't work on an empty stomach."

"Done." Tom held his hand out and shook Craig's before closing the door behind him. Watching the van drive away, he called Liz.

"I don't know what you want, but I can't do it today. I'm having some quality time with Gemma today. Mum's gone to lunch with a friend, and me and Gemma are currently making cupcakes."

"Oh no, I didn't want you to do anything other than give me advice. Craig Parker just delivered the bed and drawers we ordered yesterday. He offered to put it together, we've agreed a price and he'll be back in twenty minutes. He had a last delivery. But what do I ask him without making him suspicious? How do I broach it? He didn't recognise me from outside Denise's."

"Have you gone mad? He might be a murderer. You can't start asking him questions in your own home. Whatever possessed you?"

"Getting to the bottom of it." Tom hadn't thought of that. Craig was a strapping lad and Tom wouldn't stand a chance if things got physical. Tom had never been one for violence.

"Well, it's too late now, you don't want to change your mind. You might make him mad. Just talk about the weather or failing that, him. Blokes like talking about themselves. I might pop up, but I'll have Gemma with me. Won't be for at least an hour though."

"There's no need for that, I can look after myself. I won't wind him up. I'll talk about football if conversation is necessary. He likes football."

"Hmm. Text me and let me know how it's going. I'm going to be worried now."

Thirty minutes later, Tom was standing in his hall with Craig, and agreeing that the bed would be built first, and the other things would be put together in the hall where they'd have more room. Tom asked if he could help.

"Not yet. Might need you in a minute when I need the end lifted. Another glass of squash would be good."

Craig began cutting into the packaging with a sharp blade, and Tom decided no conversation would be necessary as he left to get Craig to get his drink. When he returned, Eddie's bedroom door was shut, and he could hear drilling. Placing the glass on the hall table he paced about a bit, before deciding to get Craig's money ready. Counting out sixty pounds, he realised that for the first time in over a year, he'd need to get some cash out of the bank. He guessed Little Compton, or possibly Greater Compton had a cashpoint, but he didn't know where. He must ask Liz. He was about to text her when the bedroom door opened.

"Pass my drink, please. I could do with you now."

Tom passed the drink and then placed the empty glass back on the table. In the bedroom, he followed Craig's instructions and within minutes the bedframe was complete.

"You start unwrapping the mattress and I'll put the slats on," Craig ordered. Craig worked relentlessly, sweat poured from his brow, but he manoeuvred the mattress onto the bed as though it were weightless. "That's that done. If I make up the drawers first, you can put the handles on while I do the carcass. I can see you want to help. If you make that sandwich you promised me, I'll have the first one ready for you." He grinned at Tom.

"No problem. What would sir like?" Tom returned the grin.

"Anything will do, ham, cheese, tuna. I like a bit of salad, but not mustard. Don't like mustard."

"I've got some nice extra mature from the cheese shop, will that do with some pickle?"

"Lovely."

While Tom made the sandwich, he considered the lottery of the parents you were born to. The young man in Eddie's bedroom wasn't angry or aggressive like his mother. She obviously brought out the worst in him. He wondered why he'd been arguing with Denise. He ate half his own sandwich, before he carried Craig's through to the hall. The first drawer had been made, and the second was well underway.

"Thanks, gov. Put it on the table, I'll finish the four for the chest first."

"You know you can sit at the table, you don't have to have it out here. Shall I put the kettle on?"

"Not for me. I don't do hot drinks. Another orange would be good though. I can sit on the stairs." Craig stood the second drawer on its side and started the next as Tom left.

The first lot of drawers complete, Tom was about to start putting the handles on when the doorbell rang. When he opened it another delivery driver smiled at him. A large box sat on the doorstep.

"Delivery." He stepped back and took a photograph of the box at Tom's feet. "Have a nice day. It's not heavy."

Tom took hold of the box. The man was right, it was big, but it wasn't heavy. "I have no idea what this is," he told Craig as he kicked the door shut. "Can I borrow your knife?" He opened the box and smiled. Lifting a polythene wrapped Simba from the box he held it up to show Craig. "It's for my grandson. I haven't met him yet. He's nearly four."

"How come?" Craig asked through a mouthful of sandwich.

"My daughter has been living in Australia, and what with Covid and everything... you know. But they're coming to live here now. We'll be a proper family. Have you got a big family?"

"Nah. Just me and my mum. My dad used to turn up every now and then, but we haven't seen him in years."

"Oh, that's a shame. I've got a small family too, really. My wife died. But I've got a sister, she's got three kids, although I've not seen them for years. But I'll have Emily and Eddie soon. Hopefully Emily will have contact with them. Have you got cousins?"

"Nope. My mum had a sister, didn't know her, but she got killed recently. She didn't have kids. Never knew my dad's family." Craig shrugged as he popped the last of the sandwich into his mouth. "I'm too young to settle down, I'd like to have kids though. I'd be a better dad than mine was." He looked sad for a moment, then shrugged and added, "But thirty will be early enough to think about that, there are a lot of girls out there who still don't know me." He winked at Tom and drank the glass of squash.

"I'll top that up. Sorry to hear about your aunt. How did she die? She couldn't have been very old."

"We were told she'd had an accident, but now it looks like someone killed her. Shame and all that, but I didn't know her. My mum didn't get on with her."

"Hang on, you don't mean Denise Knight, do you? They told me it was an accident and then changed it to murder."

Craig frowned and his head tilted as he considered Tom. "Yep. Why would they tell you anything? What's it got to do with you?"

"Nothing really. But I found her. I was out walking and there she was, dead."

"Wow. Scary. That would give me nightmares. Bet that was horrible."

"It was awful. I used to work with her in the library, so I recognised her straight away. But here's the thing, I also heard she had a daughter. When she was young, she had a daughter who she gave up for adoption. They'd recently found each other. So sad. But it means you have a cousin."

Tom could tell immediately that Craig had no idea what he was talking about. His frown was back, and he was squinting as though trying to remember something.

"Your mum might not have known. Sometimes when young girls fall pregnant and the baby can't be kept, they're sent away on some pretext."

Tom was desperately trying to get as much information as he could, without alerting Craig to the fact that he knew a lot more than he was saying.

"That's weird. A cousin. I'll ask my mum. So weird. Where is she?"

"I have no idea. We were talking about Denise in the shop and one of the women mentioned it. I'll get you another drink and get these handles done." While he was in the kitchen, Tom texted Liz.

All good. A surprisingly nice lad below the rough exterior. Didn't know he had a cousin. No need to come round. Bed done. Getting to work on the chest of drawers.

Craig was busy putting the runners in the carcass when Tom returned. Tom set about putting the handles on the drawers without further comment. Sly glances at Craig revealed the frown hadn't gone, the news of a cousin had clearly thrown him. He screwed the last handle in place.

"All done. Shall I open one of the bedside cabinets in readiness?"

"Yes. Sure. Get the fronts out, you can put the handles on those too." His smile was back, but he'd lost some of the bounce he'd had earlier.

"Will do, boss." Tom saluted him and went and did as instructed. When he returned Craig nodded towards Emily's room.

"In this one I'm guessing. Anywhere in particular?"

"Under the window I thought. What do you reckon?"

"Good a place as any." Craig looked out to the hall as the doorbell rang. "Another delivery?"

"Not that I'm expecting. Excuse me."

Tom was surprised to find Bella on the doorstep. Remembering she'd seen the murder log he didn't invite her in.

"Hello, Bella. What can I do for you?"

Bella held up a bag. "Payment. Nan thought you'd like it after your lunch if you had room."

"My cheese sandwich you mean." Tom took the bag. "Very kind. I'll have it with a cup of tea. I'd invite you in, but we're building furniture."

"I can't stop, I did want to talk to you about the churchyard though, shall I come in tomorrow after work? It's not important I... Oh, hello."

Bella flushed and Tom looked round to see Craig standing behind him. He held up the bag.

"Delivery of cake."

Craig's smile was charming. When he smiled, he wasn't a bad looking chap. He ignored Tom.

"Hello. Did you bring me some?"

"I would have if I'd known Tom had company. You're missing a treat."

"I don't think so. You're a treat without cake."

Tom couldn't have them speaking to each other. Not while Craig was still in the house. He wagged his finger.

"Much as I'd like all my heat to escape while you two flirt, I have got things to do later. Thank Alice for me, Bella."

"Will do. 'Bye." She was looking at Craig, but Tom answered.

"'Bye." He would have grinned if he weren't teetering on the edge of being caught red-handed.

Craig stepped forward. "How old are you... Bella wasn't it?"

"Eighteen, why, how old did you think I was?"

"I didn't know. But I'm going to be here another forty minutes or so, then I'm going to The Swan, I'll buy you a drink if you happen to come in."

"I might let you if I can be bothered to go. 'Bye again."

Tom started to push the door shut. Slowly. He didn't want to be rude, but his mind was whirring with how he could explain himself before an innocent conversation exposed what he'd been up to. He jumped in with both feet and mentally crossing his fingers.

"This is Craig by the way. I've just found out he was Denise's nephew. Although he didn't know her."

Bella's eyes widened. "Oh. Sorry."

"Don't worry about it. Like he said, I didn't know her."

"Oh. Okay. 'Bye again."

"Don't forget. Forty minutes," Craig called after her.

Tom wondered how well Bella had read the murder log, and whether she realised that Craig was the man seen arguing with Denise. He hoped so. Craig seemed harmless, but who knew these days. Denise had thought whoever she was meeting was harmless. He closed the door. Craig was already pulling out the first pieces he needed for the bedside cabinet.

"Better get a move on. I reckon she'll turn up."

"Do you? I'm going to put the kettle on. Do you want to share this cake with me?"

"Go on then. I'll have another squash."

Tom paced the kitchen waiting for the kettle to boil. What to do? Tell the truth, that was what, but economically. He cut the cake in half and took it out to Craig with his squash.

"Here you go. I'll put it on the table. Blimey that didn't take long." He looked at the almost complete bedside cabinet.

"No point in hanging around, especially if someone might be waiting for you. Thanks for that, I'll have it when I've finished the last one."

"I suppose not. Can I be honest with you?"

"Um, yeah. Have I done one of them wrong or something?"

"No, no. Not at all, you've done a marvellous job. It's about your aunt. Denise."

"What about her?"

"I've sort of been looking into her murder."

Craig snorted. "You, why?" He paused the unwrapping of the final cabinet.

"Because we thought it was murder. Denise had told us she was being stalked, and the police initially thought it was an accident. So we thought we'd see if we could find out anything useful for them."

"Oh." It was clear Craig thought this was weird, but he asked, "Did you?"

"We did. We found out that two things had happened between Monday morning in the supermarket and her being killed on Tuesday evening. On Monday morning, she was miserable and scared because of the stalker, on Tuesday shortly before her death she was the opposite. One of the things that made her happy was her daughter agreeing to come and live with her. We haven't found out what the other was. But, and here's the awkward thing, we know she had been seen arguing with someone at her gate a few days before, and I know that person was you. There I've said it. I've pointed to the elephant in the room."

"You've done what?" Craig looked over his shoulder to the corner of the hall.

"I've told you. What I know, I mean. This is the bit where you explain what was happening, because having met you, I think you're a nice lad, not a murdering nephew." Tom shoved his hands in his pockets. His heart was racing a little, but his hands were shaking big time. He pulled a lopsided smile.

"Oh. Right. Would have been easier if you had said that. The police did speak to me about it."

Craig picked up the drill and put in the first screw. His hands weren't shaking, and his demeanour was calm. Tom knew he was right. Craig hadn't killed Denise, but he still wanted to know what the argument was about. When Craig started on the second screw, he knew he'd have to ask more directly.

"Was it a family thing, the argument?"

"Yes, sort of. She'd had a big row with my mum. Really upset her, I don't know what was said, Mum wouldn't tell me. But whatever it was, it was bad. Mum was crying. When she calmed down, she got mad. My mum has a temper, and as it's just me and her she takes it out on me. I'm old enough to know she doesn't mean it now, but it's still a pain in the... you know. Anyway, I told her I'd go and have a word, so I did."

"But it got nasty. You don't seem like the nasty sort. A witness said you'd grabbed her hand." Tom watched colour flood Craig's cheeks.

"It was nothing. She was spiteful. She said some horrible things about my mum, and to be fair most of them were true, but she told me to ask her the truth. Ask her why she was upset. I told her to tell me because I was there, and she laughed at me. I'm not going to tell you what she said, but it was nasty. I grabbed her arm and told her they were two peas in a pod. Her and my mother. She pushed me away and I left." He looked up at Tom. "I didn't kill her. On the night she died I was—"

"You don't need to tell me that. I've already said I didn't think you did. It would be interesting to know what it was all about though. Not because I'm nosey you understand, just to get the full picture."

"I'll be glad when she's been buried. My mum is so mad about it all. She's a pain to live with. I keep out of her way most of the time. I'm looking for my own place but can't find anything I can afford."

"That doesn't sound good. But try to be patient. When my wife died, I was very angry with just about everything. Never Emily my daughter, never her. But she had to live with me. I was ill for a while, most people call it weird. Emily went to university and then off to Australia. I think the way I was stopped her wanting to come home. Your mum might need you."

"She's not upset, well, she might be, but that's not why she's mad. She thought she'd get the house. Said 'Denise divorced the waste of space, it was my mum's house, I'll get what I deserve now.' I don't think she knew about the daughter then, but I'm guessing she does now, she just hasn't told me."

"Oh dear. Families do get themselves in a mess. Talk to her, it's got to be worth a try. You never know she might just need to get whatever it was off her chest. To talk to someone."

"You've not met my mum. She does a lot of shouting, but not much talking." Craig upended the cabinet. "Nearly there."

"And a splendid job you've done too. I'll put that other one in the bedroom." Tom carried the completed cabinet into the bedroom and placed it by Eddie's bed. It was all starting to look rather splendid. When he went back into the hall, Craig was on his feet and sliding the drawer into place.

"Job done, and I'll be in the pub on time. Do you reckon she'll turn up?"

"I suspect she will. I don't know why I'm saying that, because I only met her myself yesterday, but she's a nice girl. Treat her well, and no swearing. I was told you had colourful language, you haven't here, so... you know."

"Swearing? I do, I'm not a saint. But only in circumstances which are necessary. Who said that?" Offended, Craig stood facing Tom, arms akimbo.

"Someone in the pub when you were watching Arsenal lose. They said you'd lost money, so I'm guessing that's one of the circumstances."

"Not me. My mother. Andy was winding her up too. Not that she needs any winding. I haven't got enough money to gamble, nor has she. I put the bet on for her, and she was supposed to pay me back. The bet lost, so... I've got to find somewhere to live. Don't worry about Bella, I'll be a perfect gentleman." Craig stooped and started to clear up the packaging.

"Glad to hear it. I heard you were drinking with Denise's ex. He was one of our suspects at first."

"Probably not far off the mark there. I doubt he killed her, and you didn't hear this from me, but one of the lads told me he was trying to get back with Denise and thought he'd convinced her. Then suddenly it was off again. He'd been winding her up. I didn't ask what that meant, I wasn't interested. I didn't know either of them."

"Hmm. Interesting. I'll get your money. Don't worry about clearing up. I'll do that." When he returned, Tom handed Craig some notes folded in half. "I've put a bit more than we agreed, have a drink on me. The Strangled Badger is good."

Craig fanned the notes out and looked at Tom. "This is too much. That's more than a tip."

"Take it. Buy her a pie or something. I might need a favour one day."

"Thanks. Give me a shout then, anytime." Craig jotted his number down on the pad on the table. Then picking up the cake, he ate it in two bites. "There, you've got my number now. Any odd jobs, I'm quite handy."

"So you've proved." Tom watched Craig empty yet another pint of squash and accepted the empty glass. "Have a good time."

"Will do. Thanks again, and good luck with not being nosey." Craig winked at Tom. "If you ever get to meet my cousin, give her my number, you never know we might get on."

Tom stood on the doorstep and watched Craig drive off. He was rough around the edges, but he wasn't a bad sort. He'd been right in the assessment of Karen Parker though. She didn't sound nice at all. He couldn't imagine Denise being spiteful and wondered what Karen had done or said to provoke that. As he went to close the door, Patrick Connor's car pulled up. The rain had stopped so he decided he'd have a quick word and see if he could find out what Andy Knight had had to say for himself. Walking up the road, he called a greeting as Patrick got out of the car.

"Evening, Mr Large." Patrick opened the back door and held out his hand. He took some crutches which he leaned against the car, then helped a young lady out.

Alana. Tom had forgotten she was being allowed out of hospital today. He walked forward to greet her.

"You must be Alana, I'm Tom, I live down the road. I won't keep you, it's freezing out here, just wanted to say hello. No, no. Don't shake my hand, you'll drop a crutch."

"Hello, Tom. Liz told me about you. Perhaps we can have a chat tomorrow."

Alana was a pretty girl. Very thin, and her face was pale. One leg was encased in a black plastic contraption, and Tom stood back as she turned to greet Sally, who'd also come out to meet her.

"I'd like that. See you tomorrow." Now was not the time to discuss the evidence in her mother's murder, and Tom hurried back to his own house.

Once in, he began to clear the mess left by the packaging. The polythene was rammed in the dustbin, and the cardboard ripped into a manageable size before being put in the recycling box. Tom still had more things to unwrap, and he wondered if he'd have enough room for the debris before collection day. Recycling was collected fortnightly on a Tuesday and Tom realised it had been almost two weeks since Denise had died. So much had changed in that time. He pulled the vacuum out from the cupboard in the hall. There were tiny fibres everywhere. Wouldn't be fair to leave it to Liz. He did the bedrooms again for good measure and stood back satisfied. A cup of tea first, and then he'd open the rest of Eddie's things. It would look like he already lived here.

As he went into the kitchen, his phone vibrated on the breakfast bar. It was Liz.

"Where have you been? I was just about to get Mum to come over so I could come round and make sure you were still alive. Three times I've called."

"Sorry about that. It's on silent for some reason. I've got news."

Tom told Liz what he'd gleaned from Craig, and that Alana had arrived. Then he told her how wonderful the two bedrooms looked.

"And you believed him?"

"Yes, as I said. He seems a nice lad. Don't think he likes his mother much, he's looking to move out. And that's the crucial bit. His mother. Why was Denise spiteful to her? Did she kill Denise as some sort of revenge? Don't know how a woman of that size would manhandle a dead body into a wheelbarrow or push it that distance, but if she did, I'd bet my life Craig wasn't helping her."

"I can't believe you told him what we were doing. It was a bit risky. Still is if he was a good actor."

"It's not him, Liz. But I didn't tell you what he said about Andy Knight." Tom relayed the conversation.

"It was him stalking her," Liz announced. "For whatever reason, she spurned his advances and he decided to frighten her. Doesn't mean he killed her, but he might have."

"I was going to speak to Patrick, but when I saw Alana, I didn't think it appropriate."

"No, I'm not surprised. I'm taking you to meet her tomorrow, after we've been to Oakside."

"Oakside?"

"The nursing home where Amery senior is. It's got to be worth a shot, and I doubt the police will speak to him."

"There's a reason for that. It's unethical. The man has dementia. Anything he says wouldn't stand up in court. No, Liz. It will be a waste of time, and it is immoral."

"It's not. If he's really bad, no harm done. If not, we might have another clue. I'll speak to you tomorrow. I've got to go now, Gemma wants her tea. We had dinner at half one. 'Bye."

Tom had heard the laughter in her voice, and knew she thought she'd be able to convince him. He didn't think she would. The murder log needed updating, and he probably should eat, but first he was going to unpack the rest of today's deliveries. He started by making up Eddie's bed and moved on to the toys and accessories. It didn't take long to do, and when he'd finished, he was so pleased he took photographs and sent them to Emily. She didn't respond and he realised she was probably still in bed. He set about his nightly rituals, dinner, which tonight was a lamb chop and some veg, shower, and television awaiting Emily's call. He was surprised when his phone rang at eight o'clock. He thought it might be Liz, and was surprised to find it was Emily, or when he answered it, Eddie.

"Grandad, it's me. Mummy just showed me my bedroom, it's so cool. Can I come now?"

"I wish you could, but it won't be long. I'm glad you liked it."

"I did. Didn't I, Mummy? Wait a minute."

There was a blur of red, and Emily's face appeared. "Hi, Dad, he was so excited I had to let him run off some steam before we called. It's lovely, really lovely. You shouldn't have gone to that much trouble."

"Yes, I should. I've got some bits for your bedroom too, but it's not much, I thought you'd like to choose your own."

"Well, we're most grateful. I got the tickets. We arrive in Heathrow on the tenth."

"That's fabulous. Oh gosh, Em, just a few days ago I was... Hello, Eddie."

"Look it matches." Eddie's face was replaced by a yellow blur.

"Move it back, I can't see it." Tom laughed.

Emily obliged and a Simba toy appeared. Eddie was gabbling away in the background while his mother tried to calm him down. Tom couldn't stop smiling. If he could only solve Denise's murder all would be well with the world. After a few moments Eddie reappeared.

"I've got to have breakfast before we go swimming, so I have to go. 'Bye, Grandad."

"'Bye, Eddie, love you." Tom heard him shout 'you too' as the phone was passed to Emily.

"How are you, Dad? How are things?"

"All good. I'd tell you about it, but you need to feed my grandson."

"It's okay, he'll be fine for five minutes. He's got a memory like Dory because he's so excited."

"Who's Dory?"

"If you don't know now, you certainly will by the eleventh." Emily laughed. "Oh, I was wrong, he's calling. Shall I call back later?"

"No, you've got things to do, I'll have an early night. And Em, no pills, no booze for almost a week."

Emily's eyes filled and she nodded. "I love you."

"You too, Em. Goodnight."

THE NURSING HOME

Tom was whistling when Liz arrived the next day. He'd managed to get two more returns done and get the church hall accounts into some sort of order. He was inputting a spreadsheet with the various costs when she arrived.

"Blimey someone's happy. I'd better have a look at your... Oh, Tom, he's going to be beside himself when he sees that. Well done."

"He was, I sent photos. All thanks to you, couldn't have done it without you."

"You would have managed. Looks like Craig Parker did a good job. You still falling on the side of believing him?"

Tom told her he was and explained why. "He's not stupid, but nor is he bright enough to manipulate a conversation. What you see is what you get. I think he's had a tough life, but he's keen to change that. He wants to leave home, although he still has a modicum of loyalty towards his mother. If he didn't, I think he would say more. I was so keen to know what the row between Karen and Denise had been about, I almost told him to find out. He told Bella he'd buy her a drink if she went to the pub, I told him to behave himself because she's a nice girl. Not those exact words, but you know."

"I'll take your word for it. For now. Do you want me to get on, or shall we talk about going to see old man Amery?"

Tom rolled his eyes. "I thought we'd had that conversation, but the answer to the question is get on, because I'm going nowhere until such time as I've got the church hall accounts into some sort of order. I'm on library duty this afternoon, I'm bound to be asked."

"Hmm. I'll be about an hour. Going to clean both bathrooms this morning."

"Wonderful."

Tom put all thoughts about meeting Amery senior to the back of his mind and lifting the top invoice, typed the description and amount into his spreadsheet. In no time at all, he'd got through half the pile. He was going to finish this before he let Liz talk him into another outing. He picked up the next item, it was two sheets stapled together, and he paused when he saw the detail.

In Kathy Lambert's distinctive handwriting it was noted that two hundred and thirty-six pounds had been received from the WI and banked. It was signed by Kathy and R Amery. Attached was a banking slip from several days later.

"Perhaps it's a sign I should go," he mumbled as he moved it into the receipts pile.

"You're talking to yourself. I thought we were moving away from weird." Liz grinned as she appeared with the vacuum.

"Don't do in here today, I did the rest of downstairs last night. I want to get to the bottom of this pile, and I won't be able to concentrate with that racket on."

"Yes, I noticed that. You're trying to get rid of me. I'll just put the duster around the sitting room. What were you mumbling about?"

"Signs."

"Posts or messages from the beyond? Either way, absolutely, definitely weird."

Tom laughed. "Becky Amery must be a member of the WI, she gave Kathy some money to bank, and I was wondering if seeing the name meant I should go on this waste of time trip of yours."

"In which case, of course it was a sign. Get on with that, I'm almost done. We've got to pop up and see Alana too."

"I'd rather do that. Although what do you say to someone who's lost their mother in such circumstances?"

"You talk about them, you, the weather, the state of the economy, anything but that, unless of course they bring it up. In which case you listen and mostly avoid saying much of anything. It worked for me."

"Do you know, you never cease to amaze me. Go and do your dusting."

"I'm only a cl... housekeeper for convenience, you know, I'm not thick. Just think if I were working as a high-powered barrister or the like, we wouldn't be this close to solving Denise's murder, and you wouldn't have a nice little bedroom ready for Eddie." With a flick of her duster, Liz disappeared.

When they'd both finished their respective chores, Liz hurried Tom to the car. "The sooner we get this bit done, the sooner we can get on with something more—"

"Productive?"

"That's not what I was going to say. Get in the car, it's only about twenty minutes away."

When they pulled into the nursing home carpark, Liz pulled a mask from the pocket of the dash and handed it to Tom. "Still required in these places. Same as the hospital."

Tom put his mask on and followed Liz into reception. She nodded at the young girl manning the desk. "We're here to see Mr Amery."

"Oh really, that's a surprise. He should be in the television room at this time. Not quite lunch-time. You won't have long."

"That's fine. I doubt he'll know us. Just felt we should show our faces, or not." Liz pulled at her mask.

"Why is it a surprise?" Tom asked.

"He doesn't get many visitors, I doubt even one a month. Not that he knows that. But it's sad." Realising she might just have criticised the family, the girl wagged her finger. "I mean it's sad that he doesn't realise... um." She lifted a book and opened it. "Sign in please."

"It's okay, I know what you mean." Tom smiled although she couldn't see that, and watched Liz pick up the pen.

"Shall I just do both of us or do you need individual names?"

"Doesn't matter, whichever suits, I don't think we use it unless there's a fire drill."

Writing quickly and signing with a flourish, Liz closed the book and handed it back. "Which way is the television room?"

"I'll call someone to come and get you. Can't have strangers wandering around."

Call made, a short, stout woman with a European accent came to collect them. "I am Maria. He's having a good day. He's happy today." She said without the use of any h's. She led them into a comfortable communal living room. The television was on mute, and most of the handful of residents were asleep. "He's in the window. He likes to look out."

Liz and Tom approached William Amery and took a seat on either side of him. He looked from one to the other.

"Afternoon, I don't know you two. Shouldn't you be doing something?"

Liz took his hand and clasped it between her own. "I'm Liz and this is Tom, we've come to see you."

"Have you indeed, well I'm going out in a minute, so keep it short."

"Where are you going?" Tom asked.

"Work of course. I'm never late."

"What do you do?"

"I'm an architect. I won the silver guild award in eighty-three. Is that why you're here? Please tell me you don't want an extension."

"Not at the moment, but my family is growing so who knows." Tom noticed Liz had kept hold of the old man's hand. "We're here to speak to you about Jim."

"Jim? Why? He's at school I should think. Scratch that, he will be, he's never broken a rule in his life. I know he's our boy, but he can be quite boring."

"Oh, I see. He won't be with Denise Mills then? Only we heard—" Liz gasped as William Amery slapped her before jumping to his feet. "Don't mention her name. We do not speak about her. Everyone knows that." Now in a panic, Amery looked around. "Did she hear?"

Tom checked Liz was okay and helped Amery back into his seat. "Who? Did who hear?"

"The wife, of course, she'll be lethal if she did." Amery's hands were shaking, and his eyes still scanned the room. "I think we're safe, but you'd better go before she gets back. I don't suppose I could trouble you for a lift, could I?"

"Sorry, we didn't bring the car. Why can't you—" Tom was interrupted by the return of Maria. "Mr and Mrs Smith, I must ask you to come back to reception. Say goodbye."

"But we—"

"Now. His daughter is here."

Liz and Tom looked at each other. Tom's heart sank, but Liz's eyes twinkled.

"We're in trouble," he hissed as they followed Maria back along the corridors. "You seem to be amused."

"Last time I looked there were no rules against visiting anyone, anywhere. Unless it was a prison, I suppose. This should be interesting."

"Not what I'd call it, that must be her. Look at her face. Those eyes are evil. Oh God, she's with Abi."

As they entered the reception area, Becky Amery marched over to them. A tall, broad-shouldered woman, she was immaculately presented. Liz knew her makeup would be too, if not obscured by the mask. "Mr and Mrs Smith, I presume?"

"Mrs Amery. How are you?" Liz's manner was pleasant, and although her face was still hidden by the mask she smiled. She shot a glance at Abi who was standing several feet away behind her mother. Abi gave her a thumbs up.

"How I am has nothing to do with you. Why are you visiting my father-in-law?"

"I'm not sure that's any of your business, but the short answer is because he doesn't get visitors from one month to the next. I'm surprised to see you here."

"My daughter wanted to see her grandfather. Not that it's any of your business." Behind her, Abi shook her head.

"I'm not sure what harm you thought we were doing, Mrs Amery, but I can assure you our motives are innocent. You seem to think the opposite. Why did you think we were here?"

Becky Amery deflated, her shoulders dropped, and she puffed out a sigh. "I'm sorry, I was shocked. I suppose those without families do get visitors, much like prisoners. I'd thank you if you could let us know next time you intend coming. Just looking after my father-in-law." Turning to Abi, she jerked her head. "Goodbye, and apologies once again. Maria, you may show us in."

Maria rolled her eyes and pushed the door open again. "This way."

Becky Amery marched through the door, Abi walked more slowly. "Any news?" she asked in a whisper.

Liz shook her head, and with a wave to the receptionist took Tom's arm and headed for the car. As they climbed in, they didn't know it, but they were being watched by the Amerys. "What did those people want, William?" Becky asked.

William's smile was wicked. "An extension. Growing family. What do you want?"

"This is Abi, do you remember her? She wanted to come and see you."

"Why? Does she want an extension too?"

In the car, Liz pulled off her mask and turned to Tom, her expression triumphant. "I told you it was worth it. We now know Denise's name was banned when Jim was at school. Before you say it, I know we don't know why, but a pound says they knew she was pregnant, and if they knew, Jim must have. Don't you think?"

"Never say never, and what have you. But yes, generally I agree with that. But Smith? You couldn't do better than Smith? Why did you put that anyway, if she makes a complaint, we'll be questioned about that. Lying makes it look like we had something to hide. It's lucky we have Patrick on our side.

"No one would have been any the wiser if they hadn't shown up, she won't say anything, not after I shamed her. That didn't take long, let's see Alana before I do my next client. I'll text her to let her know we're on our way."

Alana let them in with a smile. "I was going to tell you on the phone, but I thought I'd wait. In here, I need to keep my leg up." Still not competent with the crutches, Alana's journey was slow. Once she was sitting on the couch her leg stretched along its length, she told them her news. "Patrick called, no one tried to kill me. It was mistaken identity, and not even with me, but with my car. Something to do with a stolen girlfriend. Scary, but now I can relax."

"Well that is good news. Once you're more used to your crutches, we'll have to get you down to... to the house so you can see if you want anything done. You'll need the back door sorted, and some blinds at the back. I'll give it the once over first, and if you want, I'll get rid of anything you don't want to see."

"Like what?"

"Like dirty washing, and... well that's it really. I've already done the fridge and the bin."

"Thanks, but I don't want anything changed not yet. I liked it as it was. It was Denise. Weird you know, everyone keeps calling her my mum, and she wasn't, not yet. My mum died a while ago. It didn't mean I didn't love Denise, and we might have got to that point where I called her mum, but it's awkward. It's like my dad. If he's still alive, I might give him a call, I might not, but he's still my dad. I was hoping Denise would tell me who my biological father was, but I did my DNA thing anyway. Not to catch her out, but just in case. That should have come back by now. I'll check online again later."

"I do. How are you getting on with Sally?"

"Really well, she's nice. I think she apologised six times about having to go to work today, but it was nice just to be still, and quiet. In hospital they seem to be in and out every ten minutes. I'm going to start on these when you've gone." Alana tapped a pile of books.

"What are you studying?" Tom asked.

"Law. Which brings me to the question I've been dying to ask, how are you doing with your investigation? Patrick tells me it's going slowly because they can't find anyone who bore a grudge against her."

"It's moving along. I'm not going to worry you with the details, but it just got easier because we're not trying to find out who would want you both dead." Tom shook his finger. "I can see what you're going to say but I'm not going to change my mind. Are we, Liz?"

"No. I agree. Oh, are you expecting someone? I'll go." Liz got to her feet at the sound of the doorbell.

"That will be Carly I expect. She's bringing me some of my stuff."

It was, and happy Alana had everything she needed, they left the two girls to catch up. Tom was surprised when Liz turned to go into his house.

"I thought you had a client?"

"I have, but we weren't as long as expected on either of our visits. It's two weeks tomorrow, Tom. The longer it takes the less likelihood there is of catching the killer. Now we know Alana wasn't targeted, Jim Amery is right back in the frame. I knew it was possible he could have tampered with Alana's brakes, but I couldn't see a father, however remote, doing that."

"Put the kettle on. You have half an hour. I need to eat, and I must get some work done before the library."

They shared a tin of soup, and Liz drew squares on a piece of paper. In one she wrote Andy, and in the other Jim. She then listed what facts they had about each man and their connections to Denise.

"The thing is," Liz pointed her spoon at Tom "we don't know what alibi either of them gave to the police for the time Denise was killed, or when her body was moved, or how thoroughly the police checked them. Or come to that the burglary. I know everyone thinks it isn't connected but it might well be."

"I think we need to speak to Patrick on that. We're not, and I mean this, Liz, we are not going to ask them. Shall I message him now? Don't answer that, I'm doing it."

Tom sent the message, and the response came within minutes. Both had airtight alibis.

"Don't believe it. Ask him how airtight."

"No. Leave it until we see him tomorrow. Are we still going tomorrow?"

"I think so, I'll message Sally."

Sally said she'd like to go and would check with Patrick. They arranged to meet at the pub at quarter to eight. With that sorted, Tom insisted on Liz going about her own business so he could get on with his own.

The afternoon passed quickly, and Tom was glad he'd set an alarm to remind him to go to the library. He'd done well with the accounts, but there were certainly bits missing, but he'd be able to take it up with Kathy.

When he got there, a man he'd never seen before was sitting at the desk. Ruddy faced, with a shine on his bald head, Tom guessed he was in his seventies. He waved to Tom.

"Are you Tom, or are you after something?"

"I'm Tom. I don't think we've met." Tom walked to the desk and shook his hand.

"You're right, we haven't. I'm Dave I usually do a couple of morning shifts, but the vicar's wife can be very persuasive."

"That is very true. I was hoping to see her, I've also got roped into doing the accounts. I need a few more bits and pieces."

"Oh, you're that Tom."

"What Tom?"

"The one that's chasing around trying to find out what happened to Denise."

"Well, I'd like to say I'm helping the police out, but tell me, why does me doing the accounts for the church hall, tell you I'm that Tom. What have you heard?"

"I was talking to Alice in the shop yesterday, you did her posters for her. I need something run off for our skittles team, and I said I'd might ask you. She said you were probably too busy because you had your own work, the church accounts, the library, and were doing some sleuthing on Denise with Liz."

"Blimey does she know everything? How she knows I'm doing the accounts is anyone's guess."

"Nosey, and only talks to people she likes. Someone she likes would have told her. So will you do it?"

"Do what?"

"My skittles fixtures list. I only need a couple of copies. I'll pay if you're strapped for cash."

"Um. Yes. Let me know what you need. I'll take my coat off and put the kettle on."

"Good plan, white, two sugars, then you can tell me all about your sleuthing. I like a good mystery, and I liked Denise. I used to work with her dad way back when. He was taken too soon too."

Tom walked to the coat hooks trying to work out how to avoid that conversation, after all, how many people did he want knowing what they were up to? It was becoming an open secret and might put him and Liz in danger. He was saved initially by Mrs Bairstow. She'd brought her books back and was talking to Dave when he returned with the tea.

"Hello, Mrs Bairstow, you're usually a Thursday girl." Tom handed Dave his tea.

"Will you listen to this charmer, Dave? Girl. I've not been called a girl for twenty years or more."

Dave spluttered on his tea. "Make that fifty and I might believe you." Mopping up the splatters of tea with his hanky, he stamped the books back in.

"The reason I am in early is two-fold. First, you recommended short books, I want longer ones, and second, my television broke down. Or rather the box thing did, so I read more."

"Apologies. I'll leave you with Dave as I'm going to be very cheeky and pop into the vicarage to see if I can catch Kathy before we are run off our feet."

Dave gave a hearty laugh. "I told her that. Said what do you need two people for? I can count on one hand the number of times two have been needed. All she said was 'you never know' and wiggled her eyebrows. 'Know what?' I asked, and she laughed and said you'd be over at half three."

"An enigma. I'll only be five minutes."

The vicarage was on the other side of the church, and Tom took the shortest route, which was back onto the High Street and past the front of the church. As he turned towards the vicarage, a horn tooted, and Liz pulled into the curb.

"Where are you going? I thought you were on until half six."

"I am, just need a word with Kathy. Your car is headed out of the village, are you going somewhere nice?"

"I'm on the way to the chemist in GC, Gemma has chickenpox. I need to pick up her medication."

"Poor Gemma, buy her a tub of her favourite ice-cream and tell her Tom said she's only allowed ice-cream until—"

"It's you, isn't it?" A hand slapped the bonnet of the car. "Just who the hell are you, Mr and Mrs Smith?" Becky Amery stepped very close to Tom and peered at Liz. "You're a cleaner, your name isn't Smith. And you, you're the weird man that lives in Pendry's. I've just been told. I'm guessing you are also the nosey, interfering individuals who were questioning my husband. What are you up to?" She paused to look over her shoulder. "Abi, wait for me. Stay there."

Abi Amery pretended not to hear and continued to walk in the opposite direction. Becky Amery tutted as Liz climbed out of the car.

"I am a cleaner, yes. My name is Liz. It's none of your business what we were doing, but I'll tell you. We heard you father-in-law doesn't have a visitor from one month to the next. We know he'll forget us once we've gone, but a visit still broke up the monotony of his day. We have several people we—"

"He said you pretended you wanted an extension. I thought you were pulling some scam."

"Don't lie to us, we're not stupid." Tom pulled his shoulders back. "Even if he said that, which I doubt, if that were the case, we would owe him money and not the other way around. Now, I think you've embarrassed yourself enough for one day, and I've got somewhere I should be. See you tomorrow." Tom saluted Liz, shook his head at Becky, and headed for the vicarage. On the other side of the road, he watched Abi sneak into the mini-market with Bella and smiled as he heard her mother wonder where she'd got to.

Tom had been handed another bag of paperwork by Kathy, and almost wished he'd not gone to see her. As he made his way back to the library, Bella called him and trotted to catch him up.

"Hello, Mr Large, how did you get on?"

"Hello, Bella, call me Tom. Get on with what?"

"The dragon. Abi said she'd seen you with Liz and asked my nan who you were. Abi escaped. Why did you want to see her grandad? It wasn't him, he's got dementia. He doesn't know anyone. He certainly didn't kill Denise."

"It was a long shot. He thought his son was still at school and we wanted an extension." Tom smiled. "And how did you get on?"

A slight flush brushed Bella's cheeks. "Alright. He's a nice chap. He wants to help you find out what happened to his aunt. Don't know how he's going to do that. Blimey, look at the time, I've got to get back." She held up her shopping bag. "I've been on a mercy dash to make sure we've got everything ready for arts and crafts tomorrow. Mr Vaswani sells the cheapest glue sticks."

"Hello, Tom."

Tom turned to see who was calling him. He wasn't used to being in demand, especially in the street. Sally came running over.

"Thought it was you. Just a quick word, please don't phone Patrick tonight, we're going to take Alana out for a meal. She's desperate to do something normal and said she'd sit with her leg up. Oh, and she's probably coming to the quiz night tomorrow, so one of us will drive her down. We'll see you there. That was it. I must dash. Apologies for interrupting." She smiled at Bella. "Sorry, he's all yours."

"No problem, I was just leaving." With a wide smile Bella turned away as Sally ran back across the road.

Tom headed back to the library, as he passed the church, he slowed down. "I'm sorry you're gone, Denise, I wish you were here to be with your girl. But, by God, you've turned my life around. Thank you and sorry again." He grimaced, was that blasphemy? Realising people might be watching and he was being daft, he hurried up the side of the church towards the hall.

A couple of people were browsing, and Dave was still speaking to old Jane Bairstow. Tom hung the bag under his coat and went to join them. "Jackie Collins? That's a bit racy." He smiled at her.

"So he tells me, so both of you must have read it. But look at how thick it is. I've decided I'd have a change this week, I've also got this thick 'un." She held up *The Godfather*.

"And that's violent, but one of the best books I've ever read. The film's good too."

"Ah well, I can always bring them back on Thursday if I don't get on with them. You were a long time."

"I was, wasn't I?" Tom smiled, the old women in the village were very nosey. He'd decided to up his game and not feed them. When she'd gone, he apologised to Dave. "Sorry about that, I was longer with Kathy than I expected to be, and then everyone seemed to catch me on the way back."

"I've not moved. I didn't miss you, so no worries. Oh, Ken looks like he needs a hand. You go and sort him out, and I'll put the kettle on again."

They had a steady stream of readers through to closing time, although as Dave observed, that still hadn't required two of them, and as Kathy hadn't come down, Dave supervised Tom locking up before saying goodnight. Tom didn't stroll home, but nor did he dash. His house was in darkness, and he smiled as he realised in a few weeks the lights would be blazing and he'd be telling Emily to switch them off. Unless she'd changed the habits of a lifetime.

He had his dinner on a tray on his lap and flipping through the channels, stopped on a quiz show. If he did a bit of homework, they might give the grey geriatrics a run for their money. It was a replay channel so he watched three in a row, occasionally telling a contestant they should have paid more attention in school, together with more colourful insults. Emily called early, before he'd even been up to shower.

"Hello, love, everything okay? You're early." You look worried.

"I'm not really, but out of the blue Jason has suddenly decided he wants to see Eddie. He's taken him to the park. Don't get me wrong he's competent enough, but what's he up to? When we were together, I could barely get him to walk him down to nursery."

"Does he know you're coming home?"

"I haven't told him. We don't speak. He's seen Eddie three times since we split up, always here, and always because he had an ulterior motive, like picking up his cricket stuff. Anyway, they'll be back soon. How are you?"

"Before I forget, remind me to come back to nurseries. I'm fine, we're making some progress but not much. We went to see Amery's father today. He's got dementia, and Liz thought he might have information, and he did in a way, but the way he delivered it was a shock. He slapped Liz's face and told her never to mention Denise again. He also thought Jim Amery would be in school and that we wanted an extension built, so we should be careful as to how much weight we give that. How's the packing going?"

"I'm done except for a few personal things and our clothes. Eddie won't let Simba out of his sight. I'm leaving the house fully furnished, none of it is any good to me. I've got a box I'm putting Jason's bits into, and a crate I've already shipped over. The rest will go into one of the two huge suitcases I've purchased. It's quite liberating in a way, packing up and moving on.

Although there's plenty here I'll miss, I can't wait to get back now it's been decided. Did you feel like that? Oh, don't answer that if it will upset you."

"In a way, yes. I felt guilty at the memories I was leaving behind. Guilty I didn't want to keep that ugly pottery your mother insisted on collecting, and guilty because it had taken me so long to realise that one must move on. But I could see there might be a light at the end of the tunnel, so there was also a little bit of excitement, that pretty much got burned up by the anxiety." Tom laughed. "Are you glad you asked?"

"I am because you can laugh about it. And I do have a confession to make."

"Go on..." Not another confession. Tom's heart rate increased. "You know Aunt Jane packed up some bits for me that I wanted to keep."

"I do." Tom held back the smile, he knew what Emily was going to say.

"I chose five pieces of that pottery. Mum's favourite ones."

"Did you?"

"Don't panic I won't get them out there, I'll wait until—"

"I'm teasing, Emily. Of course you must get them out. But as far as the pottery goes, can we do one a month, just until I get used to them. It's funny, because I hated them I have no idea which ones were her favourite. It will be interesting to see."

"Oh wow, Dad. You're talking about her normally. It's such... hang on, that's the door. I think Eddie's back, he'll want to speak to you."

"I'm going nowhere."

Tom listened to Emily greet Eddie warmly, asking if he'd had a good time, but when Eddie ran off to use the toilet, Jason began to question her.

"He tells me you're going to see his grandad. I don't think so. No son of mine is going to be exposed to that."

"To what exactly? And it's none of your business. You barely bother with him."

"He's my son. And you'll do as you're told."

"He's my son too, and you can shove your instructions up the baker's wife's... Hello, Eddie, go and grab an apple or banana, Mummy and Daddy need five minutes."

"I know. He said we couldn't go and see the snow. We can, can't we? I told him I promised Grandad. You're not allowed to break promises, are you?"

"No, you're not. Quite right. There's some flapjack on the counter. You can have a piece of that too."

Eddie had clearly gone, as the next thing Tom heard was Emily using a voice he didn't know she possessed.

"Get off my property. Now. I'm getting a restraining order against you. Apply through the court for access to Eddie. Don't come here again. Tomorrow, there will be a box at the end of the drive with what remains of your things. It will be there at eight in the morning. I wouldn't be late, it's also rubbish day tomorrow."

"You can't do that."

"Watch me."

"Come on, Em, of course you can go and see your dad, I was just concerned. That's all."

"No you weren't, you were jealous. I have no idea what of. Perhaps it was that you hadn't given me your permission. Well as my lovely dad would say, you can stick that in your pipe and smoke it. Now get off my property, don't come here again, if you want to communicate with me, go through my solicitor in town. Browns."

"Come on, babe. There's no need for—"

"Five, four, three."

A door slammed and Tom assumed Jason had gone. Emily reappeared, there was still fire in her eyes.

"Did you hear any of that?"

"All of it. What are you going to do?"

"Nothing. Except put his box out on the street. He'll disappear again now."

"But you're not just coming for Christmas. Or have you changed your mind?"

"Oh I'm coming for good, Dad. I've already finished at work. I've signed the lease on this place, so apart from anything else, with effect from the fifteenth of December, we're homeless, or I'm in deep doo-doo. Have a chat to Eddie while I calm down. I've never been violent but I want to smash him in the face every time he calls me babe. Eddie, Grandad is on the phone."

Eddie appeared seconds later. Tom had a heart-warming conversation with him, making the nerves he felt at Jason stopping them coming home settle a little. But when Emily commandeered the phone and Eddie blew him a kiss goodbye, he didn't mention pre-school. He wasn't going to tempt fate. Emily was clearly agitated, so they brought the conversation to an end.

"Love you, Dad. Speak tomorrow, and don't go worrying about that. He's got neither the wherewithal nor the spine to do anything."

"I hope you're right, Em. Love you both. Goodnight, love."

"I am! 'Night, Dad."

Before Tom hung up, he heard Eddie ask why Emily was saying goodnight when it wasn't even bedtime. With a sigh, he decided that was enough for one day. He locked everything up and went up to bed. He didn't even shower, but knowing that oblivion was required, he took two pills with water. After an hour of thinking about every possible worst case scenario, he took another one.

Tom didn't get oblivion, he tossed, turned, and had one nightmare after the other, but he was asleep.

An Arrest

The next morning, Tom decided that as there was little he could do about the situation in Australia, the best thing for it was to get his head down and get on with some work and keep the negative niggles at the back of his mind. Emily thought all was going to be well, so he should too. Although he missed seeing her, he was glad he didn't have to discuss it with Liz. She'd had a similar idea, and had messaged to say that unless something new came up, she was going to get all her jobs done, then take her mum to the shopping centre, before picking up Gemma from her neighbour, whose children also had chickenpox, and meeting them at the pub.

Before he started, he sent a message to Emily.

Hi, Em, hope all is well there and that you and Eddie are okay. Get a good night's sleep. I'm going to the quiz night tonight and will be leaving at 7.45 UK time. If we could speak before then (not sure what time you get up), that would be great. If not please text to let me know all is well. If we don't speak before, I'll speak to you after the quiz. I should be home by ten thirty at the latest. Have a peaceful sleep. Dad. Hugs to Eddie. Love you both.

Emily had messaged straight back. They'd had an uneventful day, they'd not heard from Jason, and she WOULD be home on the tenth. He felt a little easier having received that, and as soon as breakfast was out of the way he opened his laptop and remained there until his stomach told him he needed to eat. He found little to tempt him in either the cupboard or the fridge and decided a trip to the shop would be in order. Without needing to psyche himself up, he grabbed a bag and put on his coat.

At the gate, he stood and drew in the crisp fresh air. The frost had all melted, but the chill air was welcome after a morning in front of the laptop. When he arrived at the shop, Derek Vaswani first waved through the window and then pointed across the road. Tom had been focused on the National Lottery swing board outside on the pavement, and when he looked across the road, he saw a police car parked to one side of the crossing near the pub. He hurried into the shop.

"Morning, Derek, what's going on over there?"

"I don't know. But it pulled up and two officers got out and went into the pub. Might have a drunk in there causing trouble, or perhaps they've been robbed. Times are changing, Tom. I've lived here since I was four. Other than one car accident about five years ago, and someone spraying graffiti on the bus shelter, I can't remember there ever being any trouble. In the last couple of weeks, we've had a murder, a burglary and now whatever's happening over there. I don't like it. I don't like it at all."

"Well, the murder and burglary might have been connected, but I doubt that is."

"I suppose we'll find out soon enough. Did you want anything in particular?"

"Food. I fancy something different, and I don't know what, came to see if I could be inspired."

"We've got the meal deals on again. Go and have a look in the chiller at the back. Free wine this week. If you're over eighteen of course."

"Phew, lucky I have ID on me."

Smiling, Tom headed for the cold cabinet. His basket was full when he returned.

"I was going to buy one of Alice's almond slices, but the shelf was empty. She's doing well."

"Going like hot cakes." Derek winked and started to scan Tom's shopping. "Ah the lamb korma, good choice. Now what wine do you want? White or red? It's these two that are included." Derek walked to the shelves of alcohol and lifted one of each.

"Give me both, I'm a red man, but Emily is coming home, and she likes white. While you're there, I'll have a bottle of whisky too. Just the cheap one, better start building a stock for Christmas."

Tom's heart fell. He'd given in. Christmas was an excuse to buy it, he pondered changing his mind, but thought that might look odd. He shoved it to the bottom of the shopping bag. Feeble. He was feeble. Why had he done that? Derek interrupted his thoughts.

"You coming to the quiz again tonight?" Derek handed Tom his receipt.

"I am, yes. Might have one more in the team too. Alana, Denise's daughter might be coming. It seems to be very popular. Must be the skill of the quizmaster." He managed a smile for Derek.

"Of course. But if I'm honest, I think it's two-fold. Little Compton has an aging population, and it's a way of getting out to the pub and showing off. Not sure what your motivation is."

"Definitely the former. You've got to be good to show off."

"You came second. Your team did well. Mind you, the vicar and his team weren't in last week, The God Squad we named them, and A and C haven't been there the last couple of weeks. Last week was probably out of respect for Denise. She used to be part of the team most weeks. She was good at all the popular stuff. They'll be lost now."

"Amery and Cheriton. Makes sense. Who's on their team? I popped in the other day, I only saw Jim Amery in there."

"Jim and his wife, Becky. A young lad, I can't remember his name. Molly, she used to do Denise's job and stayed on the team, and of course Denise. Awful. Molly is eighty, if she's a day, and Denise was barely in her forties. It's not right, Tom."

Derek gave a wave to a customer who had entered the shop and called out a greeting. He glanced across the road as he returned his attention to Tom. "The police car has gone. I'll have to wait to go over there before I find out why. See you later."

With a bag in each hand, Tom walked home slowly. His mind was on Denise. She'd been dead for two weeks today and they were no nearer finding out who'd killed her. He decided to chase Patrick Connor once the shopping had been unpacked. As he neared his gate, a horn sounded, and a van pulled up alongside him.

"Alright? I saw you so I thought I'd share the news." Craig Parker hung out the window.

"Hello, Craig. What news would that be?"

"Our chat got me thinking, and the more I thought the more I knew I was right. So I called that copper, the one who spoke to Bella about what she heard. He's just confirmed it." Craig smiled. "You see, I'm an upstanding pillar of the community."

"Well done, but I'm still none the wiser. If this is going to take some time, do you want a pint of squash? These bags are getting heavy."

"No thanks. Andy Knight did it. Not the murder, although he could have, but I asked around and it was him winding Denise up. He thought if he made her jumpy, she'd want someone to protect her and take him back. Something like that anyway. And when I was at the bar getting a drink for Bella, I saw him give a bloke a gold chain and take money for it. I spoke to Bella, and she said I should call the police. Now do you understand?"

"Blimey. Well done. That is a turn-up. Is that what the police car was doing earlier?"

"Yep, picking him up. DC Connor called and said they'd found some other jewellery that he couldn't explain away. And something about a drawer I didn't understand. Right, I'd better make a move, or I'll get behind. See you tonight."

"Will you? Why?"

"Because you're going to introduce me to my cousin. Bella said she's doing the quiz with you. Will you do that?"

"Of course." Tom smiled. "I'm sure she'd like that."

"I hope so. If not, it'll be like my mum says, you can't miss what you've not had."

"Not sure it works like that. How is your mum?"

"And on that note, I am going. Your fingers will snap off if you start me on that. See you later."

With a brief wave and no indication, Craig drove off. Luckily, there were no other cars about. Going inside, Tom messaged Liz with the latest news before unpacking his shopping. Liz sent back a shocked face and a thumbs up.

Tom ate his curry and got back to his accounts. The hours passed quickly and before he knew it, it was time to get ready. He wasn't starving but knew he should have something to eat but had little time. Deciding he'd eat in the pub, he put his smart trousers on and headed off. Arriving before the others, he ordered a pie and a pint and went to the same table as the week before. As the contestants trickled in, he found people waving acknowledgement, even though he had no idea who they were. That made him happy. Derek was in conversation with the landlord, a portly chap, with drooping jowls, and a shiny bald head. As Tom finished his pie, Derek came over and leaned down so he could speak quietly.

"I'm sure it will spread like wildfire, but the police were here for Andy Knight, arrested him here for burglary while we were chatting. Fancy that, poor old Denise. Never said anything about killing her, but still, it makes you wonder, doesn't it? Look at the time, I'd better get set up."

Tom hoped his face had looked suitably shocked. He didn't think he should let on that Craig had grassed up Andy. Grassed up. What an odd phrase, he must google its origins. Watching Derek set up, he pondered about life, and indeed death. Denise had had her life snatched away two weeks ago. And here they all were ready for a night of fun. They were doing their bit in remembering her, but life really does go on. Life... his thoughts were interrupted as Craig called to him.

"Can I get you a pint? I had a good tipper this week, think I owe him one." His smile was wide, and as Bella entered the pub, Tom knew why.

"I'm okay." He held up his half full glass of Strangled Badger as Liz entered.

"Look at you keen as mustard. Do you want a top up?"

Craig told her he'd just offered and bought Liz one instead. Bella and Liz came to sit with Tom while Craig awaited their drinks. Bella sat next to him and leaned in close to whisper in his ear.

"I know you know about Andy, Craig told me he'd seen you. He also tried to find out from his mum what their argument was about. She told him to mind his own business, but when he asked again, all she told him was if he asked again, she'd kick him out because bloody Billy had caused enough damage. As his cousin is coming in, he didn't want to mention it tonight." She held up her hand as Tom opened his mouth. "Don't ask me any questions, he told me that as we were walking up. I don't know any more than that. Oh this must be her."

Sally held open the door and Alana hobbled in on her crutches, Sally pointed to their table.

"Over there. Get yourself settled, and I'll take the orders. Oh, looks like we've got a new team member. That's good, Patrick is going to be late."

With five minutes to go, Alana was settled with her leg up on a stool, and having been introduced, was flanked by Craig who made it clear he was not doing the quiz, and Bella. The three seemed to hit it off and looked quite put out when Derek tapped his glass and called for silence. He made his usual announcement and had just said the first round would be on sport, when the door opened again.

"Sorry. Sorry. Can you give us two minutes? We won't get drinks first." Jim Amery held the door open, while Becky Amery, a young man and an elderly lady filed past.

Derek looked at his watch. "As it's you. There's a table free in the corner."

As the pub had already fallen silent, everyone watched the group make their way through the tables and get themselves settled.

Leaning away from Alana, Bella whispered to Tom, "Should I tell her that might be her dad?"

Tom's eyes widened. He'd not thought of that. This could get awkward. He shook his head and Bella relaxed. Tom then leaned the other way and told Liz what Bella had asked.

Liz pursed her lips and then said simply, "Later perhaps."

Tom didn't know if that was wise and was almost relieved when Derek tapped his glass again. He wouldn't have time to ponder it now.

The barmaid was sent over to take A and C's order, and Derek asked question one.

"In what year did Arsenal last win the premier league?"

There was the usual murmuring around the bar, but everyone on The Seekers' table looked at Craig, who gestured for the pen and wrote down the answer with a smirk. He kept hold of the pen for the remainder of the round, writing down each answer before the others had even had time

to think. "Second round is entertainment, and we're off, question one..."
Craig slid the answer sheet and pen across the table to Bella.

"It's like we're not even here," Liz announced and got hushed for her
trouble.

That round appeared to be easy for the youngsters, and with the third
round on ancient history, between the five of them they managed to come
up with what they thought were decent answers. At the end of that round,
Derek announced there would be a twenty-minute break for everyone to
refresh their glasses. Sally waved their voucher in the air.

"I just remembered this. Might as well use it, we're only one short. I'll get
that."

"No. I will. I need to use the toilet. What's everyone having?" Craig got
to his feet and Sally passed the voucher across as they all gave their order.

At the bar, Craig stood behind Becky Amery who gave her order.
Hearing the exchange, Craig turned around. "Alana, rioja or merlot?" he
asked and nodded at her answer. When he turned back, Becky pushed past
him, slopping red wine over his arm. "Careful," he warned her. "Lucky I
haven't got a white shirt on."

His words didn't register as Becky hurried to their table.

"I knew you were up to something. Well it won't work. I won't let it."
She spat the words at Tom and Liz and wine glass in hand, each time she
jabbed her finger a little more wine escaped. Then turning her attention
to Alana, she added, "I don't know where you came from, but go home,
you're not welcome here. As for you, Bella, what the hell are you doing
with this lot? You're not welcome in my home any—"

"Becky, come and sit down. Please. People are watching." Jim Amery
tried to turn his wife away from the table, he mumbled apologies as he did
so. "Sorry, she—"

The glass was finally emptied as Becky tried to shrug him off. "Don't you
dare apologise for me. How dare you? After all I've done. Your mother was
right. Same bloody cloth. Take me home. Now."

"What about Molly and Damien, come and... Oh for the love of... I told
you we shouldn't come. Wait outside. I'll get your coat." Becky stormed
out and Amery held up hands that shook. "Sorry about that, she's had
one too many." He stooped to pick up the glass which Becky had simply

dropped. He placed it on the table. "Not broken." The tremor in his hands was more pronounced.

"But why?" Liz asked.

"Why is she drunk? She start—"

"No, why has she taken against us, and what has she got against Alana?" She turned to Alana. "This is Jim Amery. That was his wife."

Alana looked shocked, and then struggled to her feet, holding out her hand. Her cheeks were flushed. "I'm Denise's daughter."

Tom held his breath, he thought Amery might ignore her. He was wrong. Amery clasped the outstretched hand.

"I'm so sorry about your mother. She was a wonderful person, so happy, so giving, she didn't deserve... you know what I'm saying. She was very proud of you, she told me so. But whatever else people are saying about me, I promise you, on my daughter's life, I am not your father. Although I'm sure I would have been proud to be too..." He stopped talking as the door banged open and Becky stormed back in. She took one look at him holding Alana's hand and stormed out again. "I'd better go. But I do wish you all the best." Looking across to the remaining members of his team, he called out his apologies. "You carry on without us. I'll be back to take you home." With a final smile for Alana, he hurried away.

Tom looked across at the remaining members of the A and C team. Damien looked amused and winked at Tom, but Molly was shaking her head.

"Hang on a minute." Liz was out of her chair and sitting at their table before anyone could stop her. She chose to sit next to Molly. "What was all that about? Do you two want to join us?"

"Poor Jim. Walked into the same trap as his father and look where that got him. Thank you for your offer, but we'll be okay. My hearts not in it now. Who is that young girl?"

"Alana. That's Denise's daughter," Liz explained.

Molly nodded, but all she said was 'Oh'.

"Do you know about her?" Liz pressed on.

"Denise did mention her. Caused a row that night too. You'd better go back, he's ready to start." Molly pointed at Derek who tapped his glass.

"Are we ready? Round four. Science and nature."

Knowing she wouldn't get any more information out of Molly, Liz returned. She remained quiet until the end of the round. When Derek had asked the last question, she asked Alana if she wanted to leave.

Alana shook her head. "No. Nothing's changed. For what it's worth, I believe him. Going to have to rely on the DNA now."

Bella nodded, and when the next round was underway, she whispered in Alana's ear. Tom watched. His interest in the quiz had gone, he wanted some quiet so he could work through what had happened, but he couldn't simply leave, so he sat through it. Sally and Liz did their best, but he'd lost interest and the three youngsters were whispering amongst themselves. As Derek totted up the scores, his phone vibrated. A message from Emily, that she had to go out, and she would call him before she went to bed. His mind was now in chaos. He was worried Emily was tied up with something to do with Jason, and he needed to get whatever was niggling him about the performance by the Amerys. He'd put his coat on before the winner was announced. The Grey Geriatrics had done it again, and in second place were the Ring Leaders. Thank goodness. It was over.

"Goodnight all. That was an unexpected evening. I'm going to make a move now. Liz, do you want to walk with me? Craig I'm assuming you're going to see Bella gets home safely. Alana, do you need any help getting to the car?" With everything settled, he waited for Liz to say goodbye and they set off.

"Poor Alana, what a position to be put in. What did you make of that little show?" Liz asked as they crossed the crossing.

"It's fifteen days tomorrow, a long fifteen days in some ways, but by the same token not that long to us. We've all moved on, life as usual. Only for me, it's not. For me everything has changed, for the better I might add. Yours too. Did you think two weeks ago that in between dashing from one client to the next, one school run to the other, you'd be investigating a murder, helping some weird bloke overcome his demons, and rescuing a young girl in distress? No. Did Patrick Connor and Sally Ellis think they'd be having sleepovers? No. Did Craig and Bella think they'd be seeing someone new? No. Did Alana think that she would be moving into Denise's house with a bunch of new friends ready and willing to help her out? No. Most importantly for me, did my Emily think she'd be bringing

Eddie to live with me? Absolutely no! I'm sure I could go on, but we need to finish this. Denise's murder has changed so many lives for the better she deserves to be able to rest in peace. I don't want to talk about it now, I want to go home and think. Think about what we already know, what we might know, and work it out. Because if it drags on for any longer, these fifteen days will disappear into Christmas, and then the New Year. And that's not right. Denise should be laid to rest without this left unsolved."

"No wonder we lost the quiz. But I think you're right in a way. But you know, Tom, we can only do our best. I'll go home and think about it too. Because Amery is involved, absolutely and without a doubt. But like Alana, I think he was being genuine when he spoke to her. Oh, you walked me home. I wasn't concentrating."

"That's because I'm a gentleman. A weird one, but a gentleman none the less." Tom gave a low bow. "I shall see you tomorrow. I don't care if the house is mired, which it won't be, there'll be no cleaning until this is done."

"You're right you are weird, see you tomorrow, Tom. 'Night."

"Goodnight."

When Tom got in, he added the latest news to the murder log, which by now was running to two pages. Then he sat and read it over and over again. After an hour he went to bed, but he still couldn't stop thinking about it. Knowing sleep wouldn't come alone, he took two pills out and washed them down with a small measure. Before he got back into bed, he put the bottle at the back of the cupboard in the kitchen, and rinsed out the glass, filling it with water instead. He wasn't going to let Liz know he was slipping. If he slipped again, he'd pour the stuff away. But he needed sleep. Like most people his brain functioned better after sleep.

CASE SOLVED

T om was up, showered and breakfasted by six the next morning. There'd been a sharp frost overnight and standing on the back step, looking out onto the pretty back garden, a robin landed on his fence and sang for him. Tom remembered the first In Sympathy card he'd received after Amy died. It told him loved ones were near when robins appeared. He snorted.

"What a load of rubbish. But if it is one of you, I'm working on it. I won't let you down." He closed his eyes and grimaced. He was doing it again, only this time he was talking to a robin. He needed to get a firmer grip before Emily arrived. Yesterday he'd been talking to Denise outside the church. He hurried back inside and picked up the murder log.

"Ah ha." Grabbing his phone, he checked the time. Half eight wasn't too early to call someone. He made his call, received the answer he was expecting, and smiled. Going back to his desk, he tore three sheets from his notebook and headed each one with the names of three suspects. Underneath he wrote two things: Alibi? and Motive.

He was unable to put anything against Alibi? For any of them. Not without speaking to Patrick, although that wasn't quite true. Pulling on his coat, he headed for the shop.

Derek was serving a customer and Tom waited patiently while they talked about nothing. Eventually she left.

"Hello, Tom, I'm guessing you're not buying anything, so what can I do for you?"

"I want you to cast your mind back to the quiz on the night Denise was murdered. Who was there? In general, was Andy Knight behind the bar?"

Derek thought for a moment. "He was, yes."

"Can you swear he was there the whole time, for instance, what time did you leave the pub, and was he there then?"

"He had just arrived when I got there, and he was there after round three because he made me try a new brew, strangled something or other, I didn't like it, a bit strong for me. I left about half ten. But... No, I can't say one way or the other. I was chatting to some of the others. Finished my drink and left. I didn't notice. Sorry."

"Okay, What about the A and C team. Were they there?"

"Umm, yes. Molly, the lad, and Jim. Becky wasn't, but I know they didn't stay until the end. They'd all gone by the time I totted up."

"Do you know where Molly and Damien, that's his name, do you know where they live?"

"Molly lives right at the end of Church Road, the far end, she has her Sunday papers delivered. But as far as I know, Damien lives in Greater Compton, couldn't swear to it though."

"Perfect. Thank you."

"Are you sleuthing? Did I help?"

"Yes indeed. And now I must get back. Thanks."

Tom put a proper pot of coffee on and paced about until Liz arrived. She'd barely had time to say hello before he whisked her to the table.

"Sit down. We have three suspects. We need to work out a proper motive, then prove it."

"I know that. Andy Knight, Jim Amery, Karen Parker. What's got into you?"

"Wrong. I've eliminated Karen Parker because she couldn't have moved the body on her own. She's not built for it."

"Oh. Okay. You've got my attention, fire away."

"Suspect number one. Andy Knight. He was frightening Denise in the hope she'd take him back to protect her. What if she realised and told him that? He saw her by the church, they had a row and he killed her in a fit of temper. He then left her there, went to the pub, lots of witnesses, then dumped her body later. He arrived at the pub around seven thirty, and

Derek doesn't remember if he was still there at ten thirty. He could have slipped out and moved her."

"Slipped out? I don't think any slipping would have been involved. Even running, five minutes to the churchyard and back, and at least twenty minutes to get the body to the stream, ten minutes to return the wheelbarrow at speed. That's over half an hour, you don't slip out for that length of time at that time of night. Remember, not everyone leaves as soon as the quiz finishes. Some stay for another drink."

"Okay, good point. What if he finished on the dot of eleven, twenty-five minutes to get to the body, get her in the stream, and is returning the wheelbarrow before I leave for my walk? Even a little after eleven he could have done it and I wouldn't have seen him."

"He could. We need to know where he was between half six and half seven. We need to speak to Patrick."

"We do. Write that down."

Tom slid the notepad across the table.

"Suspect number two, Jim Amery. Despite his seemingly genuine declaration to Alana, he might be her father. He knew all about her. One of the few that did. Perhaps it was him who was meeting Denise, perhaps he asked if she was going to tell Alana about him. Again, killed in a fit of temper. Leaves the body, goes home collects the others, but not Becky for some reason, and then leaves the quiz before the results are announced. Plenty of time to take the others home, go and move the body before I get there."

"Agreed. But if he's not the father, we don't have a motive, and as he was always a suspect, one assumes the police have verified his alibi."

"Another question for Patrick. Write it down."

"Come on, come on. Who's suspect number three. Not Craig, not Karen, who?"

"Becky Amery. Absolutely no idea on motive, but she wasn't at the quiz. I've checked with Kathy, and she was one of the women from the WI who were still around when Kathy bumped into Denise. She was there, Liz. At the right time. She may have a motive we've yet to find out about, it may be simply that Denise was meeting with Jim, she saw them, got jealous et cetera, et cetera. She didn't go to the quiz, why not? She had plenty of time to kill Denise, leave the body, wait till hubby had gone to the quiz, move the body and been home before Jim had dropped the others off and got home himself. If, of course, that wasn't one of his gambling nights. He might have gone to the casino afterwards."

"Do you think she's strong enough to move the body?"

"Yes, I wondered that, but I do. She's bigger than Denise, Karen and bigger than you."

"What have I got to do with it?"

"I think you could have done it. Not literally, but I think you'd be strong enough. Especially if everything was at stake. Don't forget she didn't have to rush, not particularly, so even if it took her half an hour to get the barrow along that lane, there was no one who would miss her. Certainly not Jim, and not I suspect, Abi. Abi would have been glad of her absence and not given it a second thought."

"You're right. But how do we find out?"

"The first thing we need to do is check with Patrick. I don't think they would even have checked, you know. Why would they? That would be like them checking Damien's alibi."

"Not quite, but I agree. No time like the present. Am I allowed a cup of coffee now?"

"Oh yes. Probably stewed by now. You pour. I'll call."

Tom returned moments later. "He's not picking up. Didn't even ring so his phone must be switched off, or he's got no signal at all. Damn and blast."

"Is his car outside? I didn't think to look. He was working late last night, didn't show for the quiz, doesn't mean he didn't show for Sally."

"Really? Isn't that a bit... you know?"

"No idea what you're on about. Look."

Tom came back in shaking his head. "Not there. We'll have to wait for him to call. Do we do anything in the meantime?"

"Of course. We drink this coffee and come up with a plan of what we can do."

"Right."

They mulled it over for a while, neither wished to confront Becky Amery, and as Andy Knight was in custody, they were left with Jim Amery.

"We'll have to have a ploy. You know like they do on the TV dramas. Tell him we know who, what and why, and hope he caves in," Liz decided. "Problem with that is, we'll have to make something up."

"But what?"

They sat staring at Tom's sheets for a while before Liz jumped up.

"I can't sit about doing nothing. I'm going to change your bed. I think better when I'm busy, I'm the opposite to you. You like peace, I like busy."

"I'm going for a walk. I saw a robin today, it inspired me. I'm going to walk up to where I found her. Might get some more."

Tom was out for almost half an hour. He walked much further than he intended, but in the absence of speaking to Patrick, he couldn't see what else they could do. Even if they did confront Jim Amery, he could simply deny it, and then where would they be? He walked back to the house, head down, hands in pockets. When he got back Liz was putting the vacuum back in the cupboard.

"Anything?" she asked.

"No. Only to confront Amery, and with what?"

"We have to do something. I'm going to message Sally and find out why Patrick isn't responding to us." Pulling her phone from her pocket she did just that. They were back at the table with coffee by the time Sally replied. Liz tutted before updating Tom. "He's on a training course. All day. With everything else he has on, we won't hear from him until it finishes. Sally said he thought about four this afternoon. We must go and see Amery."

"I don't think so. We could make this much worse. What would we say?"

"We'd ask him to answer the question he didn't answer last night. Why, if Alana isn't his daughter, has his wife got a bee in her bonnet. That's what. I'm going there now, I'm supposed to be doing Mr Barnham any minute, and I'll be useless until I try to do something." Liz put her coat on. "Are you coming?"

Tom closed his eyes and drew in a breath. This was going to be embarrassing, probably excruciating, but he couldn't let her do it on her own. He looked her in the eye. "I'd better keep my coat on then."

They walked down to Amery and Cheriton in silence. Liz pushed open the door and Damien jumped to his feet. When he saw who it was, he simply said, "Oh."

"Hello to you too. We're here to see Jim, I'm sure he's expecting us. Shall we go through?"

Damien had no idea what he should do, so he stood there and watched Liz open the door of the rear office. She smiled and turned to Tom.

"He's in. Come on."

Jim Amery was on his feet. "What on earth are you doing? I have clients to—"

Tom flapped his hand. "Sit down, Mr Amery, this won't take long." He was surprised when Amery did, and he pulled a chair forward for Liz and sat on the other one. "Before we go through the long version, is there anything you want to tell us, to save the additional embarrassment and heartache that will surely follow."

"I really have no idea what you're talking about. I'm sorry, you'll have to give me a clue."

"Let's start with some questions that need answering. We're awaiting DC Connor, but it will be quicker if we do it this way. Are you happy to answer our questions?"

"Will it make you leave?"

"Of course."

"Then fire away." Amery slumped back into his chair. He didn't know how, but Tom instinctively knew he hadn't killed Denise, and mentally changed the order in which he would ask his questions. He started with the most crucial one.

"Why didn't your wife join you at the quiz on the night Denise was murdered?"

"She wasn't well. She stayed at home."

"After the quiz, where did you go immediately after you dropped off Molly and Damien?"

"The casino in town. I won, me cashing in my winnings was timed on their machine. Look, the police have done all this. Can we move to something that's not already been covered? Because it would appear, as my wife has pointed out, that you have no authority and are simply interfering busybodies. You are rehashing things which have already been proven."

"We'll come back to that. Are you aware, that as far as can be ascertained, you are the only person who knew of Alana's existence? Even her sister didn't know."

"I'm afraid you're wrong. Karen certainly did because Denise told her. At least Denise told me she did."

This threw Tom as Craig certainly hadn't known. He nodded and made a note it needed to be followed up.

"Well, that means Karen's been lying too. But let's get back to you. If we accept you are not Alana's father, and DNA will prove that one way or another, but let's for now accept that you're not, why did Denise confide in you? Why not her best friend Nadine Vaswani, or Liz here. She confided in them about other things, and she wasn't ashamed of Alana, she was very much looking forward to her coming to live with her."

This wasn't true, Nadine had known, but Tom was trying to apply pressure.

"I don't know." Amery fiddled with his wedding ring. "But you're right I know she was very excited about Alana coming."

"Denise told you that too? She certainly considered you a friend."

"She did, we were friends. I'm not sure why you find that difficult to believe. She told me on Monday, the day before she died. I bumped into her when she'd finished her shift at the library. She was, as you say, very happy about it."

"Did you arrange to meet her the next day?"

"No."

"Did you tell your wife about this?"

Amery shrugged. "Why wouldn't I?"

"I don't know. But she wasn't very welcoming yesterday, quite the opposite. Why? Why would your wife worry about Alana coming here, *if* you're not the father?"

"She was drunk. You saw her."

Liz shook her head. "She wasn't drunk. She was furious. I watched you arrive, I kept an eye on you until the break, because I believed Alana might be in the same room as her real father for the first time. Becky wasn't drunk. She wasn't even furious until she realised who Alana was."

"I can't prove that one way or another, is there a point to this?"

"Yes. The point is, Denise was killed because of Alana. We know that. The question that would clear everything up is the identity of her father. Are you going to tell us?" Liz held out her hand in invitation.

"No."

"Because?"

Tom watched Amery twist his ring. He was about to lie.

"Because I don't know. I've told you that."

Tom huffed out a frustrated breath. Amery was lying and in doing so was protecting Denise's killer. He was convinced of it.

"I don't believe you. Cards on the table, Mr Amery. I know things about your family that would cause you embarrassment, and perhaps do irreparable damage. If you would just tell the truth, all that might be avoided." Tom's smile was grim.

"Listen, you tell me what you know, and I'll tell you what I know. Because I know nothing, and I don't think you do either. But you go first." Amery crossed his arms.

Amery clearly believed Tom was bluffing, and he was in part, so Tom jumped in feet first.

"Why weren't you allowed to mention Denise's name at home. Back around the time Alana was born?"

Amery slumped forward as though punched. His mouth open, he stared at Tom his head shaking slowly. Finally managing to string a sentence together.

"How did... I have no idea how you know that. My mother didn't approve of Denise. It's why we broke up and it's why I didn't come home until after Alana was born. They wouldn't let me. Do you know how much fun a student house is during the holiday season, when everyone else has gone home. I had no idea why, not until I was finally allowed to return."

"You've known about Alana all those years?" Liz's voice was almost a squeak.

"Denise told me when I came home. I was with Becky by then, my mother was arranging the wedding. Denise thought I'd like to know, she thought I deserved an explanation as to why I'd been exiled."

"Why? Why would she care?" Liz demanded. "Your mother had split you up, you'd come back with a fiancé, and she thought that? Never."

"I know. I bloody know." Tom banged the desk and fell silent.

The other two looked at Tom. His eyes were closed as he pulled all he knew together, it took a while, and at one time he even smiled. Eventually, Liz shook him gently.

"Tom, you're going to have to tell us."

Amery leaned forward. "Is he alright?"

"I'm perfectly okay. Thank you. I haven't got all the detail, and I have no idea why your wife found it necessary to kill poor old Denise. But I know it all started a while before Alana was born. I'm going to tell you why Denise put that bet on, and why it was Billy who caused a family rift that never healed."

Tom was pleased to see that although Amery looked shocked, he nodded. He wasn't playing with his ring, he knew something, but he didn't know the half of it.

"Your parents' marriage wasn't happy, was it? Your mother ruled the roost, and it was her way or hell to pay. Your father looked for relief elsewhere. I don't know how they met, possibly because you were seeing Denise. No doubt all will be revealed, but he had an affair, a liaison, I don't know what, but he did have something with Karen Parker. It didn't last long, I'm guessing your mother had something to do with that. You were a mummy's boy, and you always did as you were told. Including ending your relationship with the girl you loved. Even marrying the girl she told you to. Mummy's boy. Is that what Denise called you? Perhaps not, perhaps your father called you that. But Denise was meeting someone on Tuesday. Someone she made sure she looked her absolute best for, someone she was going to taunt if it became necessary with that bet. I'm not even sure you know about the bet, but Denise knew it would make a point."

"Now that makes sense. It's been bugging me." Liz smiled. "Carry on."

"When you went away, you met, or were you introduced to Becky? Your mother had you up the aisle at the earliest opportunity. Before you'd even finished your studies. That's not normal. I'm guessing because Becky was cut from the same cloth as her. Not, as Molly said, you and your father. Because I don't believe you would seduce young women and cast them aside. Although you do allow your wife to control your life and ruin your child's. Think about that. I know if it were you, and a girl turned up and told you they were pregnant, you would try to do the right thing, not tell them you're not interested and that they should get an abortion. I don't think you're like that, are you?"

"No." The word was snapped out.

"Did you know how much trouble Billy caused? Billy being William Amery, your father."

"Not until it was all over and done with. I don't think it was him who told her to get rid of it, it was more likely to have been my mother. When I came home and Denise told me, my mother said Denise had seduced him. She never would. I wondered for a while if he'd raped her. But she assured me he hadn't. Unsurprisingly, she didn't like to talk about that time, not until Alana found her, that was. Then she didn't care. She didn't know whether to tell Alana though. Didn't want Alana to think badly about her. She said it was bad enough that she had given her away."

"When and why did Denise come to work here?" Tom wished he had a pen and paper to write all this down.

"About five years ago because she needed a job. Her marriage was over, and she needed to earn more money. Molly was retiring, and mother, my dear, spiteful, mostly evil mother, had died. I told her there was always a job for her here, and she took it."

"How did Becky feel about that?"

"It had nothing to do with Becky. She felt nothing, why would she? She didn't know any of this then."

"She didn't know about you and Denise, or the fact that you still cared for her, or about Denise and your father?" Liz asked. "Because she certainly does now. How did she find out?"

"I told her. When Alana decided to come and live with Denise, there was every chance the paternity would be revealed, and that being the case, Becky had to know. It would embarrass her."

"Did she take it well?" Liz knew the question was unnecessary, but she thought he was trying to protect his wife from getting the justice she deserved.

Amery ran his hands over his face. "No. Even by her standards I was surprised at her reaction. I thought she'd tell me to sack Denise for lying or something. I wouldn't have. But she didn't. She just walked away from me. Like it was my fault. That was on the Monday evening. On Tuesday, she popped into the office and told me she had a WI meeting, something about flowers in the church, and she might be late home. Then she left. She's barely spoken to me since. It's why we were late getting to the quiz last night. Look, with Denise dead, I saw no point in dragging Alana into my mess of a family. My father has lost his mind, I'm told it's getting worse. Becky would never accept her, and Abi, well Abi is a law unto herself right now. I didn't want Alana to be rejected. My decision was taken out of a kindness, not out of spite."

Tom nodded. "I can see that. Which brings us to the final question."

"Why did Becky kill Denise? It can't be because the family name would be brought into disrepute. Surely she's not that shallow? Do you know?"

"I have no idea. I don't even know if you are right…" Tears welled in Amery's eyes. He swallowed and cleared his throat. "You're going to go to the police with this theory, aren't you? That being the case, I'll tell you this honestly, I don't know who killed Denise. Until five minutes ago, I didn't even consider it might be Becky. But now you've said all that, I agree it's possible. Becky has an atrocious temper, if Denise did taunt her, anything is possible, but here's my problem with that. Why would Denise taunt her? Denise wasn't like that. Why would she even agree to meet with Becky? What was the purpose? It doesn't make sense."

"Did Denise call you a mummy's boy?" Liz's voice was gentle.

"Yes. Once. The day I told her I couldn't see her anymore. She knew it hadn't been my decision. It was the last thing she said to me before I left. But I still don't understand."

"Nor do I," Tom announced. "Perhaps we'll never know what motivated either of them. But our friend is dead, and the person who killed her, Becky, must face the consequences of those actions."

"I understand that." Amery got to his feet. "I'm going to find Abi, I'm not letting anyone else tell her this. She should be in school, it might even be lunchtime. You do what you must do, but I'm going to find my daughter."

Liz stood and took his hand. "I think she might surprise you. I think she'll welcome Alana into your family with open arms."

"If that's what she wants, then I will take Abi to meet... her aunt. My sister. I'll make sure Alana gets what she should when my father dies too. What an awful mess. Why do adults create such a mess for their children?"

Tom opened the door to the front office. "I don't know, but we do. Sometimes we have no choice, but we can always put it right. Go on. Go and find your daughter. Alana is staying in Charles's Bungalow. I'm sure she'd welcome a visit."

Amery didn't need a second invitation. He left with a wave to Damien.

Tom and Liz walked back up the High Street.

"It's sad. All too sad," Liz commented. "But you did it, Tom. It's been fifteen days since Denise, and you did it."

"I think that should be, we did it. You put the kettle on, I'll try Patrick again. Oh, there's his car. I'll call him and tell him to come over. We don't want to do this in front of Alana."

Opening the door, Tom pulled his phone from his pocket. He'd missed two calls from DC Connor, and he rolled his eyes at Liz. "Mind you, probably for the best. Had we been interrupted we might never have got there. He left a message." Tom hit the play button.

"Hello, Tom, I'm not sure who your new suspect is, but I hope she's female. The heel marks at the murder site were made by two different pairs of shoes. Ha! I bet you weren't expecting that. I'm on my way to speak to the vicar's wife. They might have been hers."

Liz smiled at Tom. "He'll never believe we beat him to it. I'll put the kettle on, you give him a ring."

***

Tom was still drying from his shower when he heard his phone ringing. It was Emily. It wasn't yet six, he'd decided to get changed before he found a film to watch. With the excitement of the day, he was worried he'd fall asleep.

"Dad. Finally, I've been trying to get you."

"Is everything okay? We've had one hell of a day. We worked out that the murderer was Becky Amery, she's been arrested, and has confessed. We're still none the wiser as to why, although something was said about a will. But when she was arrested, she told Patrick she had to end it with his tart. It seems although innocent, Denise and Jim's affection for each other hadn't been missed, and she wrongly assumed he was the father. Why, I don't know, he told her Alana's father was William. It will all come out in the fullness of time, and poor old Denise can be laid to rest. Properly. Oh, why aren't you on a video call? Is everything okay? I asked but didn't wait for you to answer."

"Dad, Jason is going to contest me bringing Eddie to England. I did try to call earlier, I'm afraid... damn that beeping is my battery. I can't talk long. If you lose me, you won't hear from me until..." The line went dead, and Tom checked his phone. He'd had two missed calls from Emily, both in the last hour. She'd certainly wanted to speak to him. He tried to call her back, but it went through to her answer service.

"Hi, Emily, I'm sorry, I was in the shower. Then I prattled on. Don't panic. You will come home. I'll see to that. Give me a call as soon as you are charged. I'm not going to bed until I hear from you. You must call me back."

It was the early hours of the morning in Australia. What on earth was going on? He looked at his bedside drawer. He mustn't. He couldn't be drunk when Emily called. Instead of putting on his pyjamas, he got dressed and went downstairs. He put the television on but couldn't settle, so he paced. At eight the doorbell rang, and the door opened.

Tom went to the hall, Liz was hanging her coat on the newel post. "Liz?"

"Did she get you? Blimey what a palaver. I thought that I'd do a quick spruce up now, and then tomorrow I'll pick you up... hang on." Liz pulled her ringing phone from her pocket. "Alana, is everything okay? Um, yes. I'm at Tom's do you want them now? Oh, okay. Send him down." She stared at her phone for a moment before sliding it back in her pocket.

"What do you mean, you'll spruce up now?" Tom asked.

"Isn't it... that will be Craig. I'll get it." Liz went to answer the door, leaving a dumfounded Tom standing in the middle of the kitchen.

"Alright, Tom. Sorry about this. Did we interrupt anything?"

Tom stalked into the hall. "No. You did not! What do you want?"

"It's not my idea, but I've had a major bust up with Mum, and Alana said I could stay at Denise's. She's so cool. But you know that. Anyway, I'm here for the keys."

"I'll get them. They'll be in the car." Liz pulled her car keys from her coat pocket and left them standing there.

"Craig, while we're alone, can I establish once and for all that there is nothing going on between me and Liz. Nothing. She's come here to do a spruce up apparently. I was trying to get to the bottom of why when you arrived."

Craig held his hands up. "Got you. Nothing to do with me, none of my business."

Tom rolled his eyes. "I wasn't talking in code, I was stating a fact. Why have you fallen out with your mother?"

Sitting on the bottom stair Craig sighed. "I told her I'd met Alana and asked her why she hadn't told me about her. I was calling her bluff. I didn't know whether she knew or not. She told me it should be obvious. It wasn't. It turns out, she didn't know who knew about Alana, or if Denise had made a will. If she hadn't, Mum was intent on claiming the house as next-of-kin. It was her who sent Andy in to find out, she was going to pay him off once she'd got it. Before you ask, I have no idea how that came about because I went ballistic. Told her what I thought about her, and she kicked me out. For the record, I hope he tells the police she was in on it. Anyway, long story short, I told Bella, Bella told Alana, and she's asked me to move in. You know share with her. I can move in now, my stuff's in the van, and she'll move in once she can get up and down the stairs. She's been practicing and is much better on those crutches. What a turn-up."

"You can say that again. Liz, have you heard this?"

"How could I when I was out at the car?"

"In a nutshell, Karen put Andy Knight up to do the break-in to see if there was a will. Kept her mouth shut about Alana because she was hoping that she'd inherit as next-of-kin. Craig is moving in with Alana. Sharing. As he says, what a turn-up."

"Sure is, she thought she had no family, now she's got a cousin and a brother."

"That Jim's alright, he came up to see her with Abi. That makes Abi her niece, doesn't it? Weird."

"That's all marvellous. But I'll tell you what will be weird, shall I? Weird will be me trying to get this place cleaned up, and a big shop done tomorrow morning. I do have other clients. Now, here are your keys, I'll pop in and see you... maybe tomorrow, and show you how everything works. But if you don't go now, it will be Christmas the way things are going. Congratulations by the way."

"Thanks. I'll leave you to it." Craig took the keys and made his exit.

Tom stood arms akimbo.

"What? Come on, Tom, I've got to get a move on."

"Do I get a say in this. As it happens, spruce away, I've got stuff I need to be distracted from, but just once it would be nice if you'd explain, or let's go mad, ask, first."

Liz grinned at him. "You don't know, do you?"

"Obviously not. Know what?"

"Where your Emily and Eddie are." Liz pulled out her phone and looked at the time. "Get your laptop up and see if flights from Australia into Heathrow are on time."

"I don't even have the flight number. They're not coming until next month, or I suppose, this month now. Liz, just get on with whatever it is you want to do. Have you got time to drink tea while you work?"

"Flights into Heathrow, tomorrow. I haven't got the flight number either. But it was due to depart at six twenty our time. Takes seventeen and a half hours so they will be England sometime tomorrow morning. She did tell me, but I got so excited for you."

Tom's hands hit his head. "Tomorrow. Honestly?"

"Yes. And they'll be tired and hungry, and you need to do a big shop in preparation. I thought I'd take you to the big supermarket in the morning."

"But how will they get here? How do you know, and I don't?"

"Oh blimey, you're going to have to help me with the work the way this is going. I texted Emily my number when you told me where hers was. Just so she would get any messages I might need to send. We said hello and that was that. Then she called me earlier when we were having breakfast because she couldn't get hold of you. Her flight was due to take off, she'd been called to boarding and her phone was almost out of battery. Is that enough detail? Oh yes, and she's got a hire car waiting to pick her up. There. Now you know everything I know."

Tom grabbed Liz's face between his hands and planted a kiss on her lips. "You are the most marvellous woman, do you know that? They broke the mould when they made you. Thank you. Thank you. Thank you."

"You just kissed me. Let go of my face." Liz's face was almost the same colour as Sally's neck would have been.

Tom pulled his hands away and they fell to his side. He took a step back. "No, no I never. Not a kiss. Not a real kiss, a token of my thanks. My gratitude. My—"

"Are we both embarrassed? Yes. Shall we move on? Yes. Now get out of my way, or so help me..."

Tom gave a curt nod and went to the kitchen. What a day. What a result, on all fronts. He'd solved the murder of poor old Denise, his family would be here tomorrow, and he'd kissed Liz. He blinked. Was that a cause for celebration? He didn't think it should be, he needed to stop that line of thinking and sharpish. He could hear Liz in the sitting room.

"Cup of tea?" he called, and when the hoover went on in response, he retrieved the whiskey from the back of the cupboard and poured it away.

About the Author

AUTHOR'S NOTE

Thank you for reading The Murder. I hope you enjoyed reading this story as much as I enjoyed writing it. If you did, I'd be grateful if you would be kind enough to leave a review on Amazon when you have a moment. Constructive reviews are invaluable to authors. If you would rather contact me personally the details are below.

ABOUT THE AUTHOR

Having worked in the property industry for most of my adult life, latterly at a senior level, I finally escaped in 2010. I now work as a consultant for several independent agencies, but I dedicate the bulk of my time to writing and, of course, reading, although there are still not enough hours in the day.

I began writing quite by chance when a friend commented, "They wouldn't believe it if you wrote it down!" So I did. I enjoyed the plotting and scheming, creating the characters, and watching them develop with the story. I kept on writing, and Meredith and Hodge arrived. In 2017 the Bearing women took hold of my imagination, and the Bearing Witness series was created. I should confess at this point that although I have the basic outline when I start a new story, it never develops the way I expect, and I rarely know 'who did it' myself until I've nearly finished. Very excited about my new series, The Little Compton Mysteries.

I am married with two children, two grandchildren, and two German Shepherds. We live in Bristol, UK.

I would love to hear from you, and can be contacted here:

Website: https://www.mkturnerbooks.co.uk

Printed in Great Britain
by Amazon